A. S. Byatt

A. S. Byatt
Art, Authorship, Creativity

Christien Franken
Lecturer
Department of English
Vrÿe Universiteit
The Netherlands

palgrave

First published 2001 by
PALGRAVE
Houndmills, Basingstoke, Hampshire RG21 6XS and
175 Fifth Avenue, New York, N. Y. 10010
Companies and representatives throughout the world

PALGRAVE is the new global academic imprint of
St. Martin's Press LLC Scholarly and Reference Division and
Palgrave Publishers Ltd (formerly Macmillan Press Ltd).

ISBN 0–333–80108–3

This book is printed on paper suitable for recycling and
made from fully managed and sustained forest sources.

A catalogue record for this book is available
from the British Library.

Library of Congress Cataloging-in-Publication Data
Franken, Christien, 1961–
    A.S. Byatt : art, authorship, creativity / Christien Franken.
        p. cm.
    Includes bibliographical references (p.) and index.
    ISBN 0–333–80108–3
    1. Byatt, A. S. (Antonia Susan), 1936——Criticism and
    interpretation. 2. Women and literature—England—History–
    –20th century. I. Title.
    PR6052.Y2 Z65 2001
    823'.914—dc21

                                                00–054525

10   9   8   7   6   5   4   3   2
             07 06 05 04 03 02

Voor mijn moeder Janna en mijn broer Jan Wim

Very difficult for a novelist to have 'opinions'. To see only one side of an issue and to stay with it. The world of the novel is always inhabited by aspects of the self that relate in dialectical ways, the movements of beings in time and flux, a kaleidoscope of mirror-selves. Splinters, shards.

Joyce Carol Oates

One is so much richer for being a great number of people

A. S. Byatt

Contents

Preface

This study discusses the ideas about art, authorship and creativity in the work of one particular writer: the English critic and novelist A. S. Byatt (born 1936). This involves making a distinction between the academic and critic A. S. Byatt, on the one hand, and the novelist A. S. Byatt, on the other. Placing A. S. Byatt's critical work before her novels may seem an unconventional choice given the fact that she is much better known as a novelist than as a critic. Her critical work has seldom been the subject of sustained discussion and analysis in literary criticism.[1] When asked in interviews about the nature of her work and the type of critic she is, A. S. Byatt emphasizes that she does not see herself primarily as a critic. Her sense of herself is as a novelist whose practice and reading as a critic taught her how to write:

> I've never thought of myself as a critic. I have written an enormous amount of criticism, but all of it has been in order to earn money, not because I thought of myself as a critic with a critical reputation ... All of it was written in order to understand how to write, and most of my big critical essays are about people that the writer in me wanted to understand very badly.[2]

Although A. S. Byatt is a thoughtful and articulate critic of her own work, in this case her emphasis on the novelist persona does her criticism a disservice. In the period in which she wrote her novels she also built up a critical record which is quite exceptional in its versatility and complexity.[3] When it comes to a comparison between her critical work and her novels, Byatt's definition of her own writing practice is less useful for her reader; the fact that there are no *boundaries* between her critical and her fictional work does not mean that there may be no differences or tensions between these two fields of activity.

Indeed, in the first chapter I will show that Byatt's criticism testifies to the 'warring forces of signification' which continue to determine the content and aims of English Studies.[4] It is my aim to show that part of the interest of Byatt's criticism lies precisely in its polyvocal nature. This quality makes it futile to place her critical ideas about art, creativity and authorship in one specific category. The labels that are used such as 'humanist', 'post-structuralist' and 'feminist' are I believe reductive in this respect. Instead I will analyse the contradictory, yet highly productive ways in which Byatt's criticism moves across and in and out of Leavisite, post-structuralist and feminist debates about art, creativity and authorship, tracing an itinerary of her own.

My discussion of this itinerary serves as a framework for a new inter-disciplinary approach to A. S. Byatt's fiction. I will look at the theories of art, creativity and authorship that are imaginatively constructed in three of her novels: *The Shadow of the Sun* (1964), *The Game* (1967) and *Possession* (1990).[5] *The Shadow of the Sun* and *The Game* are her first two novels, written at the time when she was still a student at Cambridge. Until now academic literary criticism has barely paid attention to them. I hope to show that they are rich and complex sources of ideas about art, authorship and creativity and as such can be compared to Byatt's bestselling novel *Possession*.

The concept of 'gender' will play an important part in the analyses put forward in this study. Adequate readings of Byatt's novels – by which I mean readings which truly bring out the interest and quality of her oeuvre – are impossible without a discussion of the work's relationship to 'gender' and 'feminism', a relation which is far more complex and interesting than academics and literary critics have noticed. For although academic interest in Byatt's novels has steadily increased from the beginning of the 1990s onwards, such work as exists often tends to emphasize only one aspect: the traditional and receptive character of her fiction. It is seen as a sieve through which the influence of other novelists such as Iris Murdoch and Marcel Proust runs its course. The emphasis on the receptive character of Byatt's work implicitly constructs her as a traditional novelist. Michael Levenson for instance highlights the traditional aspect of the Murdoch–Byatt axis: 'Murdoch has been her literary mother. The two of them alone are enough to count as a distinct contempory lineage, nourished on the conviction that, our modernist complacencies aside, our Victorian origins are unresolved, unsurpassed'.[6] Page and Cowley's description of A. S. Byatt as 'one of the most celebrated conventional women writers' has a similar effect.[7]

Other critics actively disengage Byatt's work from feminist concerns and subject matter, stereotyping her as a non-feminist, even anti-feminist, writer. Valentine Cunningham, for instance, writes that the novelist A. S. Byatt 'stands rather alone in her refusal to ride on a politically correct bandwagon'.[8] Nancy Miller has coined the term 'the new misogyny' for this type of reasoning: it constructs an unbridgeable gap between well-known women writers such as George Eliot and Emily Dickinson – or A. S. Byatt for that matter – and feminist literary critics who argue that 'gender' matters to writing, literature and authorship.[9]

In any case, Byatt's novels are seen as more traditional than the work of experimental writers such as Virginia Woolf, Angela Carter, Christine Brooke-Rose and Jeanette Winterson. However, this traditional quality of Byatt's fiction is deceptive. The following statement by DeKoven is applicable to the three novels under discussion in this study:

> while it is an incontrovertible fact that the majority of the most successful, visible women writers employ conventional or traditional forms, it is also the case that their use of those forms is much less straigthforward and unproblematic than it appears.[10]

A. S. Byatt's 1991 foreword to *The Shadow of the Sun* already points in this direction. It is a text in which she discusses at length what it meant to her and to her writing that she was an ambitious woman writer in the 1950s. She says in the foreword that the 'battle' of writing her first novel 'fought itself out between sexuality, literary criticism, and writing'.[11] The focus of my reading of *The Shadow of the Sun* is how this battle shaped itself narratively. Combining close reading with narratological insight, I pose the question what happens when a young female novelist deploys theories of art, vision and creative identity as a medium for her anxieties about gender and generation.

The Game (1967) and *Possession* (1990) invite a further theoretical context: that of myth criticism. After flourishing in the 1950s and 1960s through the work of influential exponents such as Northrop Frye and Leslie Fiedler, the practice of myth criticism came under critical scrutiny in the 1970s, dismissed as 'a form of reductionism that neglects cultural and historical differences as well as the specific properties of literary works'.[12] In a balanced survey of the debate surrounding myths and myth criticism, Bullen mentions Voltaire, Roland Barthes, Frank Kermode and David Bidney as critics who are/were deeply suspicious of myths because of their static and conservative nature.[13] I am among those contemporary readers and writers who think it is possible to find other, less reductive ways of conceptualizing the relevance of myths to our culture. Many scholars and philosophers have analysed the ways in which myths are still formative of Western culture. They emphasize the changeability of mythic material and the agency of the writer and the critic in rewriting myths.[14] In a fascinating analysis of Tennyson's 'The Lady of Shalott', Isobel Armstrong defines Claude Lévi-Strauss, Roland Barthes, Sigmund Freud, Gaston Bachelard and Jacques Lacan as 'readers of myths who are themselves involved in the myth-making process'.[15] A. S. Byatt can be seen as such a reader. She is one of a number of contemporary novelists and critics who are deeply interested in the creative possibilities of (female) myths.[16] As a judge of the European Literary and Translation Prizes, Byatt noticed a mythical thread running through contemporary European fiction and saw her work as belonging to this tradition: 'one passion that runs right across Europe is for primitive narrative forms like classical myths and fairy tales, of which I feel myself to be a part'.[17] In interviews and reviews Byatt has often expressed her strong interest in the narrative beauty of myths and has written about the use of mythical material by novelists. Two of these myths, the Cassandra story and the Melusine mythology, structure *The Game* and *Possession* respectively. In my discussion of A. S. Byatt's revision of these myths, I will devote attention to subjects such as the ethics of art, the artist as a visionary, the difference between scientific and artistic visions, the violence of the imagination, motherhood and art and women's access to artistic subjectivity.

Thus, this study aims to question those representations of the novelist and critic A. S. Byatt which reduce her work to its traditional, conservative and non-feminist aspects. It is my intention to offer further insight into the complex interaction between an artist's creative work, her critical work and, last but not least, gender as a constitutive cultural force. My intention in this study is not to seal Byatt's work within 'the hermetic forcing-house of academic reputation' but to argue for a more nuanced criticism, one that will do justice to Byatt's patient and often ambivalent questioning of the connections between creativity, art, authorship and gender.[18] For in the case of A. S. Byatt's work, nothing is as authentic or central as her ambivalence.

Acknowledgements

I have spent years finding the words with which to investigate and explain the impact A. S. Byatt's work had on me. Although the effort was exasperating at times, the words on the page never bored me. The first person I wish to thank, therefore, is A. S. Byatt. Without the strength of her imagination this study would never have been written. As Virginia Woolf says in *A Room of One's Own* 'this is what remains over when the skin of the day has been cast into the hedge'. I would like to thank Alexa Alfer and Michael Crane for their painstaking work on the A. S. Byatt bibliography.

Excerpts from *The Game* are reprinted by permission of Sterling Lord Literistic, Inc. (© Antonia Byatt).

Extracts from *The Shadow of the Sun* (© A. S. Byatt, 1964), *Degrees of Freedom* (© A. S. Byatt, 1965) and *Still Life* (© A. S. Byatt, 1986) are reprinted by permission of PFD on behalf of A. S. Byatt.

Excerpts from *The Djinn in the Nightingale's Eye* (© A. S. Byatt, 1997), *Babel Tower* (© A. S. Byatt, 1996) and *Passions of the Mind* (© A. S. Byatt, 1991) are reprinted by permission of Random House, Inc., New York.

Excerpts from *The Shadow of the Sun, The Game, Still Life, Possession, The Djinn in the Nightingale's Eye, Passions of the Mind, Degrees of Freedom, Babel Tower*, by A. S. Byatt (Chatto & Windus) are reprinted by permission of The Random House Archive & Library.

Like any academic who sees her thoughts in print I owe an enormous debt to a number of colleagues and friends. I am grateful to my unconventional teachers Dien Muys, Inke Dam-Knook, Maureen Peeck-O'Toole and Simon Varey. Women's Studies at Utrecht University and its post-graduate seminar provided me with an intellectual environment that was truly stimulating to the development of this book. Rosi Braidotti and Maaike Meijer taught me to think longer and harder about what I had read and enjoy it at the same time. Thanks to my colleagues in Amsterdam: Theo Bögels, Richard Todd, Sinead McDermott, Lachlan Mackenzie, Diederik Oostdijk, Rod Lyall and Katrien Daemen-de Gelder. With Richard I share the fascination for A. S. Byatt's work; I thank him for his encouragement. Daniel Carroll has been a generous colleague and editor and Rieta Bergsma's wit is a gem. I have also benefited from the support of other colleagues in English Studies, especially Aleid Fokkema, Paul Franssen, Ans van Kemenade, Trev Broughton and the members of Anglo.fem.

Luck has been on my side where friends and mentors are concerned. Ank van Elk and Monique Kolfschoten asked all the right questions at crucial moments. I thank Angelique van Vondelen for her patience in managing me and my manuscript. Without the shelter and support offered by Ariadne van de Ven and John Prescott this book would have been more difficult to write. I also wish to thank my other friends: Margaret Koppejan, Maartje Los, Mischa Hoyinck, Monique de Bakker, Berteke Waaldijk, Wil Buchel, Elly Bruggink, Ben Platenkamp, Johan Pranger, Heleen van Dijk, Martin Soeters, Egbert St Nicolaas, Jan Vlaskamp, Jann Ruyters, Inez van der Spek, Marja Pruis, Jacqueline Panders, Monique Dijkman and Charles Forceville. Thanks to them I have been able to look beyond the confines of academic life. And, finally, I wholeheartedly thank my brother Jan Wim and my mother Janna for their love and encouragement.

CHRISTIEN FRANKEN
Utrecht

1
The Turtle and Its Adversaries: Polyvocality in A. S. Byatt's Critical and Academic Work

'She came, after all, not in utter nakedness but cocooned in her culture in a web of amatory, social and tribal expectations which was not even coherent or unitary'.[1]

Introduction

During the period in which she wrote *The Shadow of the Sun* (1964), *The Game* (1967) and *Possession* (1990) A. S. Byatt built an impressive critical record. The author-critic is of course a fairly well-known phenomenon in English letters. One need only think of George Eliot, Virginia Woolf, Anthony Burgess, Iris Murdoch, Malcolm Bradbury and Marina Warner to name but a few. From 1967 onwards, when her first reviews were published in *Encounter, New Statesman* and *Nova*, A. S. Byatt continually broke through the male-gender bias that dominated English literary criticism until the middle of the 1980s.

Her critical work is also quite exceptional in its versatility. As the large bibliography at the end of this study shows, one can distinguish at least eight levels in her critical work: scholarly studies, essays and articles on Romantic and Victorian writers such as Wordsworth, Coleridge, George Eliot, Robert Browning and Alfred Lord Tennyson, and on modern authors such as Ford Madox Ford, Iris Murdoch and Wallace Stevens; reviews for mainstream journals, magazines and newspapers; introductions and forewords to novels by Willa Cather, A. L. Barker, Iris Murdoch, Grace Paley, Elizabeth Bowen and Pamela Hansford Johnson; articles on her own fiction; lectures at venues ranging from the London-based Institute of Contemporary Art to public libraries across England; contributions to television and radio programmes such as *The Late Show* and *The Brains Trust* and, lastly, interviews about her own work as a novelist and a critic.

The versatility and eclecticism of Byatt's critical record are even greater when one looks at her academic career. As a student of English literature in the 1950s, A. S. Byatt developed a close acquaintance with the theories of literature developed by T. S. Eliot and F. R. and Q. D. Leavis. Byatt herself has acknowledged that her work can productively be read in the context of these theories. In 'The Pleasure of Reading' she discusses the sources of her creativity and uses the metaphor of the battle to characterize her ambivalent relationship to Leavisite criticism:

> I think, although all my books have also been fighting a more or less overt battle with Dr Leavis and the Cambridge-English school of moral seriousness and social responsibility, I have also been deeply influenced by it.[2]

Gender plays an important part in my reading of the complexity inherent to Byatt's critical approach to Leavisite criticism. Her critical work expresses a complex attitude towards the subject of 'female identity'. It shows the signs of a phenomenon which Mary Ellmann describes so lucidly in *Thinking about Women*:

> Women are like subjects of a bureaucracy in which they must read interminable and triplicated forms, whether or not they agree to sign them in the end. Their self-consciousness grows with their reading, so that educated women tend ... to walk about like sensate editorials on the Woman problem. They are not allowed to escape the sense of species, they are like giraffes reading Lamarck every morning before they stretch their necks.[3]

In negotiating the rules of this 'bureaucracy', A. S. Byatt's critical work automatically deals with the problem of 'female identity'. More specifically, the complexity of the relationship between Byatt's critical work and the Great Tradition of English criticism is in part a function of 'gender'. On the one hand, Byatt's critical work testifies to the attraction she feels towards Leavisite criticism and, on the other hand, it speaks of the difficulties she has in accepting Leavis's devaluation of 'femininity' and the personal. I will argue this last point on the basis of a comparison between Leavis's reception of George Eliot's work in his study *The Great Tradition*[4] and Byatt's own evaluation of George Eliot. I will focus on the concept of 'impersonality' because it enables me to explain how 'gender' structures Byatt's disengagement from her former teacher F. R. Leavis.

I will also discuss A. S. Byatt's critical work against the background of feminism and feminist literary theory and criticism, particularly the latter's conceptualization of female identity. Feminists have made it their task to try and conceptualize an escape from 'the sense of species' which is thrust upon women by thoroughly investigating it. This has led to a paradox in feminist thinking when it comes to female identity. In *Nomadic Subjects* Rosi Braidotti describes it thus: 'in contemporary feminist practice, the paradox of "woman" has emerged as central. Feminism is based on the very notion of female identity which it is historically bound to criticize'.[5] Byatt has defined the paradox in similar terms: 'it is one of the paradoxes of feminist thought that discussions designed to liberate women from narrowingly prescriptive, gender-based descriptions and definitions are themselves inevitably intensely preoccupied with gender and sexuality'.[6] Why then does Byatt's critical work express a strong reservation about this preoccupation, given the fact that she herself uses it in her feminist critique of Leavis's Great Tradition?

Apart from discussing the reception of feminist ideas of 'female identity' in Byatt's critical work, I will also pay attention to her views on post-structuralism. At the end of the 1960s, Byatt was present at the seminars Frank Kermode led on Barthes and (later) Derrida at University College London (UCL). From 1971 to 1983 she was a lecturer and then senior lecturer in English and American Literature at UCL. Here she experienced at first hand the changes in English Studies brought about by the post-structuralist and feminist theories of writing which were gaining prominence at English universities at the end of the 1970s and beyond. The question is why A. S. Byatt does not feel attracted to these two types of theories which succeeded Leavisite criticism. One might expect to see her own ambivalences towards 'Cambridge English' and Leavisite criticism converging with the theoretical assumptions and conclusions of the post-structuralist and feminist generation, but this is hardly the case. The question then becomes: what is at the heart of A. S. Byatt's resistance to the explicitly anti-Leavis theories of literature and criticism which feminists and post-structuralists developed? I am not raising this issue out of an uncritical enthusiasm for post-structuralism, but out of interest for what I perceive as the contradictions of Byatt's own position towards the practice of literary criticism. My questions therefore are: what stands between the academic and critic A. S. Byatt and feminist and post-structuralist theories? Why is she opposed to the portraits of writers which emerge from them while she shares their criticism of Leavisite criticism, of the school of literary thought she was academically trained in? Is it the case that the part of Leavisite criticism which *did* influence her made it difficult for her to agree with the basic tenets of feminist and post-structuralist theories of writing and literature? Can one speak therefore of a conflictual continuity between Leavisite criticism and Byatt's critical work? Considering, however, Byatt's own rather explicit rejection of the Cambridge-English school of criticism, it may be more suitable to speak of a sustained ambivalence in Byatt's relationship to Leavisite criticism. Her critical reactions towards the ideas about literature and writers expressed in Leavisite criticism, feminism and post-structuralism mean that she cannot occupy an unequivocal place to speak from as a critic.

A discussion of Byatt's critical work in the ways suggested above serves a dual purpose: first, as I already mentioned in the preface to this study I hope to counteract a narrow-minded image of the novelist-critic A. S. Byatt as somebody who is traditional, antitheoretical, high-brow and non-feminist or anti-feminist. Such terms only act as a straightjacket to the reader of her critical work. From a scholarly perspective it is impossible to place A. S. Byatt's work into one category. Secondly, a discussion of the critical trajectory followed by Byatt will enrich my readings of the connections between art, creativity and authorship in *The Shadow of the Sun, The Game* and *Possession* in subsequent chapters.

Leavisite criticism: literature, morality and the Great Tradition

When A. S. Byatt went to study English at Cambridge in the 1950s she must have known what kind of intellectual environment she was about to enter. Her mother had studied there in the late 1920s when Cambridge English was being established as a separate academic subject by pioneers such as Mansfield Forbes and F. R. and Q. D. Leavis. In one of her reviews Byatt refers to her mother's excitement at having been present at the birth of 'Cambridge English': 'my mother and her coevals certainly had a sense of sharing in a new, co-operative endeavour which brought language and thought to life'. In order to unravel what I can only describe as her daughter's ambivalence, I will first discuss the basic elements of this type of literary criticism.

F. R. Leavis attached an almost religious importance to the reading and studying of English literature. In order to understand this, one must see his ideas as part of a larger discussion about 'the condition of England', as Anne Samson has suggested.[7] In his capacity as a literary critic F. R. Leavis was a cultural theorist with bleak views on the dismal state of English society, of which the increasing number of women going to work was only one symptom. According to Anne Samson, Leavis saw this development as 'a sign of philistine times'. It is a classical point of conservatism that the dismal state of a society can be 'read off' the participation of women in its public life. Ironically, Q. D. Leavis – F. R. Leavis's wife – was allowed to be an exception to this rule.[8]

F. R. Leavis's ideas are part of a tradition of social criticism which encompasses writers such as Carlyle, Dickens, Ruskin and Arnold, the last name being most often associated with Leavis's criticism of the values of modern capitalist society. Leavis resembles Matthew Arnold in seeing 'the mechanical and human as opposed categories', that is, he held mechanization and industrialization responsible for the change from 'organic' modes of community to an inhuman mode of society riddled with problems.[9] Literature and the study of literature could function as the lighthouse leading society out of decline. Leavis believed in 'the idea of English as the one hope of renewal and growth in an otherwise irredeemable "mass-civilization" '.[10]

In raising literature and the study of literature on this pedestal, Leavis divorced both from the realm of politics, especially from the Marxist theories of cultural production which influenced debates in England in the 1930s. In 'Literature and Society', a lecture given to students at the London School of Economics in 1943, he maintained that literature yields the most valuable effect when it is approached as literature: it is of great importance to the sociological and political domain, but these fields are clearly separate and should not be conflated. In the same lecture he stresses that he does not believe in literature as a world in itself, as a purely literary domain.[11] It would be wrong to see Leavis as an adherent of the view that novels are autonomous works of art which only refer to themselves. Instead he constructs himself as the keeper of the faith in literature as the supreme repository of the lasting significance of English values and experiences, making his frame of reference a form of cultural national-ism.[12] The application of these terms is best illustrated by his famous study *The Great Tradition* in which he discusses the work of George Eliot, Henry James, Joseph Conrad and D. H. Lawrence.[13] According to Leavis, they are geniuses who make up the tradition of great English literature, because they are best at promoting 'human awareness' and 'the possibilities of life'.[14] Their work reveals 'a vital capacity for experience', 'a marked moral intensity' and 'a profound seriousness and urgent interest in life'.[15]

Leavis added to these a concept of 'impersonality' in T. S. Eliot's sense of the term. Eliot develops the concept of 'impersonality' to argue against theories which hold that art and writing are the direct expression of the artist's emotions and a direct reflection of the artist's personal life and biography. Eliot advocated non-biographical ways of reading which focussed on the poem instead of the poet. In 'Tradition and the Individual Talent' impersonality comes to mean that a 'good poet' is able to escape from the self, even destroy the self: 'the progress of an artist is a continual self-sacrifice, a continual extinction of per-sonality'.[16] F. R. Leavis adopts Eliot's concept of impersonality to praise Conrad and Austen and criticizes George Eliot's work for its lack of impersonality. I will come back to this.

These are the basic elements of the type of literary criticism F. R. Leavis advocated. His ideas about literature and writers are good examples of what Toril Moi calls the humanist type of literary criticism:

> The humanist believes in literature as an excellent instrument of education: by reading 'great works' the student will become a finer human being . . . the role of the reader or critic is to listen respectfully to the voice of the author as it is expressed in the text. The literary canon of great literature ensures that it is

this 'representative experience' which is passed on to future generations.[17]

The last element of this particular type of humanist literary criticism I want to mention here is a concept of the writer as genius. Toril Moi describes it as follows: 'the great author is great because he (occasionally even she) has managed to convey an authentic vision of life'.[18] This is, indeed, an apt gloss on F. R. Leavis's concept of the writer. Leavis also gives another twist to the old plot of the genius by emphasizing that this 'authentic vision of life' is intensely moral and therefore admirable. In his or her ability to develop such a vision the writer surpasses ordinary individuals, as Anne Samson notices:

> The writer, above anyone else, is uniquely qualified to judge his or her own world, and to reveal that world to itself, changing it into something different through the new consciousness s/he has created.[19]

Leavisite criticism and beyond

Some theorists would argue that the type of humanist criticism exemplified by F. R. Leavis saw its demise in the England of the 1990s. Anthony Easthope begins his book *Literary into Cultural Studies* with the assertion that the house of Leavis has already fallen down, like Jericho under the music: 'The old paradigm has passed ... "pure" literary study is dying ... a fresh paradigm has emerged [Cultural Studies], its status as such proven because we can more or less agree on its terms and use them'.[20]

Cultural Studies, post-structuralism, lesbian and gay studies, Marxist theories, feminism and Women's Studies, black studies, post-colonial criticism, deconstruction, reception theories, and psycho-analysis have all hammered away at the foundations of Leavisite criticism. The following assessment of F. R. Leavis by Robert Carver is representative of only one of the many kinds of criticism levelled at Leavis-inspired work:

> I always feel Leavis' theories have more to do with a very English type of moralism, almost making a secular religion from cultural

nationalism. There's a militant defensiveness about the True
Church of English literature which puts me in mind of
Savonarola: you felt Leavis would be quite happy to see the
heretics burn as well as their books. His life and his period of
influence spanned a time in which there was a great loss of
Christian faith in England, as well as a great loss of England's
international power and prestige . . . It's very Protestant, very
Puritan, very little England.[21]

Post-colonial critics have investigated how British culture asserted
its dominance in the colonies, thereby exposing the cultural nationalism inherent to Leavisite criticism.[22] Marxists have criticized
Leavisite criticism for its class-ridden assumptions, its elitism in the
advocation of the idea that because of their entrance to 'superior'
knowledge only a minority can pass on and explain the beauties of
high culture.[23] Feminists have pointed to the exclusionary practices
Leavisite criticism gave rise to, to its masculine values and the role
they play in canonizing literature and its disavowal of its own theoretical and political agenda.[24] Cultural Studies theorists have criticized the Leavisite opposition between 'high culture' and 'low
culture' as an untenable one.[25] Leavis's self-assurance about the
rightness and universal truth of his evaluative interpretations has
been replaced by deconstructionist doubts and the idea that reading
and writing are comparable forms of textual production.[26] The
strongest bastion of the Leavisite fort – the concept of literature as
'an authentic, realistic expression of human experience' – has been
criticized in all of the theories mentioned above, whether from a
feminist angle which reads 'human experience' in Leavisite criticism
as 'white middle-class male experience' or from post-structuralist
and deconstructionist angles which maintain that the 'authentic
expression of human experience' disguises the fact that subjectivity
is constituted in and through language and, consequently, is a
process without an essential core.

Given this historical and theoretical context, it is interesting to ask
what kinds of relationship exist between Leavisite criticism and
A. S. Byatt's critical work. Byatt herself describes it as a battle, and no
wonder: it sometimes seems as if the whole of British cultural theory is
fighting along *with* her. However, when one looks closer at the kind of
battle Byatt conducts with Leavisite criticism in her critical work, it

becomes clear that she is more ambivalent, not just about Leavisite criticism but also about the kind of theories that superseded it. It is possible to read her critical work as a space where Leavisite criticism and its predecessors meet in a contest about the proper function of reading and the academic study of literature. The debates concerning this issue and the influence of F. R. Leavis's ideas and like-minded literary critics are not over yet. It is true that undiluted Leavisite criticism has become an exceptional sight but it still casts its shadow over the theoretical landscape of the beginning of the twenty-first century.[27] Part of the interest of A. S. Byatt's critical work lies in the ways in which its textual strategies try to uphold a version of Leavisite criticism against theories of the Marxist, feminist and post-structuralist bent. At the same time Byatt's version of Leavisite criticism is in continuous danger of collapsing under the pressure exerted by 'gender', causing structural ambivalence in her critical work.

What one learns when young haunts one longest: A. S. Byatt as a Leavisite thinker

In a lecture given in 1991 A. S. Byatt said: 'what one learns when young haunts one longest', and certainly she encountered Leavis's Great Tradition with its emphasis on the importance of literature at a susceptible age. After more than thirty years, its effect is still evident. In 'Either a Borrower or a Lender Be', an article A. S. Byatt wrote for the *Guardian* we find her reacting against government plans for financial cuts in the budgets of British public libraries. Of course the large claims she makes for literature here partly have a polemical function. However, the Leavisite echoes are striking nonetheless. The article begins:

> If literature is the art in which the British excel, then the public libraries are the equivalent of the Tate, the Royal Opera House, the Barbican and the National Theatre . . . We are being told this week about the deficiencies in funding they face. We have been told in the past about how they must answer public demand for cassettes, CDs, videos and so on. These are all very good, but libraries are about books, and what is gained from books is quite different from what is gained from these other things, and of huge importance to our public and private lives.[28]

Placing public libraries and books on the same level as national monuments such as the Tate and its collection of modern art, Byatt implies that there is a common culture shared by the British as a people ('we have been told', 'our public and private lives').

The Leavisite overtones increase when Byatt explains why she thinks that literature is of huge importance. Like Leavis she thinks that reading literature is a way of living which contains more life, more thoughts and feelings, than a life spent not reading. This collapse of life into literature may seem escapist, exempting one from the trouble of everyday life. In A. S. Byatt's critical work, however, it has exactly the opposite effect. When looking back on her life as a young girl, she often mentions that as a child severely handicapped by asthma she spent most of her time reading in bed. She calls the illness which chained her to her bed a great blessing, which strongly indicates the importance she attaches to the books she read then. When she was slightly older she still continued to live in fantasies and myths of her own making. In 'The God I Want' she writes with humour about this period:

> At the age of six I lived almost continuously on a sandy island inhabited by an angry lion, a silver horse, twelve swans, Alexander the Great and myself. It is only just to point out – it is indicative, I am afraid, of my habit of mind – that if any of these creatures was God, it was myself.[29]

In everything Byatt writes about this period of her life, the centrality of literature to her mental well-being and to her sense of identity comes across. It was her way of living vicariously, of experiencing intensely the things of which her 'real' life was devoid. Literature and reading provided her with a knowledge of feelings and states of mind she was too young, and too restricted socially, to have access to:

> [To read] a story was to allow me explore those things I did not know about and was not constricted by, things I was desperately afraid of, or desperately needed. Its value was compensatory. In a story love and death were intensely meaningful and because they were unreal I myself was increased, satisfied, given a sense of discovery and power by undergoing them.[30]

Byatt learned to feel and think about life, sex, fear and desire from the literature she read by women writers: 'George Eliot gives one paradigms of sexual terror, Doris Lessing anatomizes dependence and independence. E. Arnot Robertson makes desire concrete'.[31] The dark sides of life acquired meaning in literature: A. S. Byatt was three years old when World War II started – her father spent five years away from his family – and she learned about insecurity, violence, panic and the fragility of life during the war. Narrative and stories helped her to see these feelings ordered, given a place in stories, mediated through narrative forms: 'I had been seduced by stories that made death seem meaningful and inevitable and acceptably final before anyone tried seriously to tell me that I had legitimate hopes of a resurrection'.[32] Literature was thus extremely important to her because of its double function: it gave her knowledge of feelings and states of mind barred from her by real life; at the same time, reading enabled her to disarm the fear and panic she truly felt by seeing them transformed by literature.

Byatt also thinks that 'to look at life from inside a story' in this way[33] – a decidedly Leavisite endeavour – has moral effects on the reader. She is intensely interested in questions of morality, especially how a de-secularized Western civilization fills the gap left behind by religion as a system of explanation. She is an agnostic who, rather than simply mourning old religious certainties, investigates their replacements from Victorian times to the present. She detects, for instance, a direct line from Victorian writers such as George Eliot and Alfred Tennyson, who struggled with the realization that religion and belief did not consist of God-given truths, to a contemporary world grappling with ways to define a 'post Christian aestheco-morality':[34]

> One of the things I most admire about Iris Murdoch is the way she understands that modern ethical debates about what is good – and whether it is possible to have any idea of good in an agnostic society – all our debates actually depend on the presence of the structure of Christian society in our world, whether or not we believe, whether or not we believe we have rejected Christianity . . . In the nineteenth century people began to think the unthinkable, that the Church might be simply about nothing . . . they were face to face with a kind of void.[35]

One of the ways in which this void may be filled is with the reading and writing of literature, both activities seen as fulfilling moral functions. This point of view can be traced back as far as Plato's *Republic* and has found adherents in writers such as Tolstoy, Murdoch and Ozick. In one interview Byatt acknowledged the direct line from the teacher F. R. Leavis to herself on this point, although she also qualified the statement somewhat: 'making works of art is moral. I'm Leavis' pupil to that extent. But it's primarily technical rather than moral'.[36] In the *Guardian* article cited above she expresses her views on the moral effects of literature in more definite terms:

> I have said that reading is private, as writing is private. I would argue that it reflects, and constructs, the inner life as nothing else does. It makes us into responsible individuals, and gives us a set of concepts and a complex language for understanding what is happening to us, exactly who we are, and what we are doing. (Such power also has its concomitant dangers, of course, of misunderstanding, of wrongheadedness. But at least it's not inert).[37]

Thus, when Byatt writes in her introduction to *Passions of the Mind* that she is in 'a sort of questioning quarrel with Leavis' vision and values' but also shares the latter, these are the two main similarities: the conviction that literature is and should remain of the utmost importance to a common culture, because we learn from it what it is to be human and to experience life in a meaningful way.[38] Secondly, reading and writing have moral effects in that these activities teach us to be morally better people and 'responsible individuals'.

Two further affinities between Leavis and A. S. Byatt concern their views on the 'impersonality' of the great writer and on the relationship between literature and politics. Byatt is adamant that writing should be 'impersonal', should be something other than an expression of the self:

> I spent most of my formative years as a writer, and indeed, as a literary critic, attempting to expunge the presence of the self, the presence of the 'I' from my idea of writing.[39]

She dislikes the idea of the writer as somebody who autobiographically expresses him- or herself in fiction and believes that writing serves as an escape from the self towards the imagination of other worlds, other people's minds, lives, feelings and thoughts. Much of her criticism of women's writing stems from this source. Byatt feels uncomfortable with what she detects as solipsistic tendencies in women's writing and expresses her criticism in terms which are I believe too general:

It is important for a writer to have a large canvas and plenty of characters, so that she can enter into other people's beings instead of just mirroring her own. That's one of the things I don't like about women's fiction, that it tends to concentrate on one or two main figures.[40]

Her critical work expresses a fear of solipsism and of writing as 'soliloqy' and favours 'ventriloquist' writers and poets such as Iris Murdoch, George Eliot and Robert Browning. Byatt explains her preference as follows:

I learned from Iris Murdoch that the kind of novel I like is the one in which there are several centres of consciousness and not just one, in which there are several ways of looking at the world, all of which have their own validity. I don't like the kind of single, intense voice, although there are great works of art which are in that form.
I've always had an instinctive dislike of the novel which is about one person only or has one central character.
[From George Eliot] I learned to invent a world peopled by a large number of interrelated people, almost all of whose processes of thought, developments of consciousness, biological anxieties, sense of their past and future can most scrupulously be made available to readers.[41]

A last similarity between Leavis and Byatt is the difficulty both have with literary theories which in their view conflate the category of 'aesthetics' with the domain of 'politics'. In 1986 A. S. Byatt agreed with those literary theorists who argued for a politically aware practice of reading. In 'Insights Ad Nauseam' she wrote, 'the proponents of political analysis of literature would argue rightly that there were always political assumptions implicit in the study of literary texts and it is best that these be brought into the open'.[42] In later years, however, her critical work shows that she changed her mind on this subject in ways which resemble F. R. Leavis's point of view. Leavis emphasized that literature could *as literature* be an important and relevant source of knowledge for sociology or politics, but that is the only relationship he could imagine, believing as he did in his critical work that the two domains could be kept apart. In 'Literature and society' there is not a trace of doubt about the incompatibility of literature and politics and as such the lecture reads as a clear and untroubled defence of the unpolitical virtues of 'High Culture'. A. S. Byatt also came to believe in the critical necessity of separating literature into a domain of its own and sees aesthetics and politics as two distinct categories of thought. She mentions often that she has felt very threatened by politically orientated literary theories and practices: 'the nature of criticism has changed a great deal since I wrote *Degrees of Freedom*. Critics have become very professional, politicized and relatively powerful, and writers have lost authority'. On 21 October 1993 she said in *The Late Show*:

> I had a terrible time in the seventies when people were laying down the law about things I ought no longer to be interested in and I still found them beautiful and interesting. I felt like a turtle that simply wanted to put its head into a shell when they threw the stones at it and think inside its shell, which is what I largely did.

The image of the turtle and its assocation with violence is typical of A. S. Byatt's observations on this subject. The image is relevant not only to her reaction towards politically orientated theories of literature, but also to her ideas about literary theory in general. Two of her main objections to the practice of contemporary academic literary theory and criticism are, first, that it is an aggressive power game and, secondly, that it bullies the reader intellectually. Byatt shares for instance Leavis's rejection of Marxist theories of literature and authorship. She views them as a threat to literature and great writers:

I am deeply troubled by the accusations of elitism that are levelled against anybody who really cares about the canon in the broadest sense as we have known it.

The culture is all fraying at the edges; a lot of powerful people in positions in teaching are saying that the canon of English literature must go and, anyway, literature doesn't matter; any piece of writing is as good as any other . . . It's the Marxist end of the teaching profession which really frightens me. It actually believes that what has been thought to be valuable in our literature was determined by class ideology and should therefore be knocked down and got rid of and expunged. You can do that very easily in a generation.[43]

This quote is striking for the way in which it dissolves all Marxist orientated types of theory – from Walter Benjamin to Terry Eagleton – into one model which is then rejected for its destructive nature. A. S. Byatt retains the Leavisite opposition between 'aesthetics' and 'politics' and therefore, ironically, accredits Marxist theories with enormous power in their ability to destroy the canon of English literature and the reputation of writers. The fact that Marxist theorists such as Terry Eagleton may spend as much time, attention and professional energy on (literary) texts as A. S. Byatt does, indeed, may take them as seriously as she does, is something that lies beyond the scope of Byatt's critical eye. It is, moreover, no coincidence that historical overviews of British literary criticism and cultural theory discuss Leavisite criticism and left-wing and Marxist theories in one breath.[44] Academic literary criticism is not exempt from the power games which always determine the distribution of knowledge, but I think that A. S. Byatt's Leavisite assumptions sometimes may lead her to perceive aggression where none is intended. A critic like Byatt, who feels that it is the task of the critic to deliver herself to the work of art, to listen quietly to it and understand what the writer 'intended' to do, is bound to recognize only violence in approaches which are less reverent towards literature than her own.[45]

Thus, A. S. Byatt has been strongly influenced by Leavisite criticism in her ideas about the great writer who is 'impersonal' in art, the moral importance of literature above other cultural products and the separation between a field of 'aesthetics' and a domain of 'politics'. The latter distinction underlies her rejection of Marxist literary theories and criticism. In other words, if one sees Byatt's critical work as an intellectual space where conflicting forces meet, the influence of Leavisite criticism acts as a stronghold against any effect Marxist ideas about literature and authorship might have had on A. S. Byatt's critical work. There is no ambivalence in her ideas about these theories and no room for a recognition of the fact that her own ideas and Marxist theories may have something in common, however small, such as the importance attached to art and the assumption that there is a relationship between morality and art.

This is, however, not the case for her reception of two other types of literary theories which have also influenced the British critical landscape: post-structuralist and feminist theories of literature and authorship. In the case of post-structuralism, Byatt acknowledges that its ideas about writing and authorship are relevant to her own thoughts. Her position is one of sustained ambivalence towards these theories. While explicitly acknowledging this ambivalence, at the same time the critical work attempts to solve it in a paradoxical way. That is, Byatt's ideas about post-structuralism are informed by two potentially conflicting speaking positions. The critic in her who affirms some aspects of post-structuralism can be juxtaposed with the 'threatened writer' who wants to defend Leavisite notions of writing and the writer. In the effort to negotiate these two conflicting positions, A. S. Byatt constructs a double-speaking position, one which is temporarily resolved when the writer 'wins' the argument. I will explain this process in my reading of 'Identity and the Writer', a lecture A. S. Byatt gave at the London-based Institute of Contemporary Art in 1986.

The self as philosopher and the self as writer: post-structuralism and 'the death of the author'

The ambivalence about post-structuralism that is present in Byatt's lecture 'Identity and the Writer' is informed by two potentially contradictionary positions. On the one hand, Byatt recognizes that there are similarities between post-structuralist ideas of authorship and the dislike she has, as a critic, of writing as the expression of 'the self'. Michel Foucault and Roland Barthes have criticized a concept of the author as the sole originator of meaning.[46] From their point of view the idea of the author as a solitary and unique individual who controls the meaning of the work of art he or she consciously produces is untenable. In his essay 'What Is an Author', Foucault makes the transition from concepts of 'the genius' and 'the author' to concepts of 'textuality' and 'readership'. Barthes also stresses the importance of the reader: 'the birth of the reader must be at the cost of the death of the author'.[47] In 'Identity and the Writer' A. S. Byatt recognizes the similarity between this critique of the author as the sole originator of meaning and her own dislike of 'the author' as somebody who narcissistically expresses herself in literature. Her aversion to solipsism and her belief that writing should serve as an escape from the self would seem to make her a natural ally of the post-structuralist critique of the author as genius who expresses himself in literature.

At the same time, however, the writer A. S. Byatt feels threatened by theories which postulate 'the death of the author' and accuses them of being aggressive towards the writer. Although she does not mention post-structuralism by name, I think that it is clearly implied in the following quote: 'a certain note of agression is common in many of the new critical disciplines, particularly towards the authors of the criticized texts who are not, in this world, their owners or originators'.[48] Elsewhere she accuses the new academic disciplines of a tendency to 'denigrate the maker of a work of art'.[49] Thus, *the critic* in A. S. Byatt begins her lecture 'Identity and the Writer' with a recognition of her own intellectual affinity with post-structuralist theories which criticize the paramount importance of 'the author'. *The writer* in Byatt feels threatened by the same post-structuralist criticism.

The step she takes to manage these opposing impulses is strikingly effective, albeit complex: she splits herself in two. She names the two components of her speaking position 'the self as philosopher' and 'the self as writer'. Thus, Byatt's statement in *Passions of the Mind* that she never felt a separation between her critical and narrative selves is qualified by 'Identity and the Writer'.[50] In this text, 'the self as philosopher' is aware that a concept of writing as the reflection and expression of an unmediated 'self' is problematic. 'The self as writer', however, is emphatic of the fact that thinking and writing do constitute 'identity'. Byatt recalls in her lecture how she was able as a very young child 'to constitute the person', that is, her sense of herself.[51] This memory is extremely important to her and goes back to the day when she was lying in a pram and on waking up became consciously aware of her own existence. She repeated the story in an interview with Tredell and in the television programme *The Brains Trust* when she was asked to describe her earliest memory:

> I remember lying on my back in my pram and making a visual construction of the edge of the pram and seeing the washhouse roof through it and the sky was blue above it and I thought 'I am here'. I must have been a baby because I had been put to sleep on the lawn in Sheffield before the war. I think of it almost every day because it was so clear and it was the moment when I thought 'I am here'.[52]

In 'Identity and the Writer' Byatt remarks that this sense of 'being there' informs the best of her writing: 'this memory is behind most of the moments when I'm quite sure what I'm doing in my work. It is to do with the working self'.[53] She maintains an 'I write therefore I am' approach, opposing the post-structuralist thought she affirms at the beginning of the lecture. In other words, Byatt simultaneously 'knows' two opposing things: first, that 'most of one's consciousness is a fiction and a tale' *and* secondly that she must defend her sense of herself as a writer against the insecurity brought about by this knowledge. In this defence her sophisticated references to post-structuralism give way to a rather oversimplified definition of post-structuralist notions of subjectivity:

> I, who was much beguiled by Eliot's idea of the impersonality of the artist, much beguiled by the idea that art was not self-expression but looking out and seeing other things which you were not, have had to bring back into my own thinking an idea, that if you have no self, there are certain things you cannot say.[54]

At the end of her lecture, 'the self as writer' A. S. Byatt wins the argument over 'the self as critic and philosopher' and resolves the ambivalence. That is, the affinity between post-structuralism and her own thought on authorship is affirmed and then again denied. There is of course the possibility that this is a rhetorical device, enabling Byatt to act out her ambivalence. Nonetheless, 'Identity and the Writer' is structured by a conceptual ambivalence which goes beyond the rhetorical. The sustained ambivalence is there at the end of the lecture, usually the place where, rhetorically, ambivalences are resolved. There Byatt defines her 'self' in ways which come close to post-structuralist thought: 'things go through us – the genetic code, the history of our nation, the language or languages we speak, the food we eat . . . the constraints that are put upon us, the people who are around us'. She is unable, however, to draw from this the conclusion that there is no 'unique individuality': 'and if we are an individual, it's because these threads are knotted together in this particular time and this particular place, and they hold'. Byatt wants to have it both ways – 'we are connected, and we are also a connection which is a separate and unrepeated object'.[55] But the concept of the artist which emerges at the end of her lecture is a traditional one. Byatt's heart-felt plea for the importance of a concept of writing as constitutive of 'identity' results in a defence of individualism, self-sufficiency, separation and isolation as creative strengths. From this follows a Leavisite definition of 'the artist' as

> someone who realizes his own separation and then starts framing and imagining the world. There isn't this desire to be fused into a collective.[56]

This traditional ending testifies to the legacy of Leavis. Byatt could have resolved her ambivalence towards post-structuralism in a different way. For instance, if read against the background of feminist thought about literature and authorship, Byatt's ambivalence about post-structuralism takes on a different meaning. Strong echoes of the feminist critique of post-structuralism and 'the death of the author' reverberate in 'Identity and the Writer', but Byatt's text makes no explicit reference to this. Many feminist critics recognize the relevance of post-structuralist thought to a dismantling of the concept of the writer as a genius. However, they also have difficulties in abandoning a concept of 'the author' altogether. That is, they recognize the potential overlap between feminist and post-structuralist critiques of traditional notions of the writer as 'genius', but they do not want to jettison the female identity of the writer into a post-structuralist void. They emphasize the importance of the fact that the author is a woman, while at the same time being aware of the dangers inherent in 'harbouring idealized, untheorized defenses of the fictions of (female) identity'.[57] What is at stake in these projects is a reinterpretation of the creative roles of women and of their presence in the art they make against post-structuralist proclamations of 'the death of the author'. Byatt does not quote feminist critics in her lecture and does not give the impression that she is aware of her being a woman writer whose 'working self' is gendered. I would like to suggest that if she had emphasized the importance of 'female identity' in her lecture instead of non-gendered 'identity', she would have had a place from which to criticize both traditional Leavisite notions of the writer as male genius and post-structuralist denials of authorship. This would have allowed her to reconcile the conflictual aspects of her thought. Again, do not mistake my position for an imposition of post-structuralist notions on Byatt's work. I am rather interested in developing a critical account of the contradictory yet highly productive ways in which Byatt's work moves across and in and out of the post-structuralist debate, tracing an itinerary of her own. In A. S. Byatt's work, more than in the average writer's, nothing is as authentic or central as her contradictions and her ambivalences.

The picture is further complicated when one looks at Byatt's critical opinions about feminist theories of literature and authorship. Here again one hears two voices. There is a voice in her work which consistently criticizes feminist literary theorists for the ways in which they use the concept of 'female identity' – a voice which defends a liberal humanist reaction to feminism. The other voice agrees that the concept of 'female identity' can be relevant to literary criticism.

A light in my darkness: gender disruption and feminist ambivalence

Let me begin to explain where one can find in A. S. Byatt's critical work a voice stressing the relevance of a concept of 'female identity' to literary criticism. The best place to hear it is in those parts of the critical work which deal with George Eliot's work. As a scholar and reviewer A. S. Byatt has devoted both passion and erudition to the explication and celebration of George Eliot's work. She co-edited a new edition of Eliot's essays for the Penguin classics and wrote a substantial introduction to it. She wrote 'George Eliot: a Celebration' and introductions to Eliot's novels *The Mill on the Floss* and *Middlemarch*.[58] Many of her reviews of books on Victorian writers and Victorian times are interspersed with references to George Eliot's life, work and intellectual background. When she writes in 'Either a Borrower or a Lender Be' that she knows George Eliot's 'inner life' better than she knows her husband's, one believes her.[59]

In her reception of Eliot's work, A. S. Byatt expresses a strong disagreement with Leavis's approach towards Eliot in *The Great Tradition*. Leavis *did* play a large part in the positive revaluation of George Eliot's work. She and her novels had acquired the reputation of being intensely old-fashioned and moralistic and Leavis's *Great Tradition* changed all that. In the process, however, George Eliot became impersonalized and thereby de-feminized. In her critical work on George Eliot, Byatt counters this critical move, not only by integrating 'the woman' Eliot with 'the artist' and 'the intellectual' but also by strongly identifying with her as a woman writer and a female critic.

Terry Lovell has pointed to the masculine imagery prevailing in Leavis's work, in which male teachers of literature are compared to 'missionaries, armies, warriors, crusaders'; 'a veritable secular church militant' as Lovell calls it. Given the fact that the readers and students of literature were mainly women, Lovell suggests that this masculine imagery served to dispel the danger of a feminization of literature.[60] A typical example of this phenomenon is the way in which F. R. Leavis turns George Eliot into a genius by 'de-feminizing' her – that is, by turning her into a non-woman. Leavis's distribution of praise and criticism of Eliot in *The Great Tradition* is structured along gender lines. He projects what he sees as George Eliot's creative 'weaknesses' unto her 'femininity'.

F. R. Leavis admires George Eliot most as an author when she is able to go beyond these 'weaknesses'. He splits George Eliot's 'genius' into two personae. One is the non-genius, the woman writer George Eliot who, according to Leavis, thwarts some of her novels by identifying with her women characters in ways that are far too autobiographical, personal, 'emotionally self-indulgent', 'immature' and 'self-ignorant'. Maggie Tulliver in *The Mill on the*

Floss, Dorothea Brooke in *Middlemarch* and Romola in the novel of the same title are all flawed in this way. According to Leavis, Maggie Tulliver is an 'idealized self-portrait': an immature girl portrayed by an immature novelist. Her lack of self-knowledge is the author's own.[61] The same argument underlies his criticism of the portrayal of Dorothea Brooke in *Middlemarch*. Leavis takes her to be the worst example of the author's 'unqualified self-identification' with her women characters:

> Dorothea is a product of George Eliot's own 'soul-hunger' – another day-dream ideal self. This persistence in the midst of so much that is so other, of an unreduced enclave of the old immaturity is disconcerting in the extreme. We have alternation between the poised *impersonal* insight into a finely tempered wisdom and something like the emotional confusions and self-importance of adolescence.[62]

The choice of words is telling: Leavis feels 'disconcert[ed] in the extreme' by Eliot's lack of impersonality. Moreover, not only does he feel disconcerted by what he sees as Eliot's uncritical identification with her heroines but also it is the emotional nature of the identification that embarasses him: 'We note it as an emotional quality, something that strikes us as the direct (and sometimes embarrassing) presence of the author's own personal need'.[63]

According to A. S. Byatt, 'embarassment' is the thing most feared by British critics. In 'Information in the Novel' she said: 'the cardinal virtue of the novel desiderated by English reviewers, some of whom are academics, is *not* to embarrass'. This observation is pertinent here, because the particular embarassment F. R. Leavis suffers from seems that of gender. It leads him to withdraw approval immediately when he thinks that he detects the 'personal needs' of *the woman* George Eliot 'directly' speaking through and in the text.

Leavis splits the personae of George Eliot in order to suppress that embarrassment: she becomes an impersonal artist and intellectual who is a genius because of her intelligence, her moral vision and the impersonal non-emotional distance she creates between herself as a writer and her characters. Leavis does approve of Mrs Transome in

Felix Holt for these reasons. It is an impersonal portrait which is not based on identification: 'the beneficent relation between the artist and intellectual is to be seen in the new *impersonality* of the Transome theme . . . She has not here, it will be noted, a heroine with whom she can be tempted to identify herself'.[64] Leavis reserves his unqualified admiration for George Eliot's portrait of Gwendolen Harleth in *Daniel Deronda*. Gwendolen is an example of Eliot's art at its 'maturest', a compliment reinforced by Leavis's comparison with Henry James's Isobel Archer in *Portrait of a Lady*. He declares George Eliot the better writer:

> As a very intelligent woman she is able, unlimited by masculine partiality of vision and only the more perceptive because a woman, to achieve a much completer presentment of her subject than James of his.[65]

This seems to counteract my argument that Leavis shrinks back at what he sees as the 'feminine quality' of Eliot's writing. Here he seems to see it as a positive aspect of her 'genius'. However, on closer inspection the compliment turns out to be backhanded for it applauds Eliot for creating an unsympathetic and selfish character in Gwendolen: 'for George Eliot the essential significance of Gwendolen's case lies in the egoism expressed here'.[66] Eliot judges Gwendolen's pre-occupation with self severely according to Leavis and, therefore, her vision of Gwendolen is more complete, disinterested and realistic than Henry James's 'indulgence' towards Isabel Archer. And she does not represent 'any possibility of the Dorothea relation to the novelist', an asset F. R. Leavis rates highly.

Leavis's evaluation of Eliot's work is based on a clear scheme of oppositions: on the one hand, there is the woman writer George Eliot who is feminine, personal, emotional, self-indulgent in her identification with her women characters. On the other hand, there is the genius George Eliot who is intelligent, impersonal, disinterested, and able to transcend her 'femininity' and the accompanying emotional quality which is 'insidious company to her intellect'.[67] Leavis's reception of Eliot's work fits Dorothea Barret's account of conservative interpretations of George Eliot which 'have tradition-ally stressed the intellectual in her work . . . seeing her in fact as an honorary man'. Leslie Stephen's inclusion of George Eliot in his book *English Men of Letters* is a case in point.[68] However, Barrett also mentions the alternative approach to Eliot's work: 'it was only through stressing her femininity . . . that it was possible to uncover her radicalism'.[69]

This is an apt hermeneutical key to assess what Byatt achieves in her critical work on George Eliot. At first sight A. S. Byatt seems to concur with Leavis's de-feminization of George Eliot. Her two essays on George Eliot in *Passions of the Mind* come under the heading 'Victorians' and are not included in the section 'The Female Voice?'.[70] This suggests that it is not important that George Eliot is a woman, that she is somehow different from the women writers Byatt discusses: Barbara Pym, Monique Wittig, Elizabeth Bowen, Georgette Heyer and Toni Morrison. However, this may be misleading, as we shall see. In her work on George Eliot, Byatt adopts a feminist view of Eliot's work and character, in explicit opposition to F. R. Leavis. Leavis tells half the story by splitting George Eliot into a woman and a genius. A. S. Byatt gives a much more rounded view of Eliot, because she presents as one integral figure the passionate woman, the artist, the intellectual and the genius. For one thing, Byatt is not embarrassed by Eliot's passion and emotionality but admires her intensely for it. Byatt sees the passion and the emotionality in Eliot's fiction as forms of positive energy, agreeing with Lerner that 'the Leavis standard of maturity underestimates the positive value of Dorothea's impulsiveness and emotional energy'.[71] In her introduction to Eliot's *Mill on the Floss* Byatt emphasizes that Eliot was quite unique in understanding the importance of sexual energy and desire in people's lives: 'of all the great English nineteenth-century novelists George Eliot best understood and presented the imperative need to come to terms with, to recognize, sexual energy and sexual desire'.[72] In 9 February 1994 edition of *The Late Show* on the BBC screening of *Middlemarch* Claire Tomalin said the same: 'George Eliot writes about sex perfectly and she never mentions it, which is always the best way to write about it. What is sex is the feeling'. Hermione Lee is another critic who, with Byatt and Tomalin, emphasizes Eliot's skill at writing about sexuality: 'Although everyone goes on about the conventions of Victorian novels, Eliot is terribly good at sex . . . [she] is truthful and authentic about the illogicality of sexuality'.[73] Byatt's admiration of the ways in which Eliot describes sexual energy and passion shows itself in her defence of Eliot's male characters, especially the ones denounced by male critics for their effeminacy. Leavis dismisses both Will Ladislaw and Daniel Deronda as 'non-men'. In an appendix to *The Mill on the Floss* Byatt refers to Leavis when she writes that George Eliot has been unlucky in her readers. Byatt, in contrast, defends the sexual interest which the passionate Dorothea Brooke and Maggie Tulliver have in Stephen Guest and Will Ladislaw: '[Stephen] is the literary descendant of other energetic, simple, sexually powerful men in novels who create quite complex problems for women whose alternative lovers are perhaps more sensitive, but less alive, forceful and exciting'. She argues that Stephen Guest arouses in Maggie Tulliver 'a hope of released physical energy, freedom, a normal life'. At the same time Byatt maintains that Eliot is more critical of Stephen than her critics give her credit for.[74]

Apart from admiring this neglected aspect of Eliot's work, Byatt also overrides her dislike of autobiographical writing as solipsistic, frequently pointing to the similarities between George Eliot's restricted life as a girl and the way she portrays Maggie Tulliver in *The Mill on the Floss*. She likes the autobiographical quality of the novel: 'it is all very well and proper for Dr Leavis to point out that George Eliot in Maggie Tulliver was paying back her own grief – but part of Maggie's life came from that too'.[75] She also takes issue with Leavis's reading of *Daniel Deronda*. While he emphasizes Gwendolen's egoism, Byatt stresses how successful Eliot is in describing the sexual terror Gwendolen experiences. In *Imagining Characters*, Ignes Sodre and A. S. Byatt bring out the ambivalence in Gwendolen's portrait, with Byatt stressing that she is 'selfish' and 'unpleasant' but also a victim: 'in many ways, of all our heroines, Gwendolen is possessed of the most energy and gets the most stopped'. Byatt recognizes in Gwendolen's fate the disadvantage of the fact that for a woman in the nineteenth century 'destiny was your sex'.[76]

Another important difference between A. S. Byatt and F. R. Leavis's reception of Eliot's work is that Eliot is the kind of intellectual and writer A. S. Byatt identifies strongly with as a woman and a writer. It goes further than appreciation – love is a more adequate word for it – and Byatt expresses it unreservedly. In the same *Late Show* both Claire Tomalin and A. S. Byatt were visibly proud of George Eliot. Tomalin explained why 'every intellectual woman warms to George Eliot',

A. S. Byatt criticized one-dimensional portraits of Eliot as a writer who is serious, moralistic and too intelligent. In the programme she constructs a more inclusive portrait of Eliot: 'the glory of George Eliot is that she is comic, intelligent, ferociously passionate and deeply sexy'. Like Leavis, she appreciates Eliot's serious side but she presents a more complete portrait of the 'other' George Eliot: the woman who was unconventional, trenchantly witty and sarcastic, who wrote and thought with intense energy and passion:

> One's idea of George Eliot is of a woman whose appearance of profound moral scrupulousness, self-discipline and intellectual rigour was not an illusion but a partial truth. She was also passionate, violent, very fierce and as extraordinarily rapid and energetic intellectually as she was minute and exact.[77]

Byatt uses feminist arguments in defending Eliot's work against the accusation that it is too intellectual or that Eliot is too intelligent for her own good. In *The Late Show* she said:

> The accusation of being too intelligent is one that is usually levelled at women and very rarely levelled at men. I do not know of any essay which says that Marcel Proust was too intelligent. What happens to intelligent women – and it still happens – is that, if you are known to be serious, if you are known to have done a lot of hard thinking, it is not supposed that you could have a sense of humour, that you could rumbustuously go off and write a passionate scene, because if you are intelligent you will not be passionate.

I want to suggest, furthermore, that this feminist argument is partly informed by identification. Byatt often compares herself to Eliot when she talks about the construction critics have made of both of them:

> I think the critics do have an idea of me as a kind of solemn intellectual woman who teaches in the university. I think somehow a sort of very simple label of the intellectual one, which means the not creative one, got attached, because the English do not like the word intellectual . . . I had a colleague

who is a South-African novelist, male, who once set an exam question on George Eliot which went: 'George Eliot is a gaunt moralistic dame. Discuss'. I said 'this isn't a question, how can you discuss it?' He said: 'of course it is, it is an accurate description'. I feel I get *that*.[78]

Thus, although A. S. Byatt has expressed reservations about the ways in which feminist criticism has established a female tradition of women writers, she acknowledges that she herself identifies strongly with Eliot. When the *Guardian* asked her with which historical figure she identified most, she mentioned Eliot 'because she thought like fury and wrote with passion, and worried a lot and got better and happier as she aged'.[79] Byatt constructs George Eliot as the literary predecessor she has learned most from:

And I, *as a woman writer*, am grateful that she stands there, hidden behind the revered Victorian sage, and the Great English tradition – a writer who could make links between mathematical skill and sexual inadequacy, between Parliamentary reform and a teenager's silly choice of a husband, between Evangelical hypocrisy and medical advance, or its absence.[80]

Clearly, A. S. Byatt's critical work on George Eliot can easily be read as feminist, not only in its explicit reaction to *The Great Tradition* in the way it emphasizes Eliot's gender but also in Byatt's strong identification with George Eliot as a woman writer and critic.

However, the feminist voice in Byatt's critical work is often drowned by another one. The structural ambivalence which is inherent to Byatt's ideas about the concept of 'female identity' comes from this troubled source. On the one hand, she projects her own feminism onto the nineteenth century in idealizing George Eliot as a model to identify with as a woman writer and critic. On the other hand, feminist theorists who emphasize the importance of 'gender' to theories of art and concepts of creative identity typically come in for heavy condemnation in Byatt's criticism. Going against the grain of Byatt's own work on George Eliot, these parts of her critical work express a disagreement with the ways in which contemporary feminist theorists and writers hold on to a feminist concept of 'female identity'. This voice is only able to define this emphasis as a limitation: 'I'm very interested in the limitations on human thought that are imposed by people seeing themselves so primarily as sexual beings'.[81]

For Byatt wants to keep writing and thinking apart from 'gender'. In a fascinating interview with Nicolas Tredell she said that as a young woman in the 1950s she hoped to

> possibly manage to be both at once, a passionate woman and a passionate intellectual, and efficient, if you just switch gear and switch gear from one to the other, but if you let them all run together organically, something messy would occur and you would get overwhelmed.[82]

She uses the word 'lamination' to explain her desire to keep these layers of identity – the passionate woman and intellectual – apart. This kind of lamination can, I believe, be compared to the step Byatt takes in 'Identity and the Writer': as I explained earlier she splits herself in two in order to try and reconcile two conflictual speaking positions towards post-structuralism. When it comes to feminist concepts of 'identity' a similar process is at work, in that 'lamination' allows Byatt to keep 'gender' apart from thinking and writing. 'The woman' and 'the intellectual' are in different categories of identity. Byatt describes 'lamination' as 'a strategy for survival' which goes a long way to explain how difficult it must have been for her to reconcile her identity as a woman with her intellectual aspirations in the 1950s.

In this context references to the gender of an author can only be taken as a lapse into restrictions and limitations. Instead, Byatt argues that the act of writing enables the woman writer to escape from 'the limits of being female' into a universalistic position, as she said in an interview: 'literature has always been my way out, my escape from the limits of being female. I don't want to have to get back in'.[83] This is the reason she often refers to Virginia Woolf's concept of androgyny:

> As a sixteen-year old I'd sat in the coal-hole of my boarding-school in the small hours reading *A Room of One's Own* by the light of the coal-furnace I'd illegitimately opened. At sixteen I'd seen it as a plea for female independence, and so it was. It was a

light in my darkness. But in my twenties and thirties I found myself more and more returning to Virginia Woolf's elegant dictum 'it is fatal for anyone who writes to think of their sex' . . . I think myself, if you're interested in art rather than in propaganda, this is a crucial thing to remember.[84]

Thus, Byatt makes use of Woolf's theory of the writer as androgynous to reinforce her own conviction that 'gender' should not be of relevance in writing and literary criticism. Byatt is, therefore, far removed from a feminist critic such as Showalter who accuses Woolf of denying the importance of female experience or a critic such as Toril Moi who uses Woolf's theory of androgyny for deconstructive and feminist purposes.

As a consequence of her identification of female identity with limitation, the critic A. S. Byatt is unable to understand why young feminist writers and feminist literary theorists would want to hold on to the concept. She calls the influence feminism has on young women writers 'a disaster' for the quality of their work.[85] As a judge for Granta's Best of Young British Novelists campaign, she expressed a dissatisfaction with the work of young women writers. Although she praises the work of specific writers such as Anne Billson, Esther Freud, Jeanette Winterson and A. L. Kennedy, her argument is marred by a lapse into generalizations and a rather ungenerous dismissal of young writers. By focussing on what Byatt decribes as 'the problem of sexuality, gender, disadvantage', women cripple their writing and impose a limitation on the subject of their novels that is 'narcissistic and sado-masochistic'.[86] In her view, their subject matter makes their novels aesthetically uninteresting. In an interview with Aragay the criticism is similarly harsh: 'there isn't one woman writer now under 40–45 that people could honourably be writing about as the best writer'.[87] This criticism is not only informed by a generational gap but also by A. S. Byatt's Leavisite assumptions about literature. The few feminist critics Byatt approves of – Elaine Showalter, Ellen Moers and Gilian Beer – are exempt from her criticism because they explain comprehensively the quality and interest of writing by women. Byatt judges their work by Leavisite standards: they show that when it comes to the making of good art, female writers are just as good or better than male writers.

In its evaluation of the work of young feminist writers Byatt's critical work overlooks the possibility that they have ideas about 'female identity' which differ from her own. There are young feminist writers who use fiction to look at 'female identity' from many directions, to think through it, and find ways out of it or subvert it from within. In this fictional practice 'gender' may serve as a microscope through which to investigate the world anew. Instead of viewing the concept as a point of ending, as a limitation, they may have chosen the problematics of 'female identity' as an enabling subject: 'no trap there, but a world opening' to use Byatt's words about English detectives by women writers. In other words, they refuse to consider the subject of 'female identity' as a depressing end to their fictional investigations or imaginative freedom. They see it as the beginning, as an enabling literary subject. For in the fictional criticism of old images lies the reconstruction of new tales of female identity.

Conclusion

I have discussed the many voices which address the reader of Byatt's critical work and the sustained ambivalence resulting from their interplay. They are, at different levels, divided within themselves: as we have seen, the first and most dominant speaker in her critical work is the Leavisite thinker. Yet this thinker who feels that her foundations are threatened by politically orientated theories, like Marxist theories of writing, coexists with the critic and essayist A. S. Byatt who recognizes that another anti-Leavis theory – post-structuralism – is relevant to her ideas. There is a convergence of interests between Foucault's critique of 'the author' as the sole originator of meaning and her own dislike of 'the author' as somebody who narcissistically expresses him/herself in literature. Her fear of solipsism and her belief that writing should serve as an escape from 'the self' should make her a natural ally of the post-structuralist critique of the author as genius who expresses himself in literature.

However, the voice of the writer intervenes. If the writer believes, like the critic, that post-structuralism is relevant, she will not be able to speak anymore from 'the self', or so the writer fears. Instead Byatt saves 'her self' by falling back on an image of the writer which is clearly Leavis-inspired. Therefore, it is the case that the part of

Leavisite criticism which *did* influence her has barred her from an agreement with the basic tenets of post-structuralist theories of writing and literature. For Byatt counteracts post-structuralism by defending the concept of creative identity, a concept which she equates with individualism, self-sufficiency, separation and isolation; in short, with a concept which bears more than a superficial similarity to the writer as 'genius'.

'Gender' does not play a role in 'Identity and the Writer', although it could have done. Feminist critiques of the post-structuralist 'death of the author' also hold on to a concept of 'identity' even though it is fraught with conceptual difficulties. A. S. Byatt is aware of these aspects of feminist thought: both of the feminist reliance on 'identity' and its difficulties. She knows that the paradox of feminist thinking is 'that our very self-definition is grounded in a concept that we must de-construct and de-essentialize in all of its aspects'.[88] Her critical work also emphasizes the relevance of 'gender' and 'female identity' in its criticism of F. R. Leavis. She uses feminist arguments in defending George Eliot against F. R. Leavis's interpretation, because she thinks that Leavis damages Eliot's greatness by de-personalizing and de-feminizing her. Moreover, A. S. Byatt also strongly identifies with George Eliot as a woman writer and a female critic.

However, as I have shown, this feminist voice is qualified by another one. Byatt's point of exit from the paradox of feminist thinking has the result that she distances herself from feminist critics and writers. Her point of exit is to be found in her definition of the great writer: it leads her argument into the area of undifferentiated literary greatness and narrows her view of women's identity to a limitation only. The critical work disavows any similarities between the work of young feminist writers and her own writing practice. Thus, there is a creative tension between the critical voice using feminist arguments to write about George Eliot, while criticizing feminism severely.

It follows from the argument developed above that A. S. Byatt's critical work partly exemplifies the relevance of the very poststructuralist thought it is so ambivalent about. As Belsey and Moore argue, post-structuralist theories of identity conceptualize the subject as 'inevitably split, unfixed, in process'.[89] Or as Donna Haraway defines it: 'the topography of subjectivity is multidimensional. The knowing self is partial in all its guises, never finished, whole, simply there and original; it is always constructed and stitched together imperfectly . . .'[90] The readings of Byatt's criticism suggested in this chapter are intended to prove the relevance of this argument. My discussion of the polyvocal aspects of Byatt's critical ideas about art, authorship and creativity does indeed lead to a notion of writing and the writing subject which depends on concepts such as fragmentation, ambivalence, complexity and gender. With these concepts in mind I will now make the transference to three of A. S. Byatt's novels: *Shadow of a Sun* (1964), *The Game* (1967) and *Possession* (1991). What are the differences and similarities between the ideas about writers, authorship and gender expressed in Byatt's critical work and her portraits of writers and of literature in these novels?

2
The Shadow of the Sun: The Lady of Shalott or the Writer as Genius

' "Sometimes", she said carefully, "I think perhaps I have no limitations". "And that is when you are most limited", Oliver said'.[1]

The anxiety of the author: looking back on writing *The Shadow of the Sun*

The source for this first chapter on A. S. Byatt's *The Shadow of the Sun* is its 1991 reprint, an edition which is quite unique.[2] It is the only novel A. S. Byatt has hitherto written a foreword for and is a fascinating text when read against the background of her critical work and the ideas she expresses about literature, authorship, gender and creative identity. The preceding chapter showed that it would be a misrepresentation of her critical work to see Byatt as somebody who is a strong advocate of feminist views on these subjects. Her work expresses too much ambivalence to warrant such a statement, though the ambivalence is also directed to Leavis-style moralism and post-structuralism. However, the foreword to her first novel is surprisingly unambivalent in its feminist analysis of the questions and problems she encountered as a female novelist in England in the 1950s. In other words, she uses the foreword to explore fully the subject about which she is so reserved in her critical work. It is one of the few texts in which A. S. Byatt discusses at length what it meant to her and to her writing that she was an ambitious woman writer in the 1950s.

When she wrote it in 1991 she did so as a successful novelist who had recently won two important awards for her widely translated bestseller *Possession*. It seems a comfortable position from which to look back at a much younger self on the brink of authorship: A. S. Byatt was 18 when she wrote the first draft of *The Shadow of the Sun*. It is a position which seems to allow for an untroubled distance from which to assess the genesis of one's writing career.

It is indeed possible to read the foreword as a condensed *Bildungsroman*, with a clear beginning, middle and end. At the beginning of this story of creative progress Byatt mentions her conviction that she wanted to be a writer: she was 'someone who *had* to write'. In the middle of the narrative she explains the problems and obstacles she had to overcome in order to be able to write at all and in order to legitimize her chosen profession. The end of the foreword records how she managed to write through the obstacles: 'but I did go on from there'. The last sentence of the foreword neatly connects the ending to her beginnings by noticing the similarities between the images she uses in *The Shadow of the Sun* and her later novels: 'It is interesting to reflect, looking back at those first suns, moons and corn how instinctively they were found, how long, although I had all the material for doing so, they took to understand and work out'.[3]

The structure of the foreword – genesis, blockage, and release – is a traditional one and lends itself well to a descriptive account of a writing career. What makes the text interesting and so unlike Byatt's critical work is the distribution of space and weight over the three separate stages. Judging from A. S. Byatt's critical work and from her position as an established novelist, one would expect her to emphasize in this autobiographical foreword the importance of the creative genesis – 'I had to write' – and the creative release into literature – 'but I did go on from there'. The middle stage of blockage would be interesting as a means to an end, the end being literature, and, therefore, less important. In the foreword, however, genesis and release are only accorded a few sentences while Byatt devotes six of the nine pages to a feminist analysis of the story of blockage.

At the beginning of her career, Byatt says, she was not at all certain whether she would be able to negotiate the conflicting meanings of 'woman' and 'novelist' in 1950s English society. England in that period was a difficult environment for any woman who aspired to the status of novelist. In an interview, the writer Michèle Roberts, who is 13 years younger than Byatt and experienced the fifties as a child, has spoken of 'the narrow fifties when it seemed monstrous for girls to want to be writers, and I felt a monster because I wanted to create'.[4] A. S. Byatt does not call her need to write monstrous, but in comparison with her critical work the foreword is refreshingly outspoken about the fact that it felt like a deviant desire. Both as a student at Cambridge where women were a minority – 'the men outnumbered us eleven to one' – and as an aspiring writer, she felt she did not conform to the norm and as a result was insecure about her chosen field. In the foreword Byatt puts the blame for her insecurity mainly on the shoulders of two people: her mother and F. R. Leavis. Leavis's theory of literature seemed to block Byatt's path to a writing career with great aesthetic and moral obstacles while her mother's strong suspicion of literature also influenced her negatively. As a consequence, she was insecure about her ability to carry off her first novel successfully:

> It is the novel of a very young woman, a novel written by someone who had to write but was very unsure whether she should admit to wanting to write, unsure even whether she ought, being a woman, to want to write (p. viii).[5]

What strikes me in these words is the distance they convey – as if Byatt is referring to another writer instead of to her younger self – while at the same time the foreword re-enacts the fear, struggle, pain and anxiety she felt at the time of thinking about and writing the first draft of *The Shadow of the Sun*:

> Reading it now [in 1991], or skimming it and remembering it, I re-experience a kind of fear . . . I always knew . . . that I must contrive to work (to think, to write). It's only now, looking back, that I see how furtive, how beleaguered, how publicly improper, I imagined this contriving was going to have to be (p. viii).[6]

Throughout the foreword such feelings are out in the open, raw on the page as it were. What dominates the foreword, though – what structures it thematically – is the theme of loneliness. It is related to the fact that, as a woman, Byatt experienced at first hand the effects of being excluded from academic pursuits because of her sex. At Cambridge she was working on a doctoral thesis on Neoplatonic creation myths, but had to give up her research and writing when she married. Her own mother before her had had to give up a career as a teacher at the end of the war when 'normal' society resumed its course. Byatt's mother acted out her frustration on her children who, as a result, were determined to lead different lives. However, Byatt's grant was taken from her upon her marriage – 'men in my position had their grants increased, to provide for their households' (p. ix). When she moved to Durham with her husband she did manage to finish *The Shadow of the Sun*, but under stressful circumstances:

> I was a very desperate faculty wife in Durham. I had two children in two years – I was 25, and thought I was old, 'past it'. I was surrounded by young men who debated in an all-male union from which the women students were excluded, though there was nowhere else for them to meet. I was lonely and frightened . . . (p. xiii).[7]

The second level of loneliness is the one which any writer has to consider. The ways in which one views oneself and one's work as part of a tradition determines partially whether one feels at home in 'the house of fiction'.[8] The critic A. S. Byatt does not have one particular home to write in. The complexity and structural ambivalence inherent to her views on literature, authorship and gender make it impossible to place her critical work into one category or within the boundaries of one critical school. Judging from the foreword, the young *writer* A. S. Byatt also had difficulties in carving a niche for herself in a writing tradition. Looking back at the beginning of her work as a novelist, she sets herself outside the tradition by emphasizing that there were hardly any writers she admired. In their influential study *The Madwoman in the Attic* Sandra Gilbert and Susan Gubar, criticizing Harold Bloom's theory of 'the anxiety of influence', point out that in assimilating the influences of their predecessors, women authors may find the burden of literary history more difficult to bear than male authors:

> The anxiety of influence that a male poet experiences is felt by a female poet as an even more primary 'anxiety of authorship' – a

radical fear that she cannot create, that because she can never become 'a precursor' the act of writing will isolate or destroy her.[9]

Authors have a myriad ways of dealing with the fear that they may have nothing to add to the tradition. One of these ways is a denial or strong dissatisfaction with the work that was created before them. In the foreword, A. S. Byatt mentions that, apart from being an ambitious woman in the restrictive society of the 1950s, she also had a literary problem. She felt she lacked literary models which she could adopt as an aspiring writer. The young A. S. Byatt disliked novels by male writers such as John Wain and Kingsley Amis for their social comedy. She does mention the great influence D. H. Lawrence's work had on her – an influence she could not escape – but in the same breath she says in the foreword that she could not 'love' him as a writer 'partly because I was a woman' (p. xii).[10] The work of women writers available to her in the 1950s – novels by Virginia Woolf, Elizabeth Bowen, Rosamund Lehmann, etc. – she found wanting. She was dissatisfied with women's novels of the nineteen fifties because she thought they were 'too suffused with "sensibility" ' (p. xi). Although A. S. Byatt writes that she felt a 'vague dissatisfaction' with Bowen and Lehmann's work at that time, she is in fact far more explicit about her rejection of their fiction: 'there is no female art I can think of that is like what I wanted to do' (p. x).[11] In this sense the young A. S. Byatt is an exception to Gilbert and Gubar's observation that in order to overcome the anxiety of authorship women writers sought female precursors 'who far from representing a threatening force to be denied or killed, [prove] by example that a revolt against patriarchal literary authority is possible'.[12] It is only later in her career that Byatt became outspoken about her strong admiration for other novelists like George Eliot, Marcel Proust, Willa Cather, Alice Munro and Iris Murdoch.[13] At the time of writing *The Shadow of the Sun* she was only certain about her admiration for Coleridge's work and she did not have women writers as role models.[14]

This is the image of the aspiring writer to emerge from the foreword to *The Shadow of the Sun*: the young writer A. S. Byatt closes herself off from literary tradition and as an ambitious woman has difficulties in constructing her identity as a novelist in the 1950s – so much so that 30 years later these difficulties strongly dominate her feminist memories of her beginnings. Given this problematic background, it is no wonder that A. S. Byatt says in the foreword that the 'battle' of writing her first novel 'fought itself out between sexuality, literary criticism, and writing' (p. xiii). The focus of my reading of *The Shadow of the Sun* is how this battle shaped itself narratively. I want to know what happens when such a young and desperate novelist goes right to the heart of her creative anxieties by writing an artist-novel in which the main characters are a male writer and a seventeen-year-old girl – the writer's daughter – who is herself an aspiring writer and one year younger than A. S. Byatt when she began to write *The Shadow of the Sun*. What theories of creative identity, authorship and art can one infer from A. S. Byatt's portraits of these people?

Introducing *The Shadow of the Sun*

A. S. Byatt's debut tells the story of a very hot summer and a stormy autumn in the life of a creative family in the North of England. The novel is divided into two parts. In the first part the characters are introduced: Caroline Severell is married to Henry Severell, a famous novelist. They have two children – Jeremy and Anna. Anna, who is 17 years old, is living at home after having been expelled from her boarding school for running away to York. She has a lot of time on her hands to consider her future; becoming a novelist is one of her options. The Severell family is joined by Margaret Canning and her husband Oliver Canning. Oliver Canning works at Cambridge University and is an expert on Henry Severell's work. During the period they stay with the Severells it is too hot to do much. Anna takes Oliver to see the stable where she has worked and spends time with him tentatively preparing for her eventual acceptance by Cambridge University. Her mother Caroline and Margaret Canning run the household together and talk. Her father Henry works in his study and leaves the house once for a long walk, his way of thinking out creative problems.

The heat continues to dominate the weather and tensions between the characters come to the surface. The writer Henry Severell and the critic Oliver Canning disagree about Oliver's reception of Henry's work. Margaret Canning worries about the problematic state of her marriage to Oliver. Anna is undecided about her future as the daughter of a famous writer; her mother and Oliver urge her to make up her mind. The first part of the novel ends when guests and family go on a seaside picnic. This is the last activity they undertake together, for during the night following the picnic a storm breaks. Anna, who is waiting in the bathroom for this to happen, is unexpectedly joined there by Oliver. He kisses her for the first time. The next morning the weather changes permanently to autumn; Oliver and Margaret Canning return to London where they live.

At the beginning of the second part of the novel Anna has been accepted at Cambridge and has a relationship with Peter Hughes-Winterton, one of her fellow students. She meets Oliver Canning again after a party when she is drunk, and spends the night with him. They start a secret affair. Unknown to Anna, Oliver's marriage to Margaret deteriorates so rapidly that Margaret has a nervous breakdown. Margaret writes to Henry and begs him to help her save her marriage. Reluctantly Henry goes to Cambridge to talk to Oliver, but he visits Anna first and finds out about the affair his daughter is having with Oliver. His mission fails miserably. Both Anna and Oliver become angry at Henry for meddling in their affairs and he leaves Cambridge without having achieved anything.

Anna does put an end to her affair with Oliver and then finds out that she is pregnant. Although she wants an abortion, Peter persuades her that the best thing she can do is marry *him*. She gives up her study, leaves Cambridge and stays at Peter's parental home to prepare herself for the wedding. She writes to her father, informing him about her plans and tells him that she has no intention of coming home again. Upon hearing this news from Henry, her mother summons Oliver to the house and tells him about Anna's pregnancy. Oliver phones Anna and after one final conversation with Henry, who dismisses him, he leaves for York. On the last page, just as Anna has decided not to marry either Peter or Oliver, the latter catches up with her in the lounge of a hotel. They discuss what to do next and at this inconclusive point the novel ends.

Samson among the women: the sublime and the writer as male visionary

The theory of creative identity and authorship which A. S. Byatt investigates in her portrayal of Henry Severell and Anna Severell, posits the writer as a visionary genius who creates through a 'sublime' experience. In her foreword Byatt refers to her idea of the writer as visionary: she describes her younger self as somebody 'who saw every-thing too bright, too fierce, too much . . . This vision of too much makes the visionary want to write – in my case – or paint, or compose, or dance or sing' (p. x). The other pole of my investigation – 'the sublime' – she does not mention in the foreword. A. S. Byatt has never talked or written about her first novel in these terms. Nor does she mention the eighteenth-century theory of 'the sublime' to which I will refer, Edmund Burke's *Philosophical Enquiry in the Origin of our Ideas of the Sublime and the Beautiful* (1757). However, Burke's theory of 'the sublime' deserves a dominant place in my reading because it is crucial to an understanding of *The Shadow of the Sun*. There are strong resemblances between the imaginatively violent ways in which Henry Severell has gathered material for his first novels and a concept of the sublime as handed down to us by Edmund Burke. The descriptions of Henry's visions and the ways in which he is 'attacked' by them present the reader with a theory of 'the creative sublime'. The narrative investigates the connection between a concept of 'the sublime' as a romantic paradigm of creativity with a concept of the artist as a genius and a visionary.

What does Burke's theory of the sublime look like? Like many eighteenth-century writers on aesthetics, Burke was concerned with the effect of aesthetic objects on the human imagination, senses and the human mind. He categorized these effects or aesthetic experiences into two main groups: 'the sublime' and 'the beautiful'. Tom Furniss's distinction of the three stages in Burke's model of the sublime experience is useful here. The first phase is 'the state of normal or habitual perception in which the relation between the mind and object . . . is one of equilibrium', a state of balance.[15] In the second phase the effect of the object is such that the individual is subjected to the ideas of fear, pain, terror and horror, to a violent aesthetic experience which threatens to overwhelm him. He feels the danger that in perceiving certain kinds of objects which suggest for instance infinity or vastness, power and magnificence, he will be unable to maintain control over himself. The subject's perception, vision and sense of self are threatened and it is as if the imagination will explode with the effort to take in entirely what looms up before the eye. In the third phase of the Burkean sublime, the individual is able to re-establish the equilibrium by mastering the effects of pain, danger and fear which threaten him. By sheer effort of will he is able 'to comprehend that which overwhelms him' and even enjoys comprehending it.[16] The outcome of the sublime is a removal of fear and pain which consequently causes aesthetic delight and a release of energy. In Tom Furniss's terms, the third phase of the Burkean sublime 'allows the subject to overcome or transcend its subjection, transforming potential annihilation into a sense of elevation', 'the sublime being the experience of the threatened self seeming to overcome or master danger through effort'.[17]

What is crucial about Burke's model of the sublime from a feminist perspective is that the rhetoric he uses in his *Enquiry* follows that of phallocentric thought as unravelled by many feminist thinkers, notably Hélène Cixous. In 'Sorties' she argues that Western philosophy is entrenched in oppositional thinking, an observation which is pertinent to Burke's adamant insistence on a rigid distinction between the beautiful and the sublime. As Burke emphasizes

the ideas of the sublime and the beautiful stand on foundations so different, that it is hard, I had almost said impossible, to think of reconciling them in the same subject, without considerably lessening the effect of one or the other upon the passions.[18]

Secondly, Cixous asks herself in 'Sorties' whether it is a coincidence that of the oppositional pairs which form the basis of Western thought, for example, Sun/Moon, culture/nature, day/night, head/heart, activity/passivity, etc., one pole is nearly always associated with 'Man' and the other one with 'Woman'.[19] The same question can be asked of Burke's distinction between the beautiful and the sublime, for throughout the *Enquiry* the sublime is associated with 'Man', the father and masculinity, and beauty with 'Woman', the mother and femininity.[20] The third step in Cixous' argument draws attention to the fact that when the separate poles of an oppositional pair are linked to Man/masculinity and to Woman/femininity respectively, the first pole is usually valued more positively than the second. That is, a hierarchical opposition is constructed between the two groups of associations. This is also true for Burke's *Enquiry* for he clearly favours the sublime above the beautiful even though he tries very hard to give a different impression. The sublime counteracts beauty's soft spots and is moulded into a framework which is pervaded with masculine associations and valued much higher than the beautiful.[21] Burke relates the sublime to labour and the work ethic, to strength, mastery of fear, to fortitude, justice and wisdom, to awe and respect. Although he emphasizes that beauty inspires the positive feeling of love, the pattern of associations attached to it in the *Enquiry* devalues it. Burke condemns beauty by turning it into a feminized concept, a label which fits a state of idle luxury, weakness, deformity and lack of masculine strength. The following example illustrates perfectly the twists in Burke: while he intends to praise beauty, he undermines its worth. For the qualities of mind which may be termed beautiful are:

> those which engage our hearts, which impress us with a sense of loveliness, [they] are the softer virtues; easiness of temper, compassion, kindness and liberality; *though certainly those latter are of less immediate and momentous concern to society, and of less dignity.* But it is for this reason that they are so amiable.[22]

Fourthly, with many critics Cixous argues that the construction of this particular ordering process is a violent one, in that the two elements of the oppositional couple can only be consigned and kept in their place by force. The binary ordering process implies that the phenomena described are forced into one or the other category: uniformity is achieved at the expense of plurality and of a disruption of categories. As Meijer writes: 'the binary opposition always offers two options, and everything which is in between or outside of these options, is forced in their direction'.[23] This is true for Burke's *Enquiry* in that he uses rhetorical and illogical force to construct the hierarchal order in which the sublime occupies a more highly valued and completely separate position from the beautiful.

How does Burke's theory of the sublime and my Cixous-inspired feminist criticism of it relate to *The Shadow of the Sun*? The novel constructs a clear connection between 'masculinity', 'genius' and 'the sublime' in its portrayal of the writer. Henry Severell needs his writing to construct his male identity and, therefore, he needs his sublime visions for through them he comes to his art: '*He felt that he was not a man without it*; after he had spent enough time away from pen and paper he lost touch with himself and had no centre to judge from' (p. 244, emphasis added). In the portrayal of his visions and the way in which he experiences them, the narrative follows the model of Burke's sublime. The onset of the sublime threatens the subject's perception, vision and sense of self. Henry Severell has attacks of vision which are violent, painful and unpredictable. He recalls that in his youth they gave him no pleasure but only hurt him. The visions seemed stronger than himself, destabilized and overwhelmed him. At that point in his life he has not found the means to sublimate his visions into art.

When he is older he is able to use his visions as a source of power for his novels, which are as violent as his visions. He does not wait patiently for inspiration. The visions stir him out of himself in a very physical way which resembles the effect of the Burkean sublime: Henry is like a battleship gearing up for action. When the vision is upon him he leaves the house for days on end. He walks for miles and exhausts himself to the point of illness. Henry is portrayed as threatening and non-human when he is under the spell of his visions, as if he is testing the claim of the sublime to 'transcend the normative, the human' (pp. 49, 57).[24] While roaming the countryside he loses his sense of his own body and identity – the second unsettling stage of the sublime experience. He feels terror at the thought that the infinity of his visions will overwhelm him. The blockage in the sublime is there in the narrator's description of Henry's state when he is nearly at the end of his powers and of his journey. He comes upon waste land with dead trees with roots looking like 'bloodless amputated wounds', land which has been violated, and there his terror is at its height (p. 62).

However, he is able to work through the sublime experience. Against breaking point he experiences pure vision. The metaphors are those of aggression and violence: trees 'hiss in the heat' and crash behind him; the air burns with 'an angry singing', the air has 'a crushing brilliance'; the light 'thunders into the silence' (p. 79). He sees light and colours which are literally alive, brimming with meaning and significance, attacking his senses: 'to see like this was to be alive, he knew, before everything else was conflagration' (p. 80). The vision washes over him and leaves him safe in the knowledge that he has overcome the terror. Terry Eagleton has called the ultimate message of the sublime 'not what we know but that we know becomes the most deepest, most delightful mystery'.[25] Henry thinks exactly the same:

> He would never, he thought, get over looking up there at the light and *knowing* that he was looking up there. He was so constantly, so consistently surprised to think, here is a man seeing and knowing – if not precisely *what* – that he is seeing (p. 85).

The sublime experience is completed and leaves a pleasurable feeling. Henry thinks with an intellectual pleasure about the creative problem presenting itself to him. Which words will he use to put the sublime experience into art.

The ambivalence of the sublime

When *The Shadow of the Sun* was published in 1964, the critics read the novel as a portrait of the artist as genius; some complained about its lack of originality.[26] However, the portrait of Henry as a genius is far from straightforward. There are places in the novel where it is undermined by the narrator and other characters. Richard Church's observation that the characters around Henry 'subscribe to his greatness' is not true, for some of this information is very critical. It is presented to the reader through five perspectives in the novel: the narrator, Caroline Severell, Anna Severell, Oliver Canning and Margaret Canning. These positions involve more ambivalence than I have accounted for in the novel's presentation of a male visionary genius. To explain this, I will return to Edmund Burke's theory of the sublime.

In *Solitude and the Sublime* Frances Ferguson provides an excellent analysis of Edmund Burke's *Enquiry*.[27] She is one of the first theorists to point out that the cause of the sublime is not determined by men's fear of the vastness and infinity of objects. According to Ferguson, Burke uses so much rhetorical force to construct the opposition between the sublime/the beautiful because of the threat which the beautiful poses to the rigid conceptual boundaries of the sublime. Given the association of the sublime with masculinity and of the beautiful with femininity, one can conclude that Burke's aesthetic theory is really a theory of masculine subjectivity under threat, as feminist theorists such as Lies Wesseling and Annelies van Heijst have argued.[28] The male subject constructed by/in Burke's *Enquiry* lives under the constant threat of that which he does not want to be: feminine, idle, weak, relaxed, luxurious, the object of love instead of awe and respect.[29]

Therefore, the sublime in Burke has a double meaning: women and femininity are conceptually excluded from it, but at the same time Burke's sublime is deeply gendered and haunted by the threat they pose to its internal coherence and rigidity. Thus, as a philosophical concept, the sublime in the *Enquiry* has strong male gender connotations, but by grounding itself so forcefully in the effort to defend the sublime/masculinity against the beautiful/femininity, the narrative exposes and makes visible that the sublime is internally unstable and bears the seeds of its own undoing.

The Shadow of the Sun reflects the instability of the Burkean sublime in several ways. At the beginning of the novel the narrator gives a long description of Henry, seemingly presenting him as a genius of 'the rugged-bearded-prophet variety'.[30] I want to bring to the fore the ambivalence of this description, because it functions as a counterpart to Henry's experience of the three stages of the sublime. The ambivalence undermines his reputation as a genius:

> The first impression of him was overwhelming – he was an enormous man, well over six feet tall, broad shouldered, with strong, wide hands, and a huge head, covered with a very thick, springing crop of prematurely white hair, which merged into an equally live, almost patriarchal beard. This had been grown originally to cover scars left by the war, but had the effect now of a deliberate flamboyance, of a pose, aesthetically entirely satisfactory, it had to be admitted, as the successful literary giant – if the idea of posing had not entailed the idea of fraud, which few people would have accused him of. He was successful, and he was generally considered to be one of the few living giants. He looked like a cross between God, Alfred Lord Tennyson, and Blake's Job, respectable, odd, and powerful all at once (p. 9).

The ambivalence is brilliantly achieved because of its subtlety and complexity. The narrator's comparison of Henry to God and Job is highly ambivalent.[31] What is more, the words 'a deliberate

flamboyance', 'the idea of fraud', 'a pose, *aesthetically* entirely satis-
factory' all increase this ambivalence. We are not certain whether
Henry does not fraudulently pose as a literary giant instead of being
one. The sentence 'he was generally considered one of the few living
giants' does not make us any more certain whether this reputation is
deserved. In this context it is remarkable that Margaret Canning's idea
of Henry as a genius is also based on hearsay: 'Henry Severell was after
all a genius, *they said*' (p. 25, emphasis added).

   In the introductory part of the novel, Henry's status as a genius and
a literary giant is further undermined by his wife's scepticism and
common sense. The reader accompanies Caroline into Henry's study
and sees through her eyes that, as a character, he bears a striking similarity to Mr Casaubon in George Eliot's *Middlemarch* and Mr Ramsay in
Virginia Woolf's *To the Lighthouse*: two men who are, however sympa-
thetically, portrayed as exemplifications of impotent male creativity
and misconceived intellectual endeavour. Henry explicitly compares
himself to Casaubon, 'dedicated and misguided' (p. 211), another
ambivalent assessment. When at the beginning of the novel the narrator presents Henry as working on his *Analysis of the English Romantic
Movement* – which, it must be admitted, sounds less grand in scope
than Casaubon's *Key to all Mythologies* – Caroline's scepticism thoroughly relativizes Henry's intellectual project (p. 8). Her view of his
fiction is also far from complimentary; from it Henry emerges as a
writer who does not care about or understand people (p. 173).
Through her, the reader gets a double and, therefore, ambivalent view
of Henry: 'Caroline was so used to looking at him that she saw both
that he was splendid, and that his shirt collar was dirty' (p. 9).[32] This
double view is reinforced by the narrator. As Eagleton notes, the dividing line between the sublime and 'the ridiculous' is very thin and the
narrator is fully aware of this.[33] Henry is descibed as 'powerful' and
'odd', an association which is repeated when he sets out on his
journey: he looks 'splendid, magnificent' *and* 'slightly silly' (p. 51).
Working in his garden he wonders whether he looks 'sublime' or
'ridiculous' (p. 167).

   Moreover, Caroline states matter-of-factly that Henry is only able
to work and disregard people because she is there to take care of the
family and other distractions (p. 173). The narrator calls Caroline 'a
sacrificially devoted wife' and also exposes the double standard
Henry applies to the sacrifice made on his behalf. He is aware that

he has accepted it, but refuses to 'be answerable for the burial of her talent' (p. 173). Through Caroline's perspective, it becomes clear that the sublime is not as autonomous as it appears. In the descriptions of Henry's visions and the way he acts on them, the sublime and the visionary do come together in a portrait of the male genius. The autonomy and stability of the sublime/masculinity are, however, illusory. In order to hold on to his idea of himself as a man who creates art through his visions, Henry is shown to be far from an independent genius. On the contrary, Caroline's presence is a necessary condition for his writing.

Thus, the narrator and Caroline both afford a critical perspective on Henry as genius. But there is a third way in which the Burkean sublime is shown to be unstable. According to Modiano, 'the sublime . . . requires a belief that the most important transformative experiences are individual and not communal'.[34] *The Shadow of the Sun* defines this individuality as an illusion: Henry thinks he can create exclusively through his sublime visions but he is dependent on his wife Caroline. The second sign that the masculine sublime is unstable can be found in the novel's portrait of the father–daughter relationship. Henry has been able to create through a denial of Anna, his daughter. His egoism and self-centredness are monumental in this regard. Given the dominance of 'vision' in *The Shadow of the Sun*, it is entirely fitting that he has neglected Anna by not seeing her: 'he hardly saw her, half the time, at all' (p. 93). The narrator mentions several times that Henry has no idea what Anna thinks, feels and does: 'he had really not the slightest idea how she lived' (p. 194); 'what Anna's thoughts were, Henry did not know' (p. 197). When they really talk for the first time in Cambridge he finally sees her and, appropriately, this is the only time when the narrator has them share the same vision of sunlight (p. 202). However, ultimately Henry is unable to see Anna as a separate human being, but constructs her as a mirror image of himself: 'You're like me, you know. Whether you like it or not. You're my daughter' (p. 200); 'she was to be like him' (p. 205); 'he wanted . . . to confirm in her the power *to see things his way* that he had decided she possessed' (p. 203, emphasis added). He is a Pygmalion who looks for a female clone to mould in his own image.

Although initially Anna takes this as long-deserved attention, she finally distances herself from him in a speech which leaves nothing to the imagination. *The Shadow of the Sun* criticizes Henry for practising artistic cloning on his daughter. The impact of Anna's criticism is great, for at the beginning of the novel the narrator presents her as a strong defender of her father against Oliver's criticism. Now she echoes Caroline's words – 'you don't like people' – when she accuses Henry of only being interested in people as material for his fiction and for being incapable of real involvement. Here we see that, through Anna, the narrative criticizes the view that art transcends moral and emotional obligations. It is a theme which returns again and again in Byatt's novels, most notably in *The Game* which will be the subject of the next chapter. In *The Shadow of the Sun* Anna's negative assessment of Henry is reinforced by the narrator who gives countless examples of Henry's cruel detachment from others, especially in the way in which he observes Margaret Canning's despair and breakdown.[35] Henry is a writer always. It is not the case that he writes one day and lives the next. Everything that happens is material for his work. He watches all the time and assesses what he sees for the relevance it may have for his work. It is what Anna dislikes.

For one brief moment, Henry himself comes to share Anna's criticism and realizes the price he has paid for art. He doubts the justice of his choices – his exploitation of Caroline and Anna and his denial of his love for his daughter. Again, the narrative uses the figure of a woman – Anna Severell – to expose the instability of the masculine sublime: Henry's awareness of his love for Anna leads to a writer's block and to a crisis in his sense of himself as a visionary and a writer. In the past he enjoyed the selflessness the sublime caused him to feel, a fictional death of the author, so to speak, after which he rose again like Lazarus from the grave to create. This is no longer possible: 'he had felt, with this love, he was heavy with a complete helplessness he had not known before. He had not been able to write' (p. 244). The fact that he continues to compare himself to Samson is very appropriate (pp. 47, 59, 171, 214, 279). Although Samson may seem the epitome of a heroic and sublime figure – inducing terror in others – his portrait is ambivalent. According to Bal's interpretation of the story, Samson brings about his own downfall out of love which makes him, like Henry, vulnerable: 'the myth is concerned with the problems of love. It is the myth of anxiety . . . Fear of the female. Fear of emotional surrender, of too strong an attachment'.[36] Henry is only able to overcome his vulnerability by repressing his love for his daughter and any sympathy he may feel for Oliver and Margaret. He does so by literally 'obliterating' from his senses – hearing, sight, smell and taste – everything about them that is painful to him, for instance 'Oliver's small, white, pleading face' (p. 278). And when he sees himself as Samson for the last time, he stresses the inevitability of Samson's violence – 'it's in the nature of things' – and calls Samson's end 'a splendid downfall', thereby neglecting the terrible aspects of Samson's revenge (p. 279). According to the biblical story, more than three thousand people die when Samson destroys the temple. Exemplary of the subtle way in which *The Shadow of the Sun* criticizes Henry is that he does not mention that Samson is *blind* when he has his revenge. Thus, the effect of the intertextual comparison between Henry and Samson is that when Henry *does* have another vision at the end of the novel we know that he really goes into it blindly. Although the narrator predicts that Henry 'would be able to continue as though there had never been a break', it is likely that he will not be able to sublimate the last vision into art.

The Lady of Shalott: the sublime and the writer as female visionary

In 1964 reviewers read *The Shadow of a Sun* as a portrait of the writer as male genius and of his daughter as a young girl who succeeds in escaping his influence. Thus, they see a narrative structure in which Oliver helps Anna to change from an adolescent into a woman by disengaging herself from her family, most importantly from her father. Contemporary critics also read Anna's portrait in this way.[37] They do not ask the question whether Byatt wanted to portray an artist in Anna, a viable question given the content of the novel. In the foreword to *The Shadow of the Sun* A. S. Byatt does discuss her own portrait of Anna in these terms. She is far more ambivalent about Anna than her critics, who have emphasized the positive aspects of her initiation into 'womanhood'. Byatt looks upon her as an artist and concludes that Anna 'is a portrait of the artist with the artist left out' (p. xii). I will adopt this definition of Anna's portrait – which has the appearance of an old-fashioned riddle – in my discussion of her portrait.[38]

If one takes Henry's visions as constituting his identity as an artist, one has to conclude that the narrative follows a different course in its portrait of Anna. She sees herself as a failure, because she is incapable of experiencing the same violent visions as her father. She accepts the figure of the visionary genius as a blueprint of the artist and concludes that she fails to come up to the requirements (p. 52).

Anna is placed into a position where she thinks she will be able to have the same visions as her father, only to conclude that she fails. The first time is in the bathroom at her parental home where she waits for the storm to break and expects to have her vision (p. 134). The second time is when she is alone at night watching a star (p. 151). The third time is when she stands on a bridge and the weather changes drastically. The lightning she sees around her makes her certain that she will finally be able to see the way Henry does:

> She was looking, into this leaping light, for what he would have seen. And then the cutting edge of the vision melted . . . I don't think I am going to know, she thought, I think I am just going to go on as I am. I can't make it. I shall never make it (p. 238).

In these three parts Anna is the subject – we are granted entrance to her thoughts and feelings from the inside. The narrator allows her a subject position in the narrative, that is, she has the power to determine our perception of her as a character. However, Anna is granted just enough subjectivity to perceive that she is unable to see as an artist. Thus, Anna may have a subject position comparable to Henry's – both characters' thoughts on the events are shown from the inside – but it is a distribution of subjectivity with a vengeance. Anna is granted the power to tell the reader about her powerlessness. At the same time Henry is the object of her view, a less powerful narrative position, but her view of him strengthens his power instead of diminishing it. Anna ascribes the sublime experience to him as if he has a right to it and she does not: 'the experience that in its real, far, unimaginable depth belonged properly to her father' (p. 238). In the foreword A. S. Byatt emphasizes that Anna does not have whole visions such as Henry experiences them, but 'partial visions': 'My Anna was not even a reflected light, she was a shadow of a light only, who had partial visions in clouds . . . or stormy moonlight, or the glare of Cambridge's blood-coloured street-lighting. I feared that fate' (p. xiii).

The second way in which the narrative constructs the absence of the woman artist in Anna's portrait is more indirect. An important difference between Anna and her visionary father is given narrative form through intertextuality. A. S. Byatt shares with many feminist critics, writers and painters a strong interest in Tennyson's poem 'The Lady of Shalott'. When asked what literature had influenced her work, she said that as a young girl she knew the poem by heart: '[its rhythm] haunts everything I write'.[39] 'The Lady of Shalott' tells the story of a woman weaving in a tower. She cannot see the world outside her tower directly, but is dependent upon her mirror for her art. She weaves 'the mirror's magic sights' and finds delight in her work. She is not allowed to look directly down to Camelot, because 'a curse will come upon her' if she does. When Lancelot comes riding by, this is what happens: The Lady looks down on Camelot and 'out flew the web and floated wide/the mirror cracked from side to side/"the curse is come upon me" cried/The Lady of Shalott' (11. 114–17). She dies in a boat floating down the river. When one reads this poem as a portrait of failed female artisthood, of the Lady's inability to experience direct unmediated visions and recreate them into art, the comparison to Anna Severell is striking. Many times she has indirect visions through glass and often the effect is a negative one, related to her writer's block for instance (pp. 17, 92, 103).

There are many instances in Byatt's work where art and the making of art are compared to 'glass' in ways which emphasize its negative or vulnerable side. Both in *The Shadow of the Sun* and Byatt's second novel *The Game*, men violently destroy glasses and make-up bottles owned by creative women. Moreover, at the beginning of her writing career Byatt was afraid of art, not only because she was uncertain about herself, but also because 'of the tyranny of art and *the glass wall* art puts between artist and life'.[40] The opposition between art and life is of course problematized here. The writer or scholar who drowns himself in his quest for knowledge and art runs the risk of becoming less human. When Henry looks for Oliver in a library he watches a scholar with a reading glass. By then aware of his neglect of Anna in his pursuit of art, Henry sees the negative image of the scholar: he calls him 'a parody of a human being' for 'looking through' his reading glass and 'not at it' (p. 214).

Where Henry experiences direct unmediated visions in the sublime mode, Anna watches through the window of the hut she hides in and only sees the face of the boy she thinks she is in love with (p. 21). Romantic love for Lancelot causes the Lady of Shalott to risk the outcome of the curse. A. S. Byatt also mentions in the foreword that 'the need to be in love' threatens the autonomy of Anna most (p. xii). I would say that Anna is threatened by Henry and Oliver who both stand in the way of her becoming an artist. Huf sees the absence of female genius in women's artist-novels reflected in the heroine's insecurity about her capacity to be an artist. Huf concludes that in these novels women do not have male Muses to help them. On the contrary, they are 'dragged down' by men.[41] Anna cannot be an artist, because Henry and Oliver function as stumbling blocks in her way. In 1964 the critics saw Oliver as Anna's saviour, but both he and Henry fulfil the opposite function. On re-reading her novel A. S. Byatt became aware of this aspect: '[Oliver] would have been the hero of any male version of this story . . . This novel does not see him quite that way. It is afraid of him, though I only understand now how much' (p. xi).

Henry neglects Anna in his selfish dedication to art. The narrator also mentions several times that Anna could have been a writer, had her father's example not been held up to her (pp. 16, 53, 91). Oliver is more dangerous to her. He threatens her privacy, first, when he comes into the hut she hides in. She is afraid of him: 'Anna shrank into a corner and watched him come in' (p. 37); secondly, when he reads her schoolwork without her knowing it and concludes that she has 'a nice little mind'. She is also described as being 'physically terrified of him' (p. 96). The narrative is most damning about him in the parts where Anna concludes that she is unable to experience the sublime. Oliver's presence hinders her from completing her vision: he enters the bathroom just when she thinks she will experience the sublime (p. 134). After the party, he passes her in the street and bullies her into going home with him – it is the night they sleep together for the first time (p. 151). The third time, when she stands on the bridge, he is not actually there, but shortly afterwards Anna finds out that, at the time of her third failed vision, she was already pregnant with their child: 'even on the bridge she had not seen, and that may have been to do with it; femina gravida, weighed down, weighed down' (p. 289). Moreover, if one accepts my association of

Anna with glass, the scene in which Oliver destroys Caroline's collection of glasses upon hearing about Anna's pregnancy acquires a sinister meaning. It is as if he wants to destroy Anna. He is an obstacle in her way until the very end of the novel. The last pages thoroughly undermine the Romantic plot and are a monument of ambivalence. They describe a hunter and his prey. As Oliver finds her in the hotel, Anna watches 'her last chance, or illusion, which? slip away as Oliver held her from it . . . Oliver's grip was like a claw on her elbow. . . . This really was the feared and expected end. At that time, she was surprisingly content' (p. 297). The narrative suggests that even this ambivalent contentment disappears in time.

Although I have pointed to Anna's insecurity and the nature of her indirect visions as signs of the absence of the woman artist, the narrative also blames Henry and Oliver for this absence. That is, *The Shadow of the Sun* not only contains a feminist critique of the male artist as visionary genius but also criticizes the lack of women's access to artistic subjectivity in a feminist way.

Water, glass, light: the presence of the woman artist

A. S. Byatt's portrait of Anna Severell can be interpreted as the absence of the woman artist and 'the failed sublime'. As the shadow of her father Anna does not seem to have a colour of her own. According to Hursthouse, the problem of shadows is that it is difficult to decide what colour they are:

> Looking across a sunbathed lawn, it may be perfectly obvious that the trees are casting shadows on it. The sun-lit grass is green all right – but what colours are the shadows? Our conscious experience is so much a matter of seeing them *as* shadows-on-grass that we may find it difficult if not impossible to see them *as* a patch of such and such a colour.[42]

However, as Willa Cather said,

> every artist knows that there is no 'freedom' in art. The first thing an artist does when she begins a new work is to lay down the barriers and limitations . . . Nobody can paint the sun, or sunlight. She can only paint the tricks that shadows play with it.[43]

Even though Anna feels that she is but a shadow of her father's genius, at some points in the novel she takes on a colour of her own. That is, A. S. Byatt is right in saying that Anna embodies 'a portrait of the artist with the artist left out'. The traditional genius is, indeed, absent, but there is a woman artist there. One can see her when one examines the nature of Anna's visions before Oliver and Henry lean on her or interrupt her. I will give three counter-examples to Anna's failed visions.

First, when Anna is in puberty she is completely surprised by changes in her vision. The description of the following vision bears the seeds of the sublime, because of its intensity and earth-shaking effect:

> Things became suddenly beautiful, intolerably beautiful, and she intolerably aware of them: she found herself, despite herself, driven to tears by the intense green she saw, looking up through the apple trees at the summer sky, unable to reduce the profusion of the gold-edged crossing twigs and the overlapping, deepening, glittering rounds of the leaves against that uncompromising midsummer blue to any order that she could comprehend. Her senses were assailed that summer, everything was disproportionate (p. 19).

My second example assumes that there is a positive version of the Lady of Shalott present in *The Shadow of the Sun*. A. S. Byatt said that in her childhood 'the enclosed weaving lady became my private symbol for my brooding and reading self'.[44] In 1994 she repeated in an interview that the women artists in her novels are

> all the Lady of Shalott: that's another image which is so deep in my very early childhood. It's to do with the thing that all my books are about: the sensuous life, childbearing, therefore men, therefore danger, and making things by yourself of exquisite beauty which can be accused of being unreal. All my books are about the woman artist – in that sense they are terribly feminist books.[45]

Anna is, indeed, described as a creative Lady of Shalott in the following quotation. When the family go to the seaside for their yearly picnic, she has a vision of herself as a writer. The narrator endorses the vision by calling it 'efficacious'. Notice that the familiar elements are there – vision and the imagination, the enclosed space, the water and the glass:

> She was submerged in her St. Anna daydream, of herself retreated to a cottage on these cliffs, writing good novels and contemplating the water. She would have rooms with little windows and deep window seats . . . She would have a table with a typewriter, in a window looking out in the direction of the sea . . . She would come and go when she wanted, no one would visit her unless invited, no one would interfere. She would have time on her side, then . . . She walked through her garden . . . in and out of all her rooms – it was an exercise of the imagination familiar and efficacious by now; she stared happily and arrogantly out over the water, amalgamating her pleasure in it with her pleasure in her hypothetical writings . . . I shall remember this, she told herself, as though a promise was contained in simply seeing it (p. 109).

In this image Anna appears as an autonomous writer, capable of vision. In her daydream she occupies 'the margin of singleness for herself' which the feminist philosopher Luce Irigaray longs for in 'Divine Women'. In this essay Irigaray is critical of a concept of female identity which only emphasizes the social roles of women:

> [a woman] is constituted from outside in relation to a social *function*, instead of to a female identity and autonomy. Fenced in by these functions, how can a woman maintain a margin of singleness for herself, a nondeterminism that would allow her to become and remain herself?.[46]

Anna may not be an artist in the sublime sense, but her daydream does create this margin of singleness for her creative self. *She* is comparable to the Lady of Shalott who, though her end is terrible, sings 'cheerly' and finds delight in her web 'with colours gay'. The ambivalence contemporary critics read in 'The Lady of Shalott' also emerges here in Byatt's portrait of Anna.[47]

My third example again modifies the image of Anna as a Lady of Shalott who is unable to be a 'true' visionary artist. I have compared Anna to the Lady of Shalott in her failure to experience vision in a direct way and transform it into art, as Henry does. In the scene below her vision is of course indirect: it is determined first by the glass and then by the water. However, this vision has a different indirectness, for this time she sees purely for herself – as in the scene at the seaside – not through an image of a man. Moreover, the description is, I think, breathtaking in its lyrical beauty. It takes place in the bathroom just before Oliver enters:

> Inside it was beautiful . . . there was nothing garish about the bathroom at all; it was a drowned world, a sunken secret world, with pillars and planes of light shining gently in its corners and the odd brightness of a tap, or the sliver of light along the edge of the basin, winking like living creatures, strange fish suspended and swaying in the darkness. The shelves were a miracle of green and silver, shadow of transparent shadow, reflected and admitted, block geometry made ideal in light . . . Shadows of light, Anna thought . . . Anna drank quickly and refilled the glass for the pleasure of watching the water. She carried it across to the window and held it so that the light was directed and split through the water onto the floor of the bath. The circle of brightness opened like a flower, with crisp, spinning petals. She curled up in the wide windowsill and turned the glass lovingly, with outstretched arms. Nothing she had ever seen had been more exquisite, or more unreal. She felt balanced and complete, between all this trapped, plotted light and the approaching storm; she said to herself, turning the glass round and round, over and over again, not knowing herself quite what she meant, 'I can do something with this. I can do something with this, that matters'. It was all so extremely important and she would, any moment now, know clearly why (p. 133).

The passage enables one to read the title of the novel differently: in this vision the meaning of shadows and, therefore of Anna as a failed visionary, is changed in a positive way. Shadows are taken to be miracuously beautiful: 'The shelves were a miracle of green and silver, shadow of transparent shadow, reflected and admitted, block geometry made ideal in light . . . Shadows of light, Anna thought'. The scene also clearly relates Anna's vision to water, light and glass in a positive sense. Anna feels balanced and complete. It is one of the first instances in Byatt's work where this is the case. The glass of water through which the light falls, guiding Anna's vision, takes on a significant and positive meaning, certainly because the association between Anna, glass and light is repeated on the next page: 'She twirled her glass, rocking the light in it. "Sometimes," she said carefully, "I think perhaps I have no limitations" ' (p. 135).[48] Often in Byatt's work the knot of associations – the water, the light and the glass – is used positively in connection to women artists and to Byatt's own sense of herself as a writer. In her introduction to *The Shadow of the Sun* she defines her writing as 'heliotropic' which means turning towards or away from sunlight. In her lecture 'Identity and the Writer' she refers to 'light' and 'glass' as images of her creative self:

> When I started writing, I had what I now see was a kind of post-Romantic metaphor for the self – and this was to do with light, rather than desire – which was the human being as a burning glass . . . And I always thought (of) the work of art as the fire that would break out if you concentrated the light, so that it went *through*; whereas if it simply all came in, and had no way out, you would be shattered.[49]

One can infer from *The Shadow of the Sun* that the most adequate concept of art should, like Anna's glass, provide both 'a way of seeing' and 'a thing seen'. This idea returns in 'The Djinn in the Nightingale's Eye' in which the feminist narratologist Dr Gillian Perholt uses 'glass' as a two-layered metaphor for art: ' "Oh *glass*", said Dr Perholt to the two gentlemen, "it is not possible; it is only a solid metaphor, it is a medium for seeing and a thing seen at once. It is what art is" '.[50] These persistent references to the dual function of glass and art as 'a way of seeing' and 'a thing seen' suggest that the writer or artist needs a distance to the making of art, needs to refrain from swallowing what she sees. However, this does not mean that she can distance herself completely from what she sees or depersonalize her self through her visions. Anna's way of seeing is not impersonal and does not distort, but is balanced and patient. There is a distance between what she sees and her perceiving eye. Her vision keeps this distance in its place 'as if a promise was contained in simply seeing it' (her thought at the seaside). She resembles the girl in Clarice Lispector's story 'So Much Mansuetude' who looks out of a window and realizes that she is content just by being there and watching the rain: 'I am at the window and only this happens: I see with beneficient eyes the rain, and the rain sees me in agreement with me'.[51] Again one is reminded of Luce Irigaray's essay 'Divine Women'. I already mentioned how her concept of the margin of singleness is relevant to a reading of Anna's daydream. Similarly Irigaray's essay contains a fruitful description of vision/the gaze as an embrace instead of as 'a weapon to ward off touching'.[52] It is a precise description of the nature of Anna's vision, one which distinguishes her way of seeing from that of her father. Henry's way of experiencing the sublime as a gateway to his violent art is one of conquest and domination. He wants to repress any threats to himself as a man and a visionary. He is unable to see Anna for herself; when he sees her, he creates her in his own image. However, the narrative shows that the stability of the sublime/masculinity is always under threat by femininity and love. Henry thinks he can repress his fear of not being able to create by denying anything that is painful to him, especially his inability to help his daughter. The narrative is ambivalent in this: Henry does experience another vision at the end of the novel, but the narrator suggests that he will never be able to write again by comparing him to the blind Samson and that the ever-present instability of the sublime will be his downfall.

Anna Severell is not presented as a visionary genius who experiences a sublime of conquest. She experiences 'a sublime of nearness' and has visions which are not violent but 'embrace' their objects without possessing them. As Cixous writes about Anna's twin in Lispector's story:

> one really has to make a big effort, and particularly one has to overrule the ego and the pretense of mastering things and knowing things . . . Perhaps this is what we call being alive. No more than this: alive. And simply alive from a serene . . . Joy'.[53]

This is the kind of visionary which may well be A. S. Byatt's ideal type of writer. As she said in an interview with Tredell in 1994, describing herself as a girl:

There are five or six childhood experiences which I always feel made me what I am, and they're all solitary and they're all to do with light or dark . . . I remember – I was a desperately unhappy child, it must be said – sitting up against a barred gate at my elementary school, trying to get away from the other children, and I was sitting very still so they would not notice me. It was a very hot, beautiful day, and on the other side of the gate was a little strip of road and then there was a huge meadow full of buttercups – it always comes back in my books . . . – absolutely full of flowers, all of which were reflecting the light back. And I remember thinking, things are amazing, they're wonderful, if one could see this in stead of having to go back in there, it would be all-right.[54]

Years later this girl wrote about Anna Severell who enjoys the aesthetic shadows of light playing across and through a glass of water, enabling her to fantasize about being a writer.

3
The Game: Cassandra or the Writer as Proto-Feminist Visionary

'Vision can be good for avoiding binary oppositions'.[1]

Introducing *The Game*

A. S. Byatt's second novel *The Game* tells the story of two women – Cassandra and Julia Corbett – and one man – Simon Moffitt.[2] Julia and Cassandra are members of a Quaker family who live near Newcastle in Northumberland. They differ two years in age – Julia is the younger sister – and find it extremely difficult to become separate individuals instead of reflections in each other's eyes. Their interdependence is symbolized by a game they devise when they are seven and nine years old: they play with armies that are made up of cards. Raised in a Quaker tradition which 'emphasizes the practical at the expense of the imaginative', as Cassandra puts it, the game serves as an outlet for their vivid imagination. It is a mutual effort: they are the only players and the game depends upon the continuation of their close cooperation. Cassandra dominates the game, though: she makes up most of the rules and nourishes the game with characters from *Morte d'Arthur* and Tennyson's poetry. It is a world of knights, romance and passion, of desire given form in words and symbols. It is also a violent world: playing 'the game' gives Julia nightmares which persist throughout her adolescence and adulthood.

They play the game for 11 years and then, when they are 18 and 20 years old, it suddenly stops. Julia wins a short story competition with a text that is based on the game and Cassandra is unable to forgive her: 'the long partnership came to an end; there was no more game' (p. 71). Their paths diverge greatly, or so it seems. Cassandra goes to study at Oxford, 'hungry for the absolutely worked drama of Lancelot and Guenevere, Tristan and Iseult', 'expecting God knew what mediaeval grace of life and significance' (p. 17). After her first year at Oxford, her relationship with her sister deteriorates when she finds out that Julia has been seeing Simon Moffit, a man whom Cassandra is in love with and fantasizes about endlessly. As a result she distances herself completely from both Julia and Simon. The novel begins in 1963 when at 38 Cassandra is still at Oxford: she is a well-known mediaevalist and leads a don's life.

Julia also leaves Newcastle but chooses a different kind of life and profession. Her romantic friendship with Simon is abruptly terminated when he suddenly goes abroad. At 20 she marries Thor Eskelund, a Quaker like her parents, and becomes a mother of a daughter, Deborah. Her professional aspirations are also different from Cassandra's: she becomes a journalist and then a writer of novels which find an eager reading public. At the beginning of the novel she leads an active social life in London. Her star is rising in the English literary firmament. She is asked to participate in a television programme on the arts and starts a secret affair with Ivan, its presenter.

Both sisters have done well in seemingly different professions, avoiding each other's company for many years. It is only when their father falls ill that they meet again at their parental home. Surprisingly, their meeting goes well. They watch Simon's appearance on television: he has become an expert on snakes and is filmed while travelling through the Brazilian jungle. Julia and Cassandra even play 'the game' again and decide that Julia will visit Cassandra at Oxford. However, their second meeting is far from successful. Cassandra feels threatened by Julia's reaction to her friends and sees her presence as an invasion of her privacy. Julia decides to break free from the influence the game still exerts on their actions. She will use her visit and Cassandra's life as material for a novel. As the novel's heroine she chooses a lady don who builds a dream world around a clergyman. This world is violated when she meets him, because his presence blurs the distinction between reality and imagination. Julia's novel *A Sense of Glory* meshes with reality in an uncanny way when Simon – whom both sisters are still in love with – returns to England. When Cassandra meets him, they pick up the pieces of their old friendship and talk about the traumatic experiences he has had to go through on his journeys.

However, when she reads Julia's novel, Cassandra is unable to separate her sister's fiction from her own lived reality. She chooses the most dramatic way out: she locks herself in her room and kills herself. Her suicide leads to an investigation and a court case in which parts of her journal are read out. In the last chapter of the novel Julia and Simon go to Oxford to collect Cassandra's papers and journals. It is Simon's last week in England: he has decided to go abroad again. Julia's marriage to Thor has broken down. *A Sense of Glory* receives the best reviews she has ever had and is selling well. Many people hold her responsible for Cassandra's death, though, and when she is alone in Cassandra's room she breaks down. On the last page of the novel she and Simon drive back to London.

Reading beyond 'the sisterly paradigm'

The Game is an early novel, the first draft of which was written when A. S. Byatt was still a student at Cambridge. Yet, this novel contains many of the themes, concerns and writerly preoccupations that return in Byatt's later work. *The Game* explores the relationship between fiction and reality, the place of the individual within the family, the dangers and rewards of art, the nature of scientific knowledge and the relation between ethics and aesthetics. Characteristically, *The Game* negotiates these issues in all their ambivalence and complexity, an intellectual sensibility it has in common with later novels such as *The Virgin in the Garden* or *Possession*.[3]

Therefore, it is unfortunate that the scant critical reception of *The Game* mainly emphasizes one particular question – the problematic relationship between the sisters Julia and Cassandra Corbett – and directly connects it to the lives of A. S. Byatt and her sister, the writer Margaret Drabble. Joanne Creighton for instance combines speculations about the relationship between the 'real life' authors Drabble and Byatt with a reading of *The Game* as a troubled account of sisterhood with a deadly ending. In doing so she thoroughly collides the author A. S. Byatt with Cassandra Corbett. Similarly

Malcolm Bradbury writes about *The Game* that it is '*unmistakably* an interpretation of [Byatt's] own competitive relationship with her sister'.[4]

The theme of problematic sisterhood which dominates their articles forces them within boundaries which A. S. Byatt investigates and *moves beyond* in *The Game*. In what looks like a pre-emptive strike on Byatt's part, the narrative anticipates the kind of reading proposed by Creighton and successfully disarms it. That is, the use of an (auto)biographical sisterly paradigm does *The Game* a disservice, because it greatly reduces the novel's richness and complexity. In order to bring some of this complexity to the fore, I shall approach *The Game* from the perspective of its discussion of 'vision', that is with an interest in the ways in which *The Game* negotiates concepts of vision in its treatment of the scientist Simon Moffitt, the academic Cassandra Corbett and the novelist Julia Corbett. 'Vision' refers to observation in the field of science as well as to the objectifying 'camera eye' mediated through (our watching of) television. These two fields of visual reference are combined in the work of the herpetologist Simon Moffitt, who makes television programmes about his scientific work in the jungle. At another level, *The Game* describes the type of imaginative and creative vision that reaches beyond (scientific) fact. It creates a new reality instead of merely reflecting a factual one. The academic Cassandra and her sister, the novelist Julia, are women who are prone to this kind of vision, who see 'too much' in a visionary way. Interestingly, A. S. Byatt once described herself as somebody 'who saw everything too bright, too fierce, too much . . . This vision of too much makes the visionary want to write – in my case – or paint, or compose, or dance or sing'.[5] Exploring and contrasting these different types of vision, *The Game* remains highly ambivalent about their advantages and disadvantages, an ambivalence which I will retrace in the following discussion of the novel.

Longing for impersonal visions: Simon Moffitt

'To find/not to impose, not to have reasoned at all/out of nothing to have come on major weather/it is possible, possible, possible. It must/be possible'.[6]

Simon Moffitt is a natural scientist whose fascination for snakes takes him to the Amazon jungle. This scientific quest unfolds over ten years of his professional life. He gives narrative form to what he sees in educational television programmes which draw a large audience, including Julia and Cassandra Corbett. The fact that as a scientist Simon passes on knowledge by letting his audience share his camera-visions is a contemporary version of a very old idea. In *The Mind's Eye*, Fox Keller describes the age-old dominance of the visual metaphor as a model for knowledge in Western thought.[7] She examines the history of the relation between visual perception and knowledge and traces it from Plato, through to Descartes and Newton. What makes Fox Keller's historical survey particularly relevant to a discussion of *The Game*'s portrayal of Simon is her emphasis on the dissociative function of the visual metaphor as a model of knowledge.[8] In Western science, vision came to be seen as creating a distance between subject and object, between the subject's eye and the object of his vision. Descartes further increased this conceptual distance between the embodied subject and the object of his vision by creating a dual split between the body and the mind. The result is an ever increasing conceptual disembodiment of vision:

> Vision is that sense which places the world at the greatest remove; it is also that sense which is uniquely capable of functioning outside of time. It lends itself to a static concept of 'eternal truths'. Although itself one of the senses, by virtue of its apparent incorpo-reality, it is that sense which most readily promotes the illusion of disengagement and objectification.[9]

Simon Moffitt is longing for this kind of disengagement, for the kind of visual perception which rests on firm boundaries between what is seen and the person who perceives it. When talking about his work, he argues that the acquisition of knowledge through visual perception should be disconnected from identity, the personal, social determinants and emotions. He would like to believe that as a natural scientist he does no more than register natural phenomena such as a snake's digestive system:

> You watch *it eating*. First you watch that . . . you might just be curious about how it does it. Why not? You might just want to know . . . Why should it be anything to do with you? It's filling

its own stomach. We don't know what it feels like. It's simply there. I - I wanted simply to – learn, to measure (p. 161).

For Simon, watching, seeing, ideally implies impersonality: 'why should it be anything to do with you?' He seeks to maintain clear-cut and well defined boundaries between himself and the object of his vision. Elsewhere, in one of his television programmes watched by Cassandra, Simon argues that a scientist need not, indeed must not, be affected or influenced by the object he watches but can merely register its existence out of a disinterested, passive and innocent curiosity:

> The scientist with a camera . . . can, as it were, rediscover inno-cence. The innocent eye, not ignorant, but trained, detached, seeing everything for itself, for what it is, with no apprehensions and very fluid preconceptions. Once one has one's own feelings in hand – once one's fears are real fears and one's needs are real needs – everything else can be seen with that pure curiosity which is one of the highest human qualities, and I would call it innocence. An achieved, an informed innocence (p. 22).

The Game asks the question whether it is possible for people to see, and even more so to watch in a way that is truly objective, and whether such objectivity can really render the eye or its gaze 'detached' and 'innocent'. *The Game* certainly suggests that Simon's concept of vision can be questioned. In the first two chapters the narrative perspective alternates between Simon's televized speeches and the thoughts and views of Julia and Cassandra while they are watching him on the box. Their views undermine his heroic status. He looks 'pompous', 'deprecating', 'secretive' (p. 13), 'anxious', having 'hairy hands with huge knuckles' and a 'lugubrious' face 'pulled into an intent pout' (pp. 20, 22). They do understand Simon's longing for innocent and detached vision, but they also criticize him for the inadequate way he handles his emotions. It is suggested that his affected emotional neutrality is intimately linked to his definition of vision as innocent, detached and disaffecting. In a letter to a friend, Julia writes that Simon is 'an emotional dabbler', 'a sexual twister, and an (unconscious?) cajoler. The sort of man who makes women feel, erroneously, that they can do things to bring him out or straighten him up' (p. 78). Through the critical perspective of Julia, a romantic plot is undermined. Although the narrator emphasizes that Julia loves Simon, her contempt stretches the concept of romantic love to its very limit. This is of course what *The Shadow of the Sun* and *The Game* have in common. Both novels do not 'give in too easily to the marriage plot and to romance', an aspect which becomes even more striking when Cassandra shares Julia's contempt of Simon's emotional illiteracy (p. 201).[10] After she has watched Simon expounding his idea of innocent and detached vision, Cassandra writes in her journal, quoting Coleridge:

> I wish I could tell you, Simon, how much I enjoy the irony of your self-projection as a scientific observer in a topsy-turvy Eden. Well, cherish your illusory neutrality; there is no love – as we both know – that does not deform and kill. We cannot combine butterfly and serpent without corrupting the butterfly (p. 25).

Simon would like to see snakes as neutral forms of life, as biological facts, but Cassandra Corbett imagines them and is aware of their symbolic meanings. She is clearly critical of Simon's concept of vision as an innocent, detached and neutral way of acquiring knowledge: 'Simon seems to have abdicated the attempt to reconcile love and suffering; he regards the order of facts as the only available truth' (p. 76). She tells him, 'I, of course, avoid facts, whereas you avoid having to imagine. Or remember' (p. 200). She knows from experience, first, that there are no fixed boundaries between the subject and object of vision and, secondly, that emotions and passion are inevitable elements of the process of perception. Cassandra knows that 'seeing' changes both those who see/learn and what is seen/learned. Yet she herself is not wholly comfortable with her visions as she tells herself: 'the discovery of facts is not enough. One has to imagine them – think about them, light them up – and one inevitably intrudes one's own personality. Ideally, one should not. Facts should speak for themselves. But they never do' (p. 68).

As the narrative progresses, Simon himself becomes increasingly uncertain about his own conceptualizations of cognitive vision. There is already a structural ambivalence in the words he chooses to defend his belief in the possibility of the innocent eye and the neutral life: he says that one 'ought to live neutrally'. The same ambivalance is evident when he muses that 'once once has one's own feelings in hand, everything else can be seen with a pure curiosity'; 'I would call it innocence' (p. 22); 'You might just want to know [how a snake eats]'; 'I hope – after a time – to make snakes seem familiar' (p. 161). His idea that the scientist with a camera can 'as it were, rediscover innocence' remains problematic not least because it implies that 'innocence' has been lost and requires an active instead of a passive effort for its archaelogical reappearance.[11] Thus, the ambivalence one finds in Simon's words argues against the theory of vision he wants to believe in.

Moreover, the narrative suggests that Simon's longing for the kind of vision that detaches him from what he sees is really the result of fear and the denial of fear. Simon has had to go through a number of traumatic experiences, among them the suicide of his father. The latter has generated in him a fear of 'meaninglessness, shapelessness, formlessness' (p. 196) and he decides to go to the Amazon jungle to face his fear in a detached way. However, the violence of nature – 'red in tooth and claw' – breaks through his detachment when he has to watch the gruesome death of his cameraman, who is eaten by piranhas.[12] At that point he is no longer able to isolate himself from what he sees and unmediated experience breaks through his emotional defences. Fox Keller's discussion of visual perception is again relevant here. The boundaries between scientific knowledge and the knowing subject, between the object of vision and the perceiving subject, are by no means clear-cut and Simon learns the hard way. He has to rethink his desire for detached knowledge, and, towards the end of the novel, grudgingly admits to Cassandra that 'detachment can't bring innocence' (p. 212). Simon does bear responsibility for making the relationship between Julia and Cassandra worse than it already is, yet he also sees himself as a victim (p. 233). His response, however, is highly ambivalent: at the end of *The Game* he again opts for detachment, but he himself calls his decision to leave England to return to the jungle 'a conditioned response . . . a flight' (p. 237).

Absolute visions: Cassandra Corbett

'I can't let you make a myth out of Cassandra' (p. 227).

It would be a misreading of *The Game* to suggest that its patient questioning of Simon's ideal of detached and disinterested vision endorses Cassandra and Julia Corbett's perspective and ideas in any straightforward way. I have described them as women who see 'too much', which is precisely why Simon feels uncomfortable under their gaze. The concepts of vision that are developed in the portrayals of Cassandra and Julia explore this excess of vision and the idea of the artist as visionary. Concepts of the artist as visionary have preoccupied A. S. Byatt throughout her writing life and their allegiances to a context of gender and myth is particularly interesting here. In the 1991 foreword to *The Shadow of the Sun*, she describes how the Greek prophetess Cassandra haunted her thoughts in the 1950s when she began to write. Her obsession with the Cassandra mythology is directly related to a concept of the writer as a female visionary. In the said foreword, Byatt compares Cassandra to male visionary writers such as D. H. Lawrence and Blake and then connects Cassandra's fate as a poor and exploited visionary to the problems she encountered in becoming a writer:

> The other thing I wrote at Cambridge, over and over, was the story of Cassandra who was loved by the sun god, also Lord of the Muses, and wouldn't give in to him, so couldn't speak, or not to be believed by anyone. Female visionaries are poor mad exploited sibyls and pythonesses. Male ones are prophets and poets. Or so I thought. There was a feminine mystique but no tradition of female mysticism that wasn't hopelessly self-abnegating. There is no female art I can think of that is what I wanted to be able to do (p. x).

The Cassandra whom she recalls here is the classical figure, the woman who is punished for rejecting Apollo and who is not believed. She spells death and disaster in vain and knows what her end will be: death in a strange country. The stories in which she appears are different from the Greek ones we are familiar with. The latter celebrate the classic hero but Cassandra is no Prometheus, Orpheus, Jason or Orestes. She lies hidden in the folds of classical adventures as a mythical figure who speaks only of silence and pain, of the futility of female vision. Byatt emphasizes that Apollo is Lord of the Muses and implies that by refusing him Cassandra cannot be an artist. It seems that for the young A. S. Byatt, who tried to become a writer in the 1950s, the mythical Cassandra functioned as a screen onto which she could project her own anxieties as a woman writer.

The image of Cassandra as a failed visionary artist returns in *The Game*. In one direct reference to the Cassandra mythology, Cassandra Corbett compares herself to her mythical namesake and stresses the impossibility of female visions: 'Cassandra who was Apollo's priestess, and – since she refused intercourse with the Lord of the Muses, *and was thus no artist* – incapable of communication. Unrelated to the world of objects around her' (p. 141, emphasis added).

The narrator makes clear that Cassandra Corbett's self-image is, indeed, that of a failed visionary and artist. She resembles Anna Severell who looks upon herself as incapable of experiencing the sublime and, therefore, thinks she is unfit to be an artist. Cassandra realizes that she will never be a writer (p. 118). She compares herself to the Lady of Shalott and stresses the impossibility of female visions:

Cassandra, like myself, a specialist in useless knowledge. The Lady of Shalott, also. The web, the mirror, the knight with the sun on him, reflected in the mirror and woven into the web. I am half sick of shadows . . . Solitude concerned with reflections . . . . . . Is it possible that one should recognize, and deliberately entertain, the harbingers of insanity' (p. 142).

In the last entrance to her journal, Cassandra again quotes 'The Lady of Shalott' when she writes, 'I am half sick of shadows': 'there is nowhere I shall not drag this grotesque shadow, our joint creature. I can choose, at least, to put out the light that throws it. I want no more reflections' (p. 230).

The Game is as ambivalent about Cassandra's failure as a visionary as it is about Simon's attempts to dispel imaginative vision from his factual gaze. For a long time, Cassandra Corbett is able to live in both a factual and an imaginary world. I already argued that Cassandra is aware of the fluid boundaries between who sees and what is seen, and she knows that she has to be careful in desiring absolute visions.

Towards the end of the novel, however, Cassandra loses herself in her imagination and suffers totalizing visions which are no longer 'heaven' but frighten her. The mythical Cassandra sees the destruction which will come over herself and the Trojans. Her visions do not speak of romance and optimism. In *The Game* Cassandra's visions are described in disturbing detail (p. 151). When she dreams that she is walking in a forest with Simon, the beauty, lightness and warmth of her surroundings give way to a panorama that resembles a painting by Hieronymus Bosch:

> she would see things she recognized; a pile of those clammy, featherless baby birds, blind reptiles with gaunt triangular heads, that fall from trees. A dead mouse, with maggots lumping themselves shapelessly across the browning flesh. A flattened hedgehog, like a blood-fringed doormat (p. 104).

When Julia publishes her own version of her sister Cassandra in her novel *A Sense of Glory*, Cassandra is finally unable to keep reality and fiction apart and commits suicide. The narrative, however, refrains from concluding unambiguously that Julia kills her sister through her art. Instead of reading the ending of *The Game* as another version of the Cassandra myth – Cassandra dying at the hands of Clytemnestra – or even as some sort of self-fulfilling prophecy, the novel maintains an ambivalent tone. What makes *The Game* such a subtle novel is that the reader cannot ultimately judge in favour of or against Julia or Cassandra. Todd rightly states that neither Julia nor Cassandra 'exerts moral superiority over the other; certainly neither is absolutely right'.[13]

In her journal, Cassandra cites as the reason for her suicide that Julia 'does a little more than simply see me, and that little is intolerable' (p. 230). However, Cassandra knows that 'to see simply' is equally impossible and her critique of Simon's concept of vision as innocent, detached and free from distortions is scathing. Yet, she is unable to see the novel as Julia's image of her, and an old one at that. Instead she explains to Simon what Julia has tried to do and agrees with her:

> It seems sufficiently clear – to me – that you can both destroy and create reality with fiction. Fictions are lies, yes, but we don't ever

know the truth. We see the truth through the fictions – our own, other people's . . . She is saying, I assume that I made too much of you. I lived off you. Well, that's true. So I'm particularly vulnerable to – to the imagination (p. 225).

Paradoxically, Cassandra transforms Julia's fiction into fact by accepting the image Julia has made of her, while the narrative makes clear that her reaction could have been different. Thus, her suicide seems a doubly desperate act. As Jane Campbell writes: '[Cassandra] finally refuses to try to live beyond her role in Julia's book . . . In killing herself, she fails to do justice to Simon's reality and to her own'.[14] While, in life, she has sought 'the freedom of imagination, but an imagination still in touch with reality', at the end of the novel, fiction – both her own and that of others – takes over completely.[15]

Both Byatt's portrayal of Cassandra Corbett and the character itself are riddled with ambivalence. On the one hand, it contains a critique of the connection between impersonality and the objectifying gaze of the (scientific or writerly) observer. Cassandra criticizes both Simon's denial of the imagination and Julia's fictions; her way of seeing contains a susceptibility to the intricate relationship between fact and fiction, and it attests to the insight that there can never be fixed boundaries between the perceiving subject and the object perceived. Interestingly this idea resurfaces 20 years later in Byatt's novel *Still Life* in which the narrator argues that 'we always put something of ourselves – however passive we are as observers, however we believe in the impersonality of the poet, into our descriptions of our world, our mapping of our vision'.[16]

In contrast, Cassandra's fragile ego-boundaries contribute to an increasing imbalance of real and imaginary worlds. These boundaries are, in turn, undermined by other people's visions of her, including the one contained in Julia's novel, and as a result Cassandra withdraws further and further from anything that resembles a 'world', be it real or imaginary. Simon urges her to occupy her place in the real world and resolve her fight with Julia, but she is unable to see herself as a separate person (*The Game*, p. 12).[17] In this sense, *The Game*'s portrayal of Cassandra draws an image of female identity which suggests that women need to achieve a certain amount of 'impersonality' and 'autonomy' in order to prevent (self-)effacement. The fact that Cassandra is a failed artist can, I believe, be explained from this perspective. The narrator describes her as longing for 'genius' but she lacks the autonomy and impersonality which are inherent in the concept of the 'great' writer. Where Henry Severell deals with his fear of dissolution through his sublime visions and turns them into art, Cassandra's imaginative visions dissolve into madness, ending in suicide. She cannot utilize art as a way of thinking through the difference between the real and the imagined and she lacks the kind of female support through which a male genius such as Henry Severell sustains the illusion that he is able to transcend reality into art. This gender-sensitive reading of the portrait of Cassandra seems to me to be more relevant than an autobiographical sisterly paradigm which only sees Cassandra as the victim of her sister Julia.

There is, moreover, a similarity between the structural ambivalence in the portrayal of the visionary Cassandra and the ambivalence about art and the writer which characterizes Byatt's criticism. The critical work affirms and criticizes a concept of the great writer and of art as the effect of 'impersonality' and 'transcendence'. It is possible to see the affirmation as Leavisite in character, while the qualification and criticism have feminist and post-structuralist elements. *The Game* is similarly ambivalent: it contains a critique of impersonality and an affirmation of 'impersonality' as a necessary element of female artistic and visionary subjectivity. This presents the reader of *The Game* with a Catch-22 situation: the moment a woman achieves the 'impersonality' needed to become a great visionary writer, she encounters the disadvantages attached to this position, such as a fear of the personal and of emotions, of gendered identity and the body. This impersonality is structurally embedded in the kind of transcendence which is achieved at the expense of other subjectivities, including the female.

Given this problem, it is highly relevant that Cassandra has a sister whose professional status as a novelist is already established at the beginning of the novel. One does not find the canonical signs of the typical artist-hero in the portrait of Julia Corbett: she is not an isolated, alienated, marginalized, suicidal outsider.[18] On the contrary, Julia seems to have it all – a publisher for her novels, a growing literary reputation, a reading public, a marriage, a lover, a daughter and a busy social life. As such, her portrait both replaces the myth of the male genius, fulfills the narrative promise which I saw exemplified in Anna Severell, and acts as a foil to Cassandra. The question is of course whether it follows from all this that *The Game* presents Julia as a woman who has been able to achieve the necessary impersonality as an artist without falling into the trap of Simon's masculine 'impersonal' visions. *The Game*'s one overtly artistic character, Julia, hardly presents the happy synthesis of Cassandra's and Simon's paradigms of vision. By adding a third layer to my reading of *The Game*, I shall explore the question as to how the 'successful' artist fares in *The Game*'s meditation on vision and art.

Proto-feminist visions: Julia Corbett

In interviews and other critical writings, A. S. Byatt has been quite negative about Julia Corbett. Images of alienation, war and waste abound in Byatt's retrospective comments on *The Game*. In her introduction to Rachel Ferguson's *The Brontës Went to Woolworths*, Byatt called *The Game* a novel 'about two sisters who were destroyed by a fantasy life which invaded or infested the real world and got out of hand'.[19] She also recounts that she 'had a lot of trouble with both Julia and Cassandra, the novelist and the Don, and felt very alienated from each of them in turn'. One can see in *The Game*'s portrayal of Julia's fiction an early reflection of the doubts A. S. Byatt entertains about feminist fiction and criticism. In an interview with Dusinberre, Byatt comments on both Julia's fiction and Ellen Moers's *Literary Women* (1978):

> I liked both [Elaine Showalter and Ellen Moers] and I thought Moers was very good on the female sexual landscape, though I'm sure I've encountered it as much in male writers as in female. What frightens me about a critic like Moers is that I'm going to have my interest in literature taken away by women who see literature as a source of interest in women. I don't need that. I am interested in women anyway. Literature has always been my way out, my escape from the limits of being female. I don't want to have to get back in. That is one of the reasons for my dislike of the women's fiction which Julia Corbett writes in *The Game*: it's self-indulgent creation, the 'waste fertility'; with which Comus tempts the Lady in Milton's 'Comus', a denial of real fertility and

real freedom. I don't want to be part of a school or movement. I have to hang on to my identity, my lone voice, because that is the source of my identity as an artist.[20]

It is, indeed, true that, at the beginning of *The Game*, Julia Corbett is presented as a writer who focusses on limitations, and the limitations of women's lives in particular. There is a historical specificity to this, of course: the story of *The Game* takes place in 1963 when Julia Corbett is 36 years old. Byatt wrote *The Game* around the same time when modern feminism had begun to make a tentative impact upon British society.[21] Julia is a writer who takes 'the trials of ordinary women' as her main subject (p. 110). Although the term 'feminism' does not enter the novel, *The Game* does present Julia as a proto-feminist novelist and is clearly critical of her exclusive interest in limitations. While Julia has turned to women's oppression as a subject, her novels do not offer a systematic analysis of its causes nor do they offer a vision of a solution, a way out. Julia feels that

women are restricted. Men have so many choices. And my books do try to say we must accept things . . . Love is a prison, it's unrealistic to suppose it's not. Everybody's possibilities solidify round them and become limitations. It's common (p. 63).

The Game seems to imply that Julia's emphasis on the limitations and restrictions of women's lives have sprung forth from her need to overcome the game she and Cassandra played as children. While the shared imaginary worlds of 'the game' once offered freedom and unlimited possibilities for constructing and reconstructing identities for herself and her sister, it also gradually exposed both of them to the riskier sides of the imagination. As an adult, Julia, it seems, has come to utilize literary realism and her subject matter to rid herself of the influence of 'the game'. Yet, perhaps paradoxically, the effects of 'the game' have proved to be limitations on her art, as she tells Cassandra: 'I didn't mean to write the stuff I write' (p. 101).

The character of the writer Julia Corbett provides a further site of structural ambivalences in *The Game*. Read against the background of A. S. Byatt's critical pronouncements, Julia seems invested with all the characteristics of a 'great' writer. Clearly, whenever Cassandra and Julia are compared the narrative presents Julia as the better writer of the two.[22] She has the same violent imagination as Cassandra – both of them play the game – but Julia is shown to be better at transforming her imaginative visions into art. When she wins a prize with a short story that originates from the game, the narrator emphasizes that Cassandra had used the same material for a story of her own. There is, however, a qualitative difference between their stories:

> Cassandra had felt outrage. She could not accuse Julia of simple theft – the story was, or had been, common property. And Julia's story, although it abounded in similarities of phrasing and passages of description, was in many ways better than her own lumpy version: it was more controlled, and had an element of amused irony that was intensified by the drawings – rather art nouveau – which accompanied it (p. 71).

Julia, it seems, is able to achieve the necessary artistic 'impersonality': as a writer, she distances herself from her material. She combines a violent imagination with the kind of detached vision needed to create art. Julia Corbett also displays other characteristics of a 'great' writer in Byatt's sense of the term. In *Imagining Characters* Byatt defines 'really great' writing as 'a form of knowledge'.[23] This, of course, is a well-known view of narrative. Kermode and Brooks have emphasized the cognitive nature of narrative and its relevance as 'a valuable mental tool'.[24] The idea that narrative is 'a specific mode of human understanding' is Leavisite in character.[25] In the first chapter I explained that the critic A. S. Byatt resembles Leavis in attaching importance to literature, because it gives people a set of concepts and a complex language for understanding what is happening to them, exactly who they are, and what they are doing. Julia also wants to have an imaginative understanding of Cassandra's inner life. Julia Corbett feels she needs to write *A Sense of Glory* in order to give shape to her experience and come to know both Cassandra and herself fully.[26] In writing *A Sense of Glory*, she seeks to lay down the ghost of the game for good precisely in order to save herself and Cassandra from mutual effacement: 'it would mean coming to grips with The Game. It would be a way of coming to grips with what's frightened me, with what I could, but don't, understand. It would be a way of seeing her as a separate individual' (p. 123). This desire recalls A. S. Byatt's words in 'Identity and the Writer' where she says that it is 'our moral duty to imagine other beings as separate, and having complex selves'.[27]

In order to reach this kind of imaginative understanding and knowledge, the writer Julia has to be curious, or so *The Game* implies. In her greedy curiosity, Julia is remarkably similar to Henry Severell, the writer in *The Shadow of the Sun*. Julia is also an astute observer with an intense curiosity in how other people live, what they think and what motives drive their actions. When Thor, her husband, unexpectedly fills their house with guests, Julia does not complain. Instead she studies these people whom she has never met before with a novelist's interest (p. 128). Like Henry, Julia is described as a collector, greedy for new impressions. When she visits Cassandra at Oxford, she sits at dinner with Cassandra and the other academics and 'collects their expressions with a speculative curiosity she would have said was akin to love' (p. 108). At the party afterwards she 'collects tones of voice' (in *The Shadow of the Sun*, Henry is described as a collector who stores and gathers in a similar sense [p. 278]). Predictably, Julia transforms 'the material' she has collected into fiction:

> Such moments of imaginative vision were rare and valuable – knowledge, any knowledge at all, was beautiful, every accident of surface or emotion related, with no effort on her part beyond *the simple will to see*. It would be a good novel, because it would not be about herself. It was a pity it couldn't be done. Julia smiled.
>
> (*The Game*, p. 123, emphasis added)

These similarities between Henry Severell and Julia Corbett are, I believe, not coincidental. Anna Severell is also described as a creative Lady of Shalott who enjoys her vision at the seaside because 'a promise was contained in simply seeing it'. From these three examples, the writer emerges as a detached and curious observer who takes possession of the object of seeing and is him/herself firmly established as a subject who remains 'detached', 'simply sees' and does not write out of a need for self-expression. She creates wholes out of fragments, meaning out of random incidents and accidents. A comparison with one of Byatt's remarks in *Imagining Characters* is illuminating in this context and suggests that the beauty of art lies in its ability to impose a formal order on an unruly world: 'with a really good book you do have the sense of discovering a kind of order in the world – or a frightening disorder which somebody has nevertheless had the courage or the power to order for you'.[28] Elsewhere a similar description can be found:

> [there's] a kind of dream I have which is most deeply to do with myself as a writer . . . where all the images fuse into a kind of intense symbolic knot or painting. In such dreams you can see everything you were worrying about laid out in beautiful objects, solid metaphors you can see and touch.[29]

Aesthetic form can, indeed, potentially act as a stronghold against 'the frightening disorder' of reality.

Can we thus read Julia Corbett as an at least potentially 'great' writer? Her detached curiosity, her desire to use narrative as a way of ordering her experience, as an entrance to knowledge and understanding, her intense pleasure in the aesthetic beauty of pattern and form certainly all have their doubles in Byatt's criticism, specifically those parts which define 'great' art and the 'good' writer in Leavisite terms.

And yet, *The Game* suggests that there are serious moral disadvantages to the perceptual position Julia assumes. Just as the character of Julia questions and undermines traditional notions of the writer as a genius and of the idea that art is autonomous, other characters expose the darker sides to her creative principles. *The Game* resembles *The Shadow of the Sun* in this respect. Anna Severell accuses her father Henry of using people as material for his fiction and for being incapable of real involvement. Her negative assessment is reinforced by the narrator who gives countless examples of Henry's cruel detachment from others, especially in the way in which he observes Margaret Canning's breakdown. Henry is a writer always. It is not the case that he writes one day and lives the next. Everything that happens is material for his work. Deborah, Julia's daughter, accuses Julia of using everything that happens in their lives as material for her fiction without thinking about the feelings of the people she writes about, Cassandra among them. It is clear that Deborah's criticisms are not without foundation. Julia reads her daughter's journal, just as she had read Cassandra's journal when they were young, and judges it 'good stuff' (p. 124), that is, well written, without giving much thought to the moral questionability of her invasion of her daughter's privacy. Her writer's mind with its dispassionate gaze determines her reaction to her husband's story about the suicide of one of his clients (p. 183). When he has an outburst of aggression in their flat and wipes her make-up bottles off the table – a scene which is reminiscent of Oliver Canning's violence – she is not afraid but merely watches him and thinks, 'it seems a little unreal to have actually to live through it, and it goes on so' (p. 185). Like Henry Severell, she prefers to stand aside and watch.

The publication of A Sense of Glory enhances the negative opinions other characters have of her. According to Caryn McTighe Musil, 'a frequent lesson for Byatt's heroines is that actions always have consequences, though they may think at first that they are acting in total freedom'.[30] This is true for Julia – the consequences of her decision to publish, if not to write her novel are disastrous. Julia's eagerness to publish A Sense of Glory and get it over and done with has blinded her to the risks she takes in exposing her sister's life. The disembodied imagination that runs into pure vision is a seductive but perilous myth. Only after publication does Julia realize that she is less free as a writer than she thinks: 'We think, Julia thought, that we are releasing ourselves by plotting what traps us, by laying it all out to look at it – but in fact all we do is show the trap up for real' (p. 208).

Contained in this one sentence is a theory of narrative which focusses on the impossible fulfilment of narrative desire. Trying to rekindle the spirit of their childhood game, Julia asks Cassandra: 'aren't you appalled that nothing we can do now can possibly measure up to the – the sheer urgency, and beauty and importance of all – all we imagined?' (p. 101). Julia's desire to return to the earlier days of 'the game' is primarily driven by the need to impose narrative closure upon it. She thinks that the writing of A Sense of Glory has enabled her to do so. However, this kind of desire for narrative closure backfires upon Julia. First, Cassandra's response to the novel shows that art may have an effect that is quite extreme. Secondly, due to Cassandra's suicide, Julia's desire to return to the imaginative beauty of the game, for whatever purpose, can never be satisfied. In

'Identity and the Writer', A. S. Byatt writes that she feels 'belea-guered' by theories of writing which privilege 'desire' as 'a sense of lack', driving narratives.[31] I would suggest that *The Game* does indeed conceptualize narrative desire as both 'the force that sets the story in motion' and as 'lack'. The novel's portrayal of Julia seems to reflect ambivalently on contemporary theories of narrative which assume that narrative desire is always 'inherently insatiable, con-demned to a restless search for an absent object'.[32]

The Game is as ambivalent about the successful artist-heroine Julia as it is about the visionary Cassandra, who fails as an artist, and about the scientist Simon, who longs for detached and innocent visual perception. The novel does not resolve these ambivalences. Instead A. S. Byatt constructs an alternative vision of art, one which neither assumes that art is a product of a totally free imagination, unrestricted by ethics, gender, personal histories and family identi-ties, nor views art as completely determined by them.

The Game does project a more open future for Julia as a writer, though. The reader can glimpse in her 'the almost miraculous shot of the – the new snake – through the skin of the old' (p. 161). She has discarded her romantic illusions about Simon Moffitt in that Cassandra's death forces her to acknowledge the true nature of her feelings for him. She realizes that they stem from 'the game's' version of Simon, a fictional character rather than an actual and separate being (p. 216). It is also suggested that she will be able to learn from her disillusion. Her outlook on life has changed consider-ably and, most importantly, she is able to improve the relationship with her daughter. Unlike Henry Severell, who loses Anna, Julia and Deborah reach some sort of understanding at the end of the novel. The following scene proves crucial and is striking in its intensity:

> Deborah turned and screamed at her, 'you take everybody's life. I hate you, I hate you, I hate you'. She launched herself at her mother. 'I hate you, too', Julia said, between blows. 'You are a censorious little bitch. You are only half-human. However, you've got to live with me' (p. 227).

Mother and daughter literally 'batter each other into a breathless and bleeding calm' and end up looking at each other 'with a kind of animal affection' (p. 227). This scene is a mirror image of the one in which Cassandra attacks Julia when they are both young (p. 310), the crucial difference being that Julia and Deborah end up understanding each other, 'seeing' each other in the cognitive sense of the visual metaphor. Campbell, too, emphasizes the importance of this scene: 'There is reason to forecast a better relationship with Deborah, resulting from the creative outburst of anger between mother and daughter as well as from Julia's realization that her daughter is the only one who has made real allowances for her'.[33]

The ending of the novel suggests that Julia has learnt that, as one of Cassandra's colleagues puts it, 'there are moral obligations that come before self-expression' (p. 220). Julia Corbett learns that both the passionate and the visionary imagination of 'the game' and an innocent and impersonal art are illusions. She can never return to 'the game'. Cassandra, it seems, knew this already. At the end of her life, she writes in her journal: 'we shared a common vision, we created a common myth. And this, maybe, contained and resolved our difficulties. This is that primitive state that has been called innocence . . . But there is no innocent vision . . .' (p. 230). Julia's new self-awareness may mean that she can become a writer who can represent, describe and re-create the object of her vision without violating it. The human need to imagine can never be innocent, but it can try to give form without aiming for closure. *The Game* itself forestalls narrative closure by pondering and projecting different types of vision in all their moral and aesthetic ambiguity. *The Game* may be read as an example of the kind of novel Julia would like to be able to write: 'modern novels, her own, amongst others – concerned themselves too exclusively with limitations. A novel ought, ideally, to balance in a perpetual juggling trick the sense of real limitation against a real awareness of human possibility' (p. 135). Still, whether Julia will eventually be able to write this kind of novel remains forever to be seen: 'Julia knew she was a new woman, but this woman had, as yet, no acts to her credit' (p. 237).

4
Possession: Melusine or the Writer as Serpent Woman

'He could not identify the Fairy Topic . . . and this gave him a not uncommon sensation of his own huge ignorance, a grey mist, in which floated or could be discerned odd glimpses of solid objects, odd bits of glitter of domes or shadows of roofs in the gloom'.[1]

Introducing *Possession*

In this final chapter on A. S. Byatt's novels, the Booker Prize-winning *Possession* will be the main focus of attention. It is a crucial novel for several reasons. Byatt's third novel *The Virgin in the Garden* (1978) and her fourth *Still Life* (1985) received critical acclaim, but *Possession* moved her into the category of eminent British novelists.[2] British reviewers hailed *Possession* as a tour-de-force, showing 'the feel of a writer who has broken bounds', and put it first on their 'Books of the Year 1990' list.[3] In the context of this study *Possession* is a crucial book, because it imagines models of female artistic subjectivity and thoughts about art and authorship which are even more fascinating than Byatt's revisions of the Lady of Shalott and the mythical Cassandra discussed before. *Possession* contains more than 80 references to the serpent woman Melusine, whose antecedents go back to the Middle Ages. Before elaborating upon the complex ways in which Melusine structures Byatt's best-known novel, I will give a brief outline of the story of *Possession*, followed by a discussion of the reception it received in Britain and of A. S. Byatt's own remarks about *Possession*.

Possession begins as a classic detective story. When Roland Michell, literary scholar and admirer of the work of the Victorian poet Randolph Henry Ash, stumbles upon a formerly unknown letter by Ash, he has no idea whom the letter is addressed to. He is able to deduce, though, that Ash must have written the letter to a woman with whom he had a lively conversation at a dinner party. Roland knows 'his' poet as a man 'whose life seemed to be all in his mind, who lived a quiet and exemplary married life for forty years, whose correspondence was . . . not of the most lively' (p. 8). The urgency of the letter and the unknown addressee intrigue Roland and he starts a literary and biographical quest on which he is joined by the feminist scholar Maud Bailey. She is one of the few experts on the work of the Victorian poet Christabel LaMotte, author of a small number of fairy tales and an epic poem *The Fairy Melusine*. Maud shares her professional interest in LaMotte with the American Professor Leonora Stern, who is convinced that LaMotte had a lesbian relationship with a painter, Blanche Glover. However, the scholars find out that their ideas about LaMotte and Ash need readjustment. The poets shared a secret life which has bypassed literary history and criticism. The quest for knowledge about a possible relationship between Ash and LaMotte leads Roland and Maud to Bailey Castle, where they find the correspondence between Ash and LaMotte; to Yorkshire where the poets spent a secret holiday together while Ash wrote loving letters to Ellen, his wife; and finally to Brittany where LaMotte fled after discovering that she was pregnant.

Maud and Roland's search becomes more urgent with every new discovery, not least because other scholars are on their heels: the deconstructionist academic Fergus Wolf; the ruthless American collector and academic Mortimer Cropper; the indomitable Professor Leonora Sterni and the downtrodden British professor James Blackadder. The narrator's descriptions of Maud and Roland's twentieth-century search alternate with a number of texts purportedly written by these academics: Leonora Stern's feminist analysis of LaMotte's epic poem *The Fairy Melusine*; a lecture by Professor Cropper and extracts of his book on Ash; academic snippets from the writings of James Blackadder, Maud Bailey and Roland Michell.

The motives of the academics are mixed, but they all want to know what happened between Ash and LaMotte when LaMotte found herself pregnant. Two questions haunt the academics: what happened to the child and did Ash know about the pregnancy? The motif of the lost child dominates the last part of *Possession*, culminating in a scene of true Gothic proportions. In the great storm which hit England in 1987 all the academics gather around the grave of Ash and his wife Ellen. There they make their greatest discovery. They find the last letter LaMotte wrote to Ash at the end of her life, in which she explains what happened to their child. Ash has not read it because his wife kept the letter from him and buried the unopened envelope with his body.

The text of the letter is included in the narrative, one of a number of nineteenth-century texts 'made up' by A. S. Byatt. *Possession* contains the correspondence between Ash and LaMotte; extracts of nineteenth-century journals and diaries written by Blanche Glover, Ellen Ash and Sabine de Kercoz, a French niece of LaMotte; fairy tales and poems by LaMotte and Ash; Blanche's suicide letter and so on. These texts constitute the nineteenth-century plot of *Possession* which is linked by two interventions by an omniscient narrator who describes Ash and LaMotte in Yorkshire and Ellen Ash at the deathbed of her husband.

At the end of *Possession*, when Maud reads LaMotte's last letter to Ash aloud, all their questions about the nineteenth-century plot are answered. LaMotte gave birth to a daughter, May, in a convent in Brittany, but did not keep her child. She was adopted by LaMotte's sister Sophie and never knew that Ash and LaMotte were her real parents. Her true origins are exposed in the letter, and so are Maud's, for it transpires that the two are directly related to one another: May is Maud's great-great-great-grandmother. Maud is, therefore, descended from both Ash and LaMotte. Without knowing it, Maud and Roland have explored Maud's own origins. After this spectacular revelation the company disperses. Maud will edit and publish the Ash–LaMotte correspondence. Roland receives three job offers from foreign universities on the strength of his work on Ash. He also finds that he is able to write poetry for the first time in his life.

By this time Maud and Roland admit that they have very reluctantly fallen in love with each other. The narrative does not provide romantic narrative closure, though. Although Maud and Roland sleep together for the first time, it is uncertain whether a relationship will survive their separate professional lives. Instead *Possession* ends with a 'postscript 1868' from which it becomes clear that Ash has seen his

child. On the last four pages an omniscient narrator describes a
meeting between Ash and his young daughter May. She forgets to tell
her 'aunt' LaMotte about the meeting and consequently it is not
recorded in letters, diaries or academic articles. It is one of the things
'which happen and leave no discernible trace, are not spoken or
written of, though it would be very wrong to say that subsequent
events go on indifferently, all the same, as though such things had
never been' (p. 508).

Nostalgia and the nineteenth-century male genius

As an exciting horn of plenty *Possession* has given rise to a great
number of interpretations. Reviewers focus on the sheer breadth of
Byatt's erudition; her treatment of the past; her skill in balancing
genres such as the Romance, the fairy tale, the campus-novel, the
detective story, and the quest; her ideas about contemporary literary
criticism and the evocation of 1700 lines of Victorian poetry. Two
related subjects dominate the reviews, though. First, the reviewers
detect qualitative differences between the Victorian Ash–LaMotte
story and the twentieth-century Maud–Roland plot. Richard Jenkyns,
for instance, finds Maud and Roland unconvincing characters:
'Roland remains shadowy, and Maud never comes alive'.[4] He sees a
difference between the vividness of the nineteenth-century plot and
the relatively 'conventional' and 'cardboard' twentieth-century plot
of *Possession*. Secondly, the reviewers 'know' the intentions
A. S. Byatt had in devising the two plots in this particular way. They
argue that *Possession* is evidence of her exclusive love of the nineteenth century and its history, culture and literature. The reviewers
assume that as a writer she prefers this historical and literary period
to contemporary life, morals, literature and literary criticism. The
reviews construct an image of a nostalgic recorder of a time long past
who dislikes the twentieth century and its modern literary theories.
Possession becomes the book of a writer 'more robustly reactionary
than she knows, longing to burst out and declare that traditional
country life is best, and the modern world is scruffy and smutty, and
what a girl needs is a strong, handsome man to look after her'.[5]
According to the reviews, the novel's main character is the Victorian
poet Randolph Henry Ash who is modelled on the artist as a genius.
The reviewers read *Possession* as a fictional eulogy in which the

nineteenth century and the nineteenth-century male genius speak
A. S. Byatt's mind.

Interviews published just after A. S. Byatt had won the Booker
Prize reinforce the image of the writer adduced by reviewers. The
interviewee A. S. Byatt agrees with critics that there is a qualitative
difference between the nineteenth- and twentieth-century plot of
Possession. She calls it a conscious aesthetic choice on her part. The
nineteenth-century story about the two poets Ash and LaMotte is
meant to be more vivid aesthetically than the plot which contains
the two scholars Maud and Roland.[6] As a writer Byatt disengages
herself from the twentieth-century plot by saying that she found the
writing of this part relatively boring: 'I kept thinking I'm not going
to have to describe Maud and Roland doing something again. How
can I get interested in this'.[7] The writing of the nineteenth-century
plot, in contrast, was a far more emotional and involved activity:
'the most remote things were actually the closest'.[8] Byatt said she
used *Possession* to challenge a modern view of Victorian poets as
'dead, respectable boring figures'. She needed her nineteenth-
century characters Ash and LaMotte 'to be terribly urgent, interesting and complicated', living in a past which 'is more alive and more
violent than the present, somehow more full of wonderful words
than the present'.[9]

Another form of disengagement from the twentieth-century plot
is A. S. Byatt's explicit identification with the Victorian genius
Randolph Henry Ash. It is an identification which has old roots. As
a young girl A. S. Byatt was influenced by her mother's love of the
Victorian poets Tennyson and Browning. Both Henry Severell, the
writer in *The Shadow of the Sun*, and Randolph Henry Ash are
modelled on those Victorian men of letters. Tennyson's 'The Lady
of Shalott' strongly influenced *The Shadow of the Sun* and, to a lesser
degree, *The Game*. Alfred Lord Tennyson was the inspiration for
Henry Severell; Ash is a composite portrait of Matthew Arnold,
Tennyson, George Eliot's husband G. H. Lewes and, most importantly, Robert Browning. A. S. Byatt admires the ventriloquist nature
of Browning's poetry. She compared herself to him when she said
that *Possession* allowed her to 'invent a poet in a novel' in the same
way Browning said 'he could bring people back to life . . . by
breathing life into them'.[10] According to Byatt, Ash resembles
Browning in his greed for knowledge about other people and his

ability to use the writing of poetry for other ends than self-expression. The latter artistic principle is applauded in Byatt's critical work, as I showed in the first chapter.

Byatt's attitude towards the nineteenth-century poet Christabel LaMotte is different. *Possession*'s portrait of LaMotte also has composite elements: she and her work are inspired by nineteenth-century poets such as Emily Dickinson, Charlotte Brontë, Christina Rossetti and Elisabeth Barrett Browning. In an interview Byatt said that Christabel LaMotte has been named after the British suffragette Christabel Pankhurst and after the heroine of Coleridge's unfinished poem 'Christabel'.[11] In the period just after she won the Booker Prize, Byatt's statements about LaMotte seem almost to imply that she is an auto-generational character, as if she created herself and was suddenly there, independent of the writer. A. S. Byatt explicitly creates a gap between Christabel LaMotte and herself and identifies herself with Ash – 'Ash carries my thoughts whereas Christabel carries her own'.[12] Byatt further creates a distance between LaMotte and herself by saying that she did not write LaMotte's poems, notably the 'Spilt Milk' poem. Since A. S. Byatt emphasizes that this poem is 'feminist at its deepest level', it seems logical to infer from this that it is the feminist nature of LaMotte's work which causes the disengagement:

> and I remember thinking, of course, she would write a poem about spilt milk. Now that is a feminist poem at its deepest level. It really is a blasphemous feminist poem because it's set against the male Christ figure who in every icon pours forth blood and water from his side which feed the people, and here is a woman who has lost her child and is expressing this useless milk which any woman who has given birth to a child that has been taken away from her has got to do, and it's very painful. Two male editors have tried to take that out because they were worried by it, and I said, 'it's because you haven't biologically imagined it'. But a woman ought to.[13]

The verb 'ought to' conveys the ambivalence which is so typical of A. S. Byatt's thoughts about gender and feminism. While she acknowledges the relevance of female experience to writing and reading, at the same time she disengages herself from Christabel LaMotte and the feminist nature of LaMotte's work. For she also said of the 'Spilt Milk' poem 'it's actually a very wicked poem and it was hers not mine in a sense, I couldn't have written that from me'.[14]

Feminist literary theory and 'parrot writing'

'Perhaps as Nietzsche once observed, we must choose our enemies carefully, for we come to resemble them'.[15]

In some of the interviews in which she discusses *Possession* A. S. Byatt creates a gap not only between herself and Christabel LaMotte but also between herself and modern theories of literature such as feminism, deconstruction and post-structuralism. In interviews she has discussed *Possession*'s portraits of late twentieth-century literary scholars by focussing mainly on Leonora Stern – the American professor of Women's Studies. Leonora's portrait is a caricature of a lesbian feminist who follows every theoretical trend there is, in A. S. Byatt's words, and who invades Maud Bailey's life, wreaking havoc there. Elaine Showalter, herself an American professor of English at Princeton University and a feminist, commented upon Leonora Stern in 'Feminists under Fire'. She gives a lucid and ironical overview of the stereotype of the feminist critic in English satire from the nineteenth century onwards to the present time. According to Showalter, one of the characteristics of the genre is that American feminists 'fare worst of all'. Showalter's good-humoured conclusion is that 'Leonora is a wonderful comic creation' and that 'hostile stereotypes are perhaps to be expected during a period of gender crisis'.[16] Although I agree with the latter, I also think that the word 'comical' disguises the satire in Leonora's portrait. Abrams's definition of satire is I think relevant to Byatt's portrait of Leonora: 'satire is the literary art of diminishing a subject by making it ridiculous and evoking toward it attitudes of amusement, contempt, indignation or scorn. [Satire] uses laughter as a weapon, and against a butt existing outside the work itself'.[17] When read against the background of A. S. Byatt's critical work it is possible to argue that the satire in Leonora Stern's portrait is, indeed, directed at a butt outside *Possession*, namely feminist literary criticism of a very specific kind: in the description of Leonora's writing the narrator ridicules the ideas of Luce Irigaray, the French philosopher of sexual difference whom I already referred to in

Chapter 2. What is meant with the term sexual difference? According to Buikema and Smelik, sexual difference:

> refers to psychoanalytic ideas of sexual identity and sexuality. More specifically, the notion of sexual difference is linked to a debate which has primarily taken place in French theory. Theories of sexual difference start from the fact that a subject is born with a female or male body, and develops a related psycho-sexual identity. Where gender theorists understand the construction of femininity and masculinity as more determined by cultural and social processes, sexual difference theorists understand it as more determined by (unconscious) intra-psychological processes.[18]

Given the nature of A. S. Byatt's criticism of feminist literary theories, it is not wholly coincidental that Leonora Stern's use of this philosophy is satirized in *Possession*. One can find the clearest example of the novel's satirical approach to Leonora in the description of her analysis of LaMotte's poem *The Fairy Melusine*. Leonora's reading of LaMotte's poem contains direct references to Irigaray's *This Sex Which Is Not One* and can, therefore, be considered as a form of pastiche. Maud Bailey gives Leonora Stern's study to Roland Michell to read; he dislikes it and finds it compelling at the same time (p. 246). A. S. Byatt expresses her dislike in less ambiguous terms:

> [Leonora's] style is revolting in the extreme. Leonora writes feminist descriptions of the landscapes of my poet Christabel LaMotte and she says that these landscapes represent female sexuality and the female body. She cannibalizes several sentences from Luce Irigaray about the female sexual structure, 'ce sexe qui n'en pas un' . . . The truth is I can't bear Leonora's style because she reduces everything to sex and gender as though there was nothing else in the world.[19]

When Sonia Zyngier asked A. S. Byatt about the motivation for her satirical portrait of Leonora Stern, Byatt again criticized Women's Studies for what she believes is its separatism, its advocacy of women writers whatever their quality, its 'bad' influence on young women writers and its interest in the woman behind the writer.[20] There is a similarity here between A. S. Byatt's remarks on Leonora Stern and those parts of the critical work in which Julia Corbett is mentioned. A. S. Byatt mentions her dislike of the proto-feminist writer Julia Corbett and her doubts about feminist literary criticism in one breath, emphasizing a Leavisite idea of the writer as an individual who has a non-political 'lone' voice. However, in my reading of *The Game* I also argued that the novel is far more ambivalent about Julia and Cassandra Corbett than A. S. Byatt's remarks about Julia's fiction suggest. Generally it can be said that Byatt's criticism and fiction also express doubts about a Leavisite concept of the writer which come close to post-structuralist and feminist theories of writing and creative identities. The result is a sustained ambivalence which structures the critical work in important ways.

Byatt's remarks about *Possession* are similar sites of structural ambivalence. In fact, the distinction which I read in 'Identity and the Writer' – between the writer A. S. Byatt who feels threatened by post-structuralism and feminism and the critic who acknowledges the relevance of contemporary literary theories – is also valid here. That is, in the interviews in which A. S. Byatt talks about *Possesson* two voices address the reader. It is the threatened writer who disengages herself from Christabel LaMotte and from modern feminist literary theory: 'my instinct as a writer is to distance myself from it'.[21] It is this voice which constructs feminist literary criticism as a monolithic block in order to defend an idea of the writer as an individual who must be original, unlike literary theorists who practise a form of 'parrot writing'.[22] This voice reinforces the reception of the novel sketched earlier. Both construct an image of *Possession* and of its writer which work by way of opposition: between Randolph Henry Ash/Byatt and Christabel LaMotte; between nineteenth-century poets and contemporary scholars; between the greedy and curious nineteenth-century masculine imagination and the critical twentieth-century mind inspired by other ways of thinking such as deconstruction and feminism; between the writer A. S. Byatt and contemporary literary scholars.

At the same time A. S. Byatt denounced comments on *Possession* for their sexism: 'As for the bloody Birmingham Post', she said, 'the headline was "Mother's novel wins prize". As if one did not spend all one's time writing. When did you last see "Father's novel"? Anyway it is wrong. I am a mother of four'.[23] *The critic* A. S. Byatt is also aware of the fact that she exaggerates the dismal nature of feminist literary criticism. As she tells Zyngier: 'I exaggerate, but that is because I do feel threatened and so I hit out'. She also explains in an interview with Aragay that she likes literary theory: 'I like theory. My attitude to theory is very complicated, because I have a naturally theoretical mind and I can read theoretical books with a kind of intense pleasure . . . I myself find the theory absorbing, I get very excited'.[24] The next quote is most revealing in that here the writer and critic are simultaneously at odds with each other. Byatt followed Kermode's seminars on literary theory at the end of the nineteen-sixties:

> I was at that stage a full-time writer with two very small children and perenially exhausted and I said 'I need my mind to go fast'. We did Derrida and we did Barthes at the time when nobody was doing them and it was very exciting. At the same time it frightened me as a writer. I would go out of these seminars and write a list of words that were not amenable to being used in the seminars. Roland's lists are words that you can't possibly turn into literary theoretical words.[25]

There is one particular reading of *Possession* which adds another layer to the ambivalence about literary theories and about the writer, authorship and gender mentioned above. The critical reception sketched above suffers from partiality and gives an inadequate representation of *Possession*. What disappears completely behind the image of the nostalgic writer A. S. Byatt who identifies herself with Ash and disengages herself from LaMotte and modern literary theories, especially of the feminist kind, is that *Possession* also contains a counter-figuration of artistic female subjectivity. The narrative contains more than 80 references to the serpent woman Melusine, whose antecedents go back to the Middle Ages.

A. S. Byatt first encountered the Melusine mythology when she attended a feminist conference on Melusine in Italy.[26] She then read the essay 'Divine Women' on the Melusine mythology by Luce Irigaray, the philosopher she is critical about in her interviews. Irigaray investigates what Melusine has to tell contemporary readers about love, motherhood, femininity and divinity. I will read A. S. Byatt's revision of the Melusine mythology in the light of

Irigaray's essay in order to show that both writers imagine Melusine in feminist ways.

'La serpentine victime'

The nineteenth-century plot of *Possession* resists an age-old paradigm which constructs Melusine as an evil woman and an unnatural other. The serpent-woman Melusine is probably best known from a text written by the medieval writer Jean d'Arras: *Le Roman de Melusine ou l'Histoire des Lusignan*.[27] The story of Melusine as rendered by d'Arras is part of a number of fairy tales and myths which has as its subject the impossible love between mortals and supernatural beings. Here is a brief outline of its basic elements: a fairy, Presine, sees her marriage destroyed when, contrary to his promise not to visit her in childbed, her husband Elinas enters her room. As a consequence she is banned to an island with her three daughters, one of whom, Melusine, chooses to avenge her mother by imprisoning Elinas. Instead of being grateful, Presine punishes her daughter by changing her appearance: Melusine is destined to be part woman, part snake. She needs a mortal man in order to live a woman's existence and die a natural death or else she will be imprisoned in eternal pain. She finds this man in Raymond, who has to promise her that he will never pry into her supernatural powers and will not visit her on Saturdays when, unknown to him, she changes into a snake from her waist to her toes. If his gaze falls upon her then, she will lose the appearance of a woman. They marry, Melusine gives birth to ten boys who all have some defect, but perform heroic deeds against the Saracens. Due to Melusine's other fertile powers the country and its inhabitants enjoy great prosperity. All is well until goaded on by evil rumours, Raymond discovers Melusine's secret. He spies on her when she takes a bath and uses his knowledge to denounce her publicly, thus confining her to an eternal life as a snake. She may only visit the castle to feed her two youngest children. She circles around the towers of the castle, predicting death and disaster and uttering horrible cries: 'les cris de la fée'. Like the mythical Cassandra and the Lady of Shalott, Melusine meets her predetermined fate – 'un échec inévitable'.[28]

Melusine's punishment and death became even more important as the Melusine mythology changed with history. Stuby writes that d'Arras based his story on folk tales, the content of which he changed considerably.[29] Gone is the powerful, unromantic, wild serpent woman. She is presented in a more outspoken Christian framework, that is, she is subjected to Christian sacraments surrounding mass, marriage and christenings. She is also described as a (suffering) mother in a much more pronounced way: she bears ten boys and is only allowed access to the castle to feed her two youngest children. Her unnatural powers are a burden and a defect to her. And finally, her ill-fated existence is closely bound to one man whom she must love eternally, even when the rewards of this love are permanently out of reach anyway and no longer relevant.

This is the kind of plot which many Melusine versions share. Le Goff and Le Roy Ladurie show that, from the seventeenth century onwards, Melusine's character becomes, indeed, more and more diabolical, evidence of 'la diabolisation progressive du myth'.[30] Lundt argues that myth criticism which followed d'Arras has 'a tendency to overemphasize Melusine the demon. The story tends to be read as a warning against female seduction and against the danger the woman presents to men's spiritual welfare and salvation'.[31] In fiction a similar kind of interpretation – Melusine as the embodiment of evil – has resulted in stories and poems which share the following themes: an obsession experienced by men with Melusine's secret; the complete dependence of the woman on a female existence legitimized by the love for one man; and men's fear of Melusine's unnatural powers, resulting in a desire to domesticate her. If this fails, which it is bound to do in these narratives, the woman Melusine has to die, a fate which some writers let her choose willingly.

Judging from *Possession*, Byatt is acutely aware of the ways in which Melusine has been portrayed and represented in literature and literary criticism. One does not find the emphasis on the monster Melusine in her novel, though. On the contrary, *Possession* changes this particular historical paradigm. The nineteenth-century story about Ash and LaMotte resists an image of Melusine as an evil woman and a monster by emphasizing the fact that Melusine is both a mother and a daughter. References to both these roles can be found in *Possession*'s portrait of Christabel LaMotte.

The first comparison – between the daughter LaMotte and Melusine – is an implicit one. In the story of Melusine as recorded by Jean d'Arras, Melusine is punished by her mother Presine.

Instead of being grateful, Presine punishes her daughter by changing her appearance: Melusine is destined to be part woman, part snake. Like Cassandra and the Lady of Shalott, she has to live with a curse upon her. If Raymond discovers her true nature Melusine will have to live in eternal pain.

Like Melusine, the Victorian poet Christabel LaMotte is alienated from her mother. In the Britanny part of *Possession*, LaMotte's cousin Sabine quotes from a conversation she has with LaMotte about the latter's parents. Like other artist-characters such as Benjamin Disraeli's Contarini Fleming, Mme de Staël's Corinne and Barrett Browning's Aurora Leigh, LaMotte has a mixed nationality: her father is French and her mother English.[32]. The narrator constructs a strong opposition between LaMotte's parents. LaMotte is positive about her French father who is a famous scholar of mythology: she owes her interest in the Melusine mythology to him because he told her over and over again about Melusine. He also gave her 'the desire to write' and a strong interest in language (p. 174). She is negative about her mother: LaMotte writes in English – her mother's language – but describes it as a handicap: 'my mother is not a spiritual woman, and her language is that of household minutiae and female fashion' (p. 348). Sabine concludes from their conversation that LaMotte's mother is still alive, but that LaMotte has not turned to her for help when she found out she was pregnant. This is the only place in *Possession* where LaMotte's mother is mentioned and she is presented as an absence in her daughter's life.

The portrait of the daughter–mother relationship in the nineteenth-century plot of *Possession* is a tragic one. The cycle of alienation repeats itself when LaMotte herself bears a daughter. When she decides to accompany Ash on his journey to Yorkshire, she knows what the consequences may be. She is punished terribly for her decision. She becomes pregnant with an unwanted child, calling her pregnancy 'a monstrous catastrophe of body and soul' (p. 500). She prohibits the people in her acquintance from discussing the pregnancy. She gives birth in a convent in Britanny, separated from Randolph Ash and Blanche Glover, the two people she knows and loves. She loses Blanche Glover, who feels betrayed and kills herself, causing LaMotte terrible anguish and guilt. As a 'fallen woman', LaMotte is precluded from bringing up her child. Her sister Sophie adopts May; LaMotte is forced to distance herself from her own child, who will remain in ignorance of her true origin. May is even afraid of her 'aunt' and does not share her love of literature: 'She cared nothing for books, nothing. I wrote her small tales, and they were bound and printed, and I gave them to her, and she smiled sweetly and thanked me and put them by. I never saw her read them for pleasure' (p. 502).

Thus, the nineteenth-century plot of *Possession* presents LaMotte as a Melusine figure who is condemned to an existence as a mother without her child. Moreover, as a tragic mother figure LaMotte is not an exceptional character in the nineteenth-century plot. As Byatt said of Victorian women: 'the problem of the fact that sex for women leads to childbearing is . . . central to the whole question of sexual equality and women's freedom'.[33] Ellen Ash is one of 15 children of whom 4 survive. She fires Bertha because the latter is unmarried and pregnant and will bring scandal to Ash's house. Sabine de Kercoz, who is determined to be a writer, dies in childbed. When at the end of her life LaMotte compares herself to Melusine, even insisting that she *is* Melusine, she specifically refers to the mother who has been banished and expelled: 'I have been Melusina these thirty years. I have so to speak flown about and about the battlements of this stronghold crying on the wind of my need to see and feed and comfort my child, who knew me not' (p. 501). The narrator presents LaMotte as a victim of social circumstances and, thus, writes beyond Melusine's fate as an evil woman in charge of her own fate.

In doing so, the nineteenth-century plot of *Possession* interprets the Melusine mythology in ways which are similar to contemporary feminist interpretations of d'Arras's story, many of which postdate *Possession*.[34] In the readings of feminists theorists such as Stuby, Irigaray and Vincenot, the Melusine mythology becomes the vehicle for an analysis of a creature who is thoroughly victimized as a woman, a mother and a wife. Keeping Bal's idea in mind that, in myth criticism, every version of a myth is produced by/in the subjective preoccupations of the interpreter, it seems that Stuby, Irigaray and Vincenot are preoccupied by Melusine as exemplary of the unfulfilled condition of women.[35] They successfully resist an easy identification with this kind of female character and have not gone along obediently, as it were, with a masochistic interpretation of the story. Anger speaks from their essays: they never forget that Melusine's fate need not have been an inevitable element of the narrative, had another imagination and another culture shaped her.

In 'Divine Women' for instance, the essay which A. S. Byatt read for *Possession*, Luce Irigaray discusses what the Melusine mythology tells us about motherhood. The myth exposes and portrays painful inadequacies, according to Irigaray. Inadequacies which are partly enacted and caused by men and women, partly inherent to the systems of beliefs and symbols they are born into.[36] According to Irigaray, the Melusine mythology is a story about the lack of a female genealogy between women. Muraro explains Irigaray's concept of female genealogy as follows: it is a 'genealogy based on procreation which binds us to the mother, to her mother, and so on, maternity functioning as the structure of a female continuum that links us to the origins of life'.[37] According to Irigaray, the mythical Melusine is not embedded in such a maternal continuum. She is cursed by her mother and has to leave her own children behind. Vincenot also reads the Melusine mythology as a story about motherhood which is full of contradictions. On the one hand, motherhood is considered women's true existence and, on the other hand, Melusine's life is turned into a 'sad fate'. Vincenot acutely remarks that whereas, in fairy tales, boys are usually sent out in the world protected by 'amulet, incantation, or memorial', Melusine is unprotected and, therefore, an easy victim.[38]

Thus, what the nineteenth-century plot of *Possession* has in common with Irigaray and Vincenot's readings is that it presents the story of Melusine as a tragic portrait of motherhood. In *Possession* LaMotte lacks the presence of a mother and cannot be a mother to her child, due to nineteenth-century social circumstances which are presented as far more limiting to women than they are to men. In this sense, *Possession* gives a feminist analysis of the tragic social and historical background of Victorian women's lives. Although A. S. Byatt is adamant that she does not want to be 'ghettoized by modern feminists into writing about women's problems', I would like to conclude this part by suggesting that she already does so in *Possession*'s revision of the Melusine mythology.[39] Moreover, this revision bears a resemblance to Luce Irigaray's feminist argument in 'Divine Women'. According to Irigaray, Melusine's fate goes against the grain of the idealization of motherhood which is an integral part of Western culture. Melusine's motherhood is not fulfilled; she is a tragic figure and her marriage to Raymond is incomplete and ends in disaster. It is that kind of tragedy which also determines the nineteenth-century plot of *Possession*.

The nineteenth-century artist-novel plot

However, when it comes to Irigaray's interpretation of Melusine's 'unnatural' side, *Possession* chooses another perspective. Irigaray interprets the narrative as an enactment of male fear of motherly power and a desire to master the latter, because it is experienced as 'amorphous, unformed, a dangerous abyss'.[40] She reads the stories of Melusine as narratives of punishment in which the serpent woman or water woman is castigated for the possession and exertion of powers which are unavailable and closed to men, motherhood being one of them. Irigaray also reads the mythology as evidence of the fact that women are hindered from successfully reconciling the triple identity 'daughter-woman-mother'.[41] She interprets the inhuman part of Melusine's appearance as a sign of the ways in which women have been represented as the other, as strangers to themselves:

> The impotence, the formlessness, the deformity associated with women, the way they are equated with something other than the human and split between the human and the inhuman (half-woman, half-animal) . . . they are forced to comply with models that do not match them, that exile, double, mask them, cut them off from themselves and from one another, stripping away their ability to move forward into love, art, thought, toward their ideal and divine fulfilment.[42]

According to Irigaray, we may call ourselves 'women' but all the possible dimensions contained in that word are still in a symbolic future: hence her interpretation of Melusine's unnatural side as monstrous and as a symbol of her incomplete nature as a woman. She represents femininity as an, as yet, unfinished symbolic process in which all women are enveloped. Melusine does not have a 'real self' yet her monstrous side bears evidence of this lack. As the Dutch theologian Mulder puts it: 'Luce Irigaray discusses what is hidden by/in all the transformations Melusine goes through. These incarnations are partial, these shapes are partial. Her full birth is constantly delayed and deferred. Melusine is not yet a woman, born as a woman'.[43]

While *Possession* shares Irigaray's analysis of Melusine as the tragic daughter and mother, it also adds a different perspective on female subjectivity. A. S. Byatt uses the Melusine mythology to write a woman artist's story. *Possession* is quite unique in imagining Melusine as a mother *and* as a woman artist. Irigaray for instance is not specifically interested in the Melusine myth as a story of female creativity. Vincenot does mention Melusine's creativity but is critical of what d'Arras's story has to say about it. Melusine's 'endless production, of children, castles, harvests, towns etc. is only directed towards one aim: the care for offspring and a husband'. LeGoff, Le Roy Ladurie and Hallissey mainly emphasize the economic importance of Melusine's building power.[44] *Possession* opens up the Melusine paradigm by constructing a relationship between the artist LaMotte and Melusine. That is, the novel reappropriates Melusine, and the stories which hold her, as a way of writing a woman artist's story. Melusine is a counter-figuration of female artistic subjectivity which informs *Possession* as strongly as the portrait of the Victorian genius Randolph Henry Ash. In its portrait of the poet LaMotte, the narrative connects motherhood, love and creativity in its rewriting of the Melusine mythology.

How does the narrator of *Possession* construct the relationship between the artist LaMotte and Melusine? First, in the letters which Ash and LaMotte write to each other. Their correspondence shows that LaMotte is seduced by the fact that Ash is also a poet and understands what she is trying to do. They talk as equals and share a writer's understanding in their letters. The beginning of their friendship is based on art, the intellectual life and an interest in Melusine. She functions as a creative bridge between Ash and LaMotte and her life is an important theme in the letters they write to each other. As Ash says: 'and yet she it was who caused this correspondence to be opened' (p. 172). LaMotte discusses with Ash how to incorporate the Melusine motif in an epic poem; what the technical problems are in this writing process; which elements of the mythology might be useful to her creative imagination. They disagree about the possible interpretations of Melusine's character. In one of his first letters to LaMotte Ash quotes Paracelsus: 'The Melusinas are daughters of kings, desperate through their sins. Satan bore them away and transformed them into spectres, into evil spirits, into horrible revenants and frightful monsters' (p. 171).

LaMotte criticizes Ash for thinking Melusine a monster. She intends to represent Melusine as an ambivalent figure: 'an Unnatural Monster – and a most proud and loving and handy woman . . . a combination of the orderly and humane with the unnatural and the Wild' (p. 174, 179). In describing Melusine in this way, LaMotte has distance and empathy in mind:

> I would write, if I undertook it – a little from Melusina's – own – vision. Not as you might, in the First Person – as inhabiting her skin – but seeing her as an unfortunate Creature – of Power and Frailty – always in Fear of returning to the Ranging of the Air (p. 175).

Thus, Christabel LaMotte thinks about using the Melusine mythology in an artist's way. When she discloses her poetic plans to Ash, it is clear she is determined to use the licence art allows her to save Melusine from negative interpretations. Since this is exactly what the writer A. S. Byatt does in *Possession*, she has much more in common with LaMotte than she suggests in the interviews.

LaMotte is also intrigued by what the Melusine mythology has to say about the relationship between autonomy and creativity. She is obsessed with Melusine, not only because she wants to rewrite her as a poetic figure and save her from negative interpretations, but also because she is intrigued by the space the Melusine mythology does provide for a concept of autonomy and creativity and a relationship between the two. The fact that Melusine owns her own space on Saturdays in which she is left alone and the fact that she creates madly and is applauded for it is attractive to LaMotte. She is not interested in Melusine's motherhood: it is the creative, productive Melusine which initially draws her attention. This particular emphasis is reinforced when the narrator closes the gap between LaMotte, the analytical artist judging her material, and Melusine, the figure which is the object of her attention. Many of LaMotte's allusions are to Melusine as a creative woman who is autonomous sometimes and escapes to a free space. This free space opens up undreamt possibilities, as LaMotte tells her young cousin Sabine de Kercoz:

> She said, in Romance, women's two natures can be reconciled. I asked, which two natures, and she said, men saw women as double

beings, enchantresses and demons or innocent angels. 'Are all women double?', I asked her. 'I did not say that', she said. 'I said all men see women as double. Who knows what Melusina was in her freedom with no eyes on her?' (p. 373).

The Melusine mythology in the nineteenth-century plot of *Possession* is used to investigate the subject of a woman artist's autonomy. It revises the usual idea of the nineteenth century, confining women to their homes, imprisoning them. LaMotte prefers it this way, because it enables her to live the only life she wants to have: the life of the mind, of language, of art. She is able to secure this by living out her ideal with another artist, Blanche Glover. Reviewers of *Possession* overlook this fact and largely concentrate their analyses on the relationship between Ash and LaMotte. Richard Todd is the only commentator to pay attention to Blanche Glover and compares her portrait to that of Val, Roland's girlfriend.[45] Most critics neglect LaMotte's relationship with Blanche and, hence, LaMotte's bisexuality. When Ash and LaMotte have slept together for the first time, Ash wonders about LaMotte's 'delicate skills' and 'informed desire' which contradict her virginity: 'he could never ask . . . It was like Melusina's exhibition, and no narrative bound him, unlike the unfortunate Raimondin, to exhibit indiscreet curiosity' (p. 285). Here the narrative relates LaMotte/Melusine's unknown side to lesbian sexuality. The narrator sketches an artistic utopia in Bethany, Blanche and LaMotte's artistic community. LaMotte describes it as 'a sealed pact', allowing her to live without 'the usual female Hopes (and with them the usual Female Fears) in exchange for – dare I say Art' (p. 187). Bethany is the space which is comparable to Melusine's room, to the Lady of Shalott's tower and to Anna Severell's bathroom. Here LaMotte can be what she truly is and wants to be: a poet to the core. Thus, the narrator subverts the monstrosity attached to Melusine's private space for it is presented as a strength. It is this representation of artistic autonomy which makes *Possession* different from the interpretation Irigaray gives of Melusine's monstrous side. Irigaray reads the mythology as evidence of the fact that women are hindered from successfully reconciling a triple identity: 'daughter-woman-mother'. She interprets the inhuman part of Melusine's appearance as a sign of the ways in which women have been represented as the other, as strangers to themselves. According to Irigaray, Melusine does not have a 'real self' yet her monstrous side bears evidence of this lack. Vincenot also wonders whether Melusine's Saturdays are a blessing in disguise to her, providing her with solitude and calm, but she concludes that they are no compensation for the fate which finally befalls her: 'in no way is she protected against intruders' or against the rumours about infidelity which circulate around her. The fact that she is not unfaith-ful on Saturdays but just herself – half woman, half snake – makes it worse. She is there for herself which poses a threat to a concept of femininity which emphasizes, as Vincenot puts it: 'the adoration, the worship of the male sex'.[46]

The narrator of *Possession*, in contrast, uses the analogy between the artist LaMotte and Melusine to present the space of Melusine's deviancy as liberating, as the place where she can really be herself. The usual artist–novel's opposition between art and life is deconstructed when LaMotte says: 'the need to set down words – . . . words have been all my life, all my life – this need is like the Spider's need who carries before her a huge burden of silk which she must spin out – the silk is her life, her home, her safety' (p. 108). LaMotte's life *is* her art and vice versa, and the image of the spider constructs her obsession with art as a natural necessity. Willa Cather uses a similar image in her artist-novel *The Song of the Lark*:

> Your work becomes your personal life. You are not much good until it does. It's like being woven into a big web. You can't pull away, because all your little tendrils are woven into the picture. It takes you up, and uses you, and spins you out; and that is your life.[47]

This is then the second way in which the nineteenth-century plot of *Possession* uses the Melusine mythology. Melusine comes to stand for the figure of the woman artist who wants to break through the opposi-tion of life and art and wants to live for her art. Therefore, the figure of Melusine can be compared to the Lady of Shalott, who functions as a symbol of female creative subjectivity in *The Shadow of the Sun* and, to a lesser degree, in *The Game*. Lamotte compares herself to Melusine and to the Lady of Shalott in a letter to Ash:

> think of me if you will as the Lady of Shalott – with a Narrower Wisdom – who . . . chooses to watch dilligently the bright

colours of her web . . . to make – something. You will say, you are
no Threat to that . . . I know in my Intrinsic Self – the Threat is
there (p. 187).

LaMotte has a feminist desire for artistic autonomy which Ash
threatens when he becomes more insistent. It is not coincidental that,
when LaMotte looks back on her affair with Ash, she misses the
correspondence rather than the passion: 'but now I am old I regret
most of all not those few sharp sweet days of passion – I regret . . . our
old letters, of poetry and other things . . .' (p. 501). Ash and LaMotte
are part of a Romance plot but it is a plot which has quite deterministic overtones. The narrator emphasizes LaMotte's final willing-
ness in participating in the affair and her unromantic down-to-earth
execution of her decision to join Ash on his trip to the North of
England: 'this is necessity . . . I'm afraid, of course. But that seems to
be of no real importance . . . Of course I shall regret . . . But that, too,
is of no importance at this time' (p. 276). La Motte has taken a
decision to go away with Ash and sleep with him and stands by it,
although she knows that she will suffer under the consequences. As
Byatt said in an interview: 'She is the most interesting character in the
book. She makes a lot of decisions rather powerfully. She is morally
extremely interesting'.[48] The moral decision concerns the question
whether she should sleep with Ash; the decision destroys her autonomy. Up to that point she has been able to hold her own, to preserve
her autonomy and be a woman and a writer, but after she has slept
with Ash the similarities between her life as an artist and Melusine
turn into a different direction. Thus, while many reviewers found Ash
too good to be true as a lover and poet I think that the narrative is
quite ambivalent about him. As long as Ash and LaMotte share their
interest in art LaMotte does not feel threatened. This changes
gradually as the letters show (pp. 137, 170, 187, 195, 199, 502). At
some places in the narrative, Ash is presented as an intruder. Blanche
writes in her journal: 'so now we have a Prowler. Something is
ranging and snuffing round our small retreat . . . This Peeping Tom
has put his eye to the nick or cranny in our walls and peers shame-
lessly in' (p. 47). Indeed, the threat Ash poses to LaMotte's creative
autonomy resembles the effect Oliver Canning has on Anna Severell
in *The Shadow of the Sun*. Ash uses the Melusine myth as an excuse:
'on the levels of tales, you know, all prohibitions are made only to be

broken, must be broken – as is indeed instanced in your own Melusina with striking ill-luck to the disobedient knight' (p. 181). Like Raymond, Ash breaks the prohibition and the nineteenth-century plot of *Possession* is ambivalent about the results. It rewrites the Melusine mythology in two ambivalent ways, using it to portray LaMotte's life as part of an artist-novel plot. This plot becomes entangled with a tragic nineteenth-century mother–daughter plot. LaMotte is a woman artist who uses Melusine's deviancy as liberating, as the place where she can really be herself, and a mother who has to suffer when Melusine's prohibition is broken.

Female genealogies: the twentieth-century artist-novel plot

Byatt's new construction of Melusine as a symbol of female creativity spills over into the twentieth-century plot of *Possession*. As I said before there are critics who found this plot unconvincing, but the reader who pays attention to Melusine will notice that the twentieth-century plot of *Possession* also connects Melusine, motherhood and art. LaMotte's art forms a textual bridge from the nineteenth- to the twentieth-century story. The fact that these poems are partly included in the narrative makes *Possession* a true heir of the first British eighteenth-century artist-novels published by women writers. Not only did they choose artists as their central characters, they also mixed genres by including poetry in their prose. These samples of poetry were presented as art made by the artist-heroine, as is the case in *Possession*.[49] The inclusion of the spilt milk poem and parts of *The Fairy Melusine* in the narrative works well for a rewriting of the Melusine mythology as a woman-artist's story. The narrator of the nineteenth-century plot constructs the woman LaMotte as 'la belle inconnue'. We only know LaMotte through her letters and the perspective of her cousin Sabine de Kercoz, Ash and so on. At the same time, LaMotte does live on in her work and can be known through it. The reader learns most about her through her letters to Ash and her poems. Such a narrative structure forces the reader's attention towards the artist LaMotte. The relationship between LaMotte, Melusine and art in the ninteenth-century plot spills over into the twentieth-century story and it is here that *Possession* changes the dismal ending of the Melusine mythology. LaMotte's poem *The Fairy Melusine* is feminist in the sense that she writes beyond the deadly ending of the Melusine mythology. Chronologically, LaMotte writes the epic poem about the fairy Melusine after she has given birth. She describes Melusine the mother and her pain and also calls a female Muse to tell the story of a proud and autonomous Melusine who has a face 'self-contained and singing to itself' (p. 298).

In the twentieth-century plot LaMotte's letters and her poem *The Fairy Melusine* are discovered, read and interpreted by twentieth-century feminist scholars such as Leonora Stern, Maud Bailey and Ariane Le Nimier. The narrator quotes at length from the feminist discussions and presents the reader with an overview of feminist interpretations of the Melusine mythology and of LaMotte's poem. Readers arc, thus, drawn into a highly theoretical discourse and are asked to participate in an intellectual and theoretical discussion about the possible meanings and interpretations of the figure of Melusine. I would argue that, even though a feminist scholar such as Leonora Stern is satirized in *Possession*, she and Maud Bailey are 'the discerning readers' LaMotte hopes for in her last letter to Ash: 'I think she will not die, my Melusina, some discerning reader will save her?' (p. 501). The male academics such as Cropper and Blackadder are only occupied with Ash, who is already established.[50]

The connection between feminism, the mythical figure of Melusine and art is established even more strongly at the end of the novel, when it becomes clear that Maud Bailey descends from both Ash and LaMotte. *Possession* writes beyond LaMotte and Melusine's ending by creating Maud. It is fitting that Maud is a feminist expert on LaMotte's work and shares LaMotte's passionate interest in words. This narrative development establishes a female genealogy in Irigaray's sense of the term described earlier. It is a female genealogy which gives Maud an exciting foremother and LaMotte a daughter who loves her work. It evokes art as a bridge, as 'a labor of love, a continuation of the . . . impulse of a thwarted parent, an emotional gift for family, child, self, or others'.[51] In this sense *Possession* is different from *The Shadow of the Sun*, for instance. The difficulties between the male genius Henry Severell and his daughter Anna and the fear of art are absent from *Possession*. *The Game* already contains the first contours of a mother–daughter relationship in the portraits of the novelist Julia

Corbett and her daughter Deborah. *The Game* is critical of the writer who makes the ethical mistake of thinking that 'art' is more important than 'life' and family. However, where Henry Severell loses his daughter Anna, Julia Corbett and Deborah literally fight it out between them and are able to reach some sort of reconciliation. *Possession* takes up again the mother–daughter relationship and constructs a female genealogy between Christabel LaMotte and Maud Bailey, using the Melusine mythology to do so. Elaine Feinstein is the only English critic who notices the narrative connection between Melusine, LaMotte and Maud Bailey: 'it is on Maud Bailey that the wish for freedom LaMotte so beautifully articulates in her reading of the mermaid fairy story is focussed'.[52] As such, *Possession* contradicts Huf's observation that in contemporary artist-novels by women writers, the artist-heroine lacks a real or symbolical mother and, therefore, has to go through the painful process of giving birth to herself.[53] On the contrary, it reinforces Blau DuPlessis' observation that the presence of a stimulating mother is the outstanding characteristic of twentieth-century artist-novels by women writers. The mother is 'a nurturing source, not an impediment, she replaces the negative influence of a thwarting partner by a positive influence, she becomes her daughter's Muse'.[54] LaMotte and Melusine take on a presence which reminds me of a narrative feature of novels by black women writers. As Toni Morrison has said, 'there is always an elder there. And these ancestors are not just parents, they are sort of timeless people whose relationships to the characters are benevolent, instructive, and protective, and they provide a certain kind of wisdom'.[55] Or, as the woman tells the eldest princess in one of A. S. Byatt's fairy tales:

> There is always an old woman ahead of you on a journey, and there is always an old woman behind you too, and they are not always the same, and may be fearful or kindly, dangerous or delightful, as the road shifts, and you speed along it. Certainly I was ahead of you, and behind you too, but not only I, and not only as I am now.[56]

Conclusion

To conclude this chapter on *Possession* and the Melusine mythology I will return to the ambivalence that is such a structural aspect of

A. S. Byatt's ideas about art, creativity and authorship. This study has shown that Byatt's novels may be read as portraits of the Lady of Shalott, Cassandra and Melusine and the meanings they have as symbols of female artistic subjectivity. In more recent interviews A. S. Byatt has pointed to the similarities between the Lady of Shalott and her own creative female characters such as Cassandra Corbett and Christabel LaMotte:

> Cassandra and Christabel are very close to each other. They're the woman closed in the tower who has given her soul for her writing but is also somehow destroyed. They're all the Lady of Shalott . . . It's to do with the thing that all my books are about: the sensuous life, childbearing, therefore men, therefore danger, and making things by yourself of exquisite beauty which can be accused of being unreal. All my books are about the woman artist – in that sense they're terribly feminist books – and they're about what language is. Because of course, if language is as much nature as childbearing, you're all right.[57]

In this chapter I have read A. S. Byatt's critical remarks about *Possession* and the text of the novel itself as more ambivalent than the quote above suggests. Byatt's disengagement from Christabel LaMotte and her satirical portraits of feminist literary critics such as Leonora Stern exist alongside *Possession*'s feminist revision of the Melusine mythology. *Possession* acknowledges the deterministic undertones of the Melusine mythology and at the same time uses it to write another story. Byatt rewrites the usual nineteenth-century woman's plot which ends in marriage or death and changes it into a woman-artist's story, a story in which the juggling of female autonomy, love and creativity are the main themes as Byatt herself recognized:

> Elaine Feinstein, in her review of the book, rightly saw the true point of contact between Maud and Christabel as the moment when Christabel gives a cry which is my cry throughout the book: 'you're taking away my autonomy, you're giving me something wonderful that I regard as secondary, my work is what matters'; and nevertheless she falls heavily in love because she is a very powerful and passionate woman.[58]

This story spills over into the twentieth-century plot and gives fictional form to a female genealogy, the nature of which bears remarkable similarities to feminist ideas about 'genealogies', notably those of Luce Irigaray. *Possession* can be read as a narrative revenge on Melusine's ending and the little mermaid's pain: a reappropriation of a seemingly inevitable fate. As Andre Brink writes: 'Melusina is restored to her position of benign power through an act of historical correction'.[59] Like feminist writers such as Irigaray and Stuby, Byatt does not go along with a masochistic interpretation of the story. *Possession* writes beyond the ending of Melusine's dismal fate, in Blau DuPlessis' sense of that concept: 'the invention of strategies that sever the narrative from formerly conventional structures of fiction and consciousness about women is what I call writing beyond the ending'.[60] Melusine rises from the ashes, so to speak, and becomes a woman artist, instead of a monster. The reader is asked to step back and reflect upon all these forms while being given the possibility to realize that there can be positive elements to this story. *The Game* is quite pessimistic in its use of the Cassandra mythology in that Cassandra Corbett is described as a failed female visionary. *Possession* rewrites a myth that is potentially just as destructive in more affirmative terms. As such, *Possession* is the most exciting and optimistic of the three novels discussed in this study. Byatt's rewriting of Melusine shows the relevance of Helen Dunmore's remark that myths and fairy stories 'come about because they are containers into which we can pour the shapelessness of grief, loss and joy. In the best of Byatt's fairy stories there is always this drive of necessity beneath the fine surfaces of the writing'.[61] Byatt appropriates a mythical figure whose representations seem to speak only of female impotence and pain, to develop alternative conceptions of art, creativity and a female genealogy.[62]

Art Made Me: Conclusion

'Life, she wants to say, though it is books she is talking about . . .'[1]

This book contains a critical account of the contradictory, yet highly productive ways in which Byatt's fiction and criticism move across and in and out of Leavisite, post-structuralist and feminist debates about art, creativity and authorship, tracing an itinerary of her own. One of the main conclusions to be drawn from my investigation is that in the case of A. S. Byatt's work, nothing is as authentic or central as her ambivalence. In other words, A. S. Byatt's descriptions of male writers such as Henry Severell and Randolph Henry Ash and female visionaries such as Anna Severell, Christabel LaMotte, Julia and Cassandra Corbett are of great interest, precisely because they *are* so ambivalent. They are fictional frameworks which allow us to think better about the complex nature of creativity and its ambivalent relation to gender because A. S. Byatt's novels perfectly describe where the seduction of literary genius lies. She describes male and female characters who long for artistic genius because of the promises it contains, for instance the transcendence of the limitations of gender, the achievement of excellence and the wholeness of art which may act as a stronghold both against the disorder and the dullness of reality. In *Love's Knowledge* Martha Nussbaum points to this transcendent potential of art, citing the work of Henry James and Marcel Proust as specific examples:

Both James and Proust compare excellent literary works to angels that soar above the dullness and obtuseness of the everyday, offering their readers a glimpse of a more compassionate, subtler, more responsive, more richly human world. That is a view about transcendence. And I believe that it is extremely important to make the aspiration to that sort of transcendence central to a picture of the complete human good.[2]

This is the kind of positive transcendence which one finds in A. S. Byatt's novels, one that may still be relevant to anyone interested in the potential of art. I also read in Byatt's novels a further advantage: they conceptualize the 'great' writer as an observer who may follow a desire to use narrative as a way of ordering experience, as an entrance to knowledge and understanding, who may experience an intense pleasure in the aesthetic beauty of patterns and form. One can find this 'ideal' type of writer in both Byatt's fiction and criticism, specifically in those parts which define 'great' art and the 'good' writer in Leavisite terms.

What makes A. S. Byatt's work even more interesting to debates about art and the nature of creative identity is the fact that it also qualifies a concept of the great writer and of art as transcendence in ways which have feminist and post-structuralist elements. This aspect of her work constitutes its relevance to English Studies in a greater way than has been assumed thus far. A. S. Byatt's criticism testifies to the attraction she feels towards 'Leavisite' ideas about the writer as a genius but it also speaks of the difficulties she has in accepting Leavis's theory of impersonality and his devaluation of 'femininity'. This is why I believe that 'ambivalence' as a critical term of analysis is relevant to any scholarly reading of A. S. Byatt's work, generating rich rewards for us as readers. As a critical term 'ambivalence' foregrounds the ways in which both Byatt's fiction and her criticism agree with and differ from Leavisite criticism, feminism and post- structuralism. Literary scholars working with the critical ideas developed in these fields may benefit from the ambivalent light A. S. Byatt's work throws on them, certainly in the light of the re-evaluation of F. R. Leavis's work which is currently taking place in England.

Moreover, A. S. Byatt's work also makes us aware that even though the seduction of genius and the transcendence of art have their rewarding sides, both can also have dismal effects. Martha Nussbaum explains that a human desire for transcendence may come forth from motivations that are quite negative, for instance when it leads to 'forms that involve withdrawing love and concern from that which cannot be stably controlled, or admitting as valuable only that which is immune from change and alteration'.[3] A. S. Byatt's novels are critical of this type of transcendence because it leads the male genius to separate himself and his art from love, women and gendered identity. In other words, Byatt's novels offer a critical perspective on the relationship between a concept of art as transcendent and the construction of male identity. They describe such a concept of art as closely allied to, indeed structurally embedded in, the idea that male artistic identity is achieved through disembodiment, alienation and a separation from women. In criticizing the effects of a masculine pursuit of genius and transcendence, *The Shadow of the Sun*, *The Game* and *Possession* offer us alternative visions of art and creative identity, which do not assume that art is a product of a totally free imagination, unrestricted by ethics, love, gender, personal histories, family identities, nor are they completely determined by them. A. S. Byatt's novels are susceptible to the promises contained in the transcendence of art while also pointing to their dangers. This is the second level on which the term 'ambivalence' is of relevance as a category of analysis, pointing to the moral nature of Byatt's novels. The latter show the dangers of a concept of art and the imagination which denies the ethical boundaries it is bound to run up against and do not follow the idea that, in the last resort, art is a force which transcends morality. As such, they construct a definition of transcendence that is similar to the one described by Martha Nussbaum: 'what is recommended is a delicate and always flexible balancing act between the claims of excellence, which lead us to push outward, and the necessity of the human context which pushes us back in'.[4]

More generally, I would like to conclude that from my readings of *The Shadow of the Sun*, *The Game* and *Possession* A. S. Byatt emerges as a far less traditional novelist than she is usually given credit for. From a gender-sensitive perspective, it is important that her novels criticize the lack of women's access to artistic subjectivity and construct counter- figurations of creative women, such as the mythical serpent woman Melusine and the Lady of Shalott. Thus, A. S. Byatt's novels prove the relevance of Patricia Yaeger's observation that instead of being a form of constraint, the novel may 'celebrate . . . capaciousness as a form', containing emancipatory strategies which are 'a force of praxis and change'.[5] Adequate readings of the emancipatory strategies in Byatt's work – by which I mean readings which truly bring out the interest and quality of her oeuvre – are impossible without a discussion of the work's relationship to 'gender' and 'feminism', a relation which is far more complex and interesting than academics and literary critics have allowed for.

There is clearly much more to be learnt from A. S. Byatt's criticism and fiction. For instance the relevance of science to an adequate understanding of her fiction asks for a separate investigation. The relation between aesthetic pleasure, sensuality and rationality is another subject which I believe will provide an adequate hermeneutical key to Byatt's fiction. What interests me most in terms of future research is the question in which ways A. S. Byatt's novels and criticism can be related to fields outside literature and literary theory. For instance, the knot of associations which structure her portraits of writers – water, light and glass – has a relevance that goes beyond literature. They are metaphors of creativity which deserve further investigation, for instance in the context of philosophy and aesthetics. It will be exciting to look in more detail at how Byatt's 'obsession' with light and shadows can be read in the context of Plato's myth of the cave, for instance. The idea of glass as solid matter and transparent liquidity can also be read productively in the context of aesthetics. I have already explained how the metaphors of water, light and glass enable Byatt to represent the problematics of the (creative) female subject in her fiction. It seems to me that Luce Irigaray's work on metaphors of identity and creativity and A. S. Byatt's ideas could be read alongside each other in productive and interesting ways, as I hope Chapter 2 already proves.

And finally I would like to return one last time to the concept of 'ambivalence' in order to emphasize its relevance for a textual ethics of reading. The quality of the reception of A. S. Byatt's work benefits from the kind of reading which focusses on the many kinds of complexities and ambivalences to be found there. Such practice will make us better readers of Byatt's work. That is, I would like to continue the kind of work which stresses the relevance of the concepts of gender, fragmentation, ambivalence and ambiguity to an understanding of her novels. For I am suspicious of the idea that 'good art' and 'fragmented art' are mutually exclusive terms, as Maureen Freely suggested in a review of Ozick's *Portrait of the Artist as a Bad Character*: 'like most fiction writers (and, I suspect, even most post-modernists) [Ozick] believes that fiction has no point unless it has an emotional and moral centre – especially at a time when so many culture vultures refuse to call it art unless it is fragmented'. In this study I suggest that the fragmented and structurally ambivalent nature of A. S. Byatt's novels and criticism partly constitutes its moral nature. Moreover, the different types of ambivalence discussed in this study make Byatt's fiction and criticism such rich sources for anyone interested in the theoretical and imaginative potential of the novel. For as Toni Morrison writes:

> [the novel] should be beautiful, and powerful, but it should also *work*. It should have something in it that enlightens; something in it that opens the door and points the way. Something in it that suggests what the conflicts are, what the problems are. But it need not solve those problems because it is not a case study, it is not a recipe.[6]

As such, a textual ethics of reading also has political relevance, in offering us ways of coming to terms with the necessary fragmenta-tions and complexities that are part of our lives as women and men, heeding the words of Barbara Johnson who said: 'I find that a lot of feminist criticism is very shy of ambiguity, not interested in unde-cidability, as a provisionary exploratory situation. So my tendency would be to inject more suspicion of answer into feminist criticism, rather than less'.[7] What I am arguing for, therefore, is that 'ambiva-lence' should be part of the critical categories we have at our disposal because of its relevance to the moral, political and aesthetic questions of our time.

Notes

Preface

1. Exceptions are Robert Carver, 'In Pursuit of the Fugitive Good: Criticism and the Arts on the Air. A. S. Byatt in Conversation with Robert Carver', Robert Carver (ed.), *Ariel at Bay: Reflections on Broadcasting and the Arts* (Manchester: Carcanet, 1990), pp. 45–54; Nicolas Tredell, 'A. S. Byatt', *Conversations with Critics* (Manchester: Carcanet, 1994), pp. 58–74; Richard Todd, *A. S. Byatt* (Plymouth: Northcote House in Association with the British Council, 1997).
2. Mireila Aragay, 'An Interview with A. S. Byatt' (Barcelona, 1992). Unpublished.
3. See the bibliography at the end of this study and Part I of Alexa Alfer and Michael D. Crane, with contributions by Michael J. Noble and Christien Franken, *A. S. Byatt: an Annotated Bibliography* (address: http://asbyatt.com/biblio/index.htm, 1999).
4. Barbara Johnson, *The Critical Difference: Essays in the Contemporary Rhetoric of Reading* (London: Johns Hopkins University Press, 1980), p. 5.
5. A. S. Byatt, *The Shadow of the Sun* (London: Chatto & Windus, 1964); *The Game* (London: Chatto & Windus, 1967); and *Possession* (London: Chatto & Windus, 1990).
6. Michael Levenson, 'The Religion of Fiction', *New Republic* (2 August 1993), pp. 41–4 (42). Reprinted in A. S. Byatt, *Degrees of Freedom* (London: Vintage, 1994). In her study of Etty Hillesum's philosophy, Denise de Costa notices that there are disadvantages to the kind of literary reading which only focusses on similarities. According to de Costa, the main disadvantage is that comparative readings disguise the authenticity of women's work. Denise de Costa, *Anne Frank and Etty Hillesum: Inscribing Spirituality and Sexuality*, trans. Mischa F. C. Hoyinck and Robert E. Chesal (New Brunswick: Rutgers University Press, 1998).
7. Adrian Page and Julian Cowley, 'The Twentieth Century: Fiction', in Elaine Treharne (ed.), *The Year's Work in English Studies 1992* (Oxford: Blackwell, 1995), pp. 486–91 (488) . On hearing about their description of her work, A. S. Byatt did not waste words: 'conventional is *ludicrous*. Must write novel' (letter to the author 1996).
8. Valentine Cunningham, 'In a Little Room', *British Book News* (July 1993), p. 422.
9. Nancy Miller, *Getting Personal* (London: Routledge, 1991), pp. 101–7. Griffin *does* compare A. S. Byatt and Iris Murdoch from a perspective which pays attention to gender: 'Both writers are a generation apart but they underwent similar experiences, being students, scholars and novelists

as well as women in post-war Oxbridge and London. Both have academic and novelistic interests in an intellectual world dominated by men, and both have a very intellectual, ideas-approach to their fiction'. Gabriele Griffin, 'A. S. Byatt', in Janet Todd (ed.), *Dictionary of British Women Writers* (London: Routledge, 1989), pp. 116–17. Nicci Gerrard and Michèle Roberts have also written about Byatt's work from a feminist perspective. Nicci Gerrard, *Into the Mainstream* (London: Pandora, 1989). Michèle Roberts' review of *The Matisse Stories* is a model of subtlety and intelligence, not least for the attention she pays to gender. Michèle Roberts, 'Matisse: All the Nudes That's Fit to Print', *Independent* (22 January 1994). See also 'The Passionate Reader: Possession and Romance', *Food, Sex & God* (London: Virago, 1998), pp. 47–69.

10. Marianne DeKoven, 'Male Signature, Female Aesthetic: the Gender Politics of Experimental Writing', in Ellen Friedman and Miriam Fuchs (eds), *Breaking the Sequence: Women's Experimental Fiction* (Princeton: Princeton University Press, 1989), pp. 72–84 (80).

11. Byatt, *Shadow of the Sun*, p. xii.

12. Chris Baldick, 'Myth Criticism', *Concise Oxford Dictionary of Literary Terms* (Oxford: Oxford University Press, 1990), p. 144.

13. J. B. Bullen, *The Sun Is God: Painting, Literature and Mythology in the Nineteenth Century* (Oxford: Clarendon Press, 1989). In *Mythologies* Barthes emphasizes the ahistorical nature of myths: 'myth deprives the object of which it speaks of all history. In it, history evaporates. It is a kind of ideal servant: it prepares all things, brings them, lays them out, the master arrives, it silently disappears: all that is left for one to do is to enjoy this beautiful object without wondering where it comes from. Or even better: it can only come from eternity'. Roland Barthes, *Mythologies* (London: Paladin, 1973), p. 165.

14. See for instance Hélène Cixous, 'The Laugh of the Medusa', *Signs* 1/4 (1976), pp. 857–93; Mary Lefkowitz, 'Feminist Myths and Greek Mythology', *TLS* 22 (28 July 1988), pp. 804–8; Teresa de Lauretis, 'Desire in Narrative', *Alice Doesn't: Feminism, Semiotics, Cinema* (Bloomington: Indiana University Press, 1984), pp. 103–57; Estella Lauter, *Women as Mythmakers: Poetry and Visual Art by Twentieth-Century Women* (Bloomington: Indiana University Press, 1984); Ellen Handler Spitz, 'Mothers and Daughters: Ancient and Modern Myths', *Journal of Aesthetics and Art Criticism* 48/4 (Fall 1990), pp. 411–20; Agnès Vincenot, 'Genèse', *Renaissance* (Amsterdam: Perdu, 1990), pp. 46–89; Drucilla Cornell, 'Feminine Writing, Metaphor and Myth', *Beyond Accomodation: Ethical Feminism, Deconstruction and the Law* (London: Routledge, 1991).

15. Isobel Armstrong, 'Tennyson's "The Lady of Shalott": Victorian Mythography and the Politics of Narcissism', in Bullen, *The Sun Is God*, pp. 49–108.

16. One could also think of novelists such as Toni Morrison, Marina Warner, Salman Rushdie and Michèle Roberts.

17. Richard Todd, 'Interview with A. S. Byatt', *NSES: Netherlands Society for English Studies* 1/1 (April 1991), pp. 36–44. See also A. S. Byatt's essay on

fairy tales, *Fairy Stories: the Djinn in the Nightingale's Eye* (Address: http://www.asbyatt.com/essays.htm [1999]).

18. Mark Rawlinson, 'Single Author Studies', *The Years Work in English Studies 1992* (Oxford: Blackwell, 1995), p. 510.

1 The turtle and its adversaries: Polyvocality in A. S. Byatt's critical and academic work

1. A. S. Byatt, *Still Life* (Harmondsworth: Penguin, 1986), p. 127.
2. A. S. Byatt, 'The Pleasure of Reading', in Antonia Fraser (ed.), *The Pleasure of Reading* (London: Bloomsbury, 1992), pp. 127–32 (132).
3. Mary Ellmann, *Thinking about Women* (London: Harcourt, 1968), p. 187.
4. F. R. Leavis, *The Great Tradition: George Eliot, Henry James, Joseph Conrad* (London: Chatto & Windus, 1950).
5. Rosi Braidotti, *Nomadic Subjects* (New York: Columbia University Press, 1994), p. 17.
6. A. S. Byatt, 'Hearths in the Wilderness', *TLS* (15 May 1987), pp. 507–8 (507).
7. Anne Samson, *F. R. Leavis* (London: Harvester, 1992), p. 6. See also Andrew Milner, 'Culturalism', *Contemporary Cultural Theory* (London: University College London, 1994), p. 20.
8. The influence Q. D. Leavis had on her husband's work and on the content of 'Cambridge English' is interesting. See P. J. M. Robertson, 'Queen of Critics: the Achievement of Q. D. Leavis (1906–1981)', *Novel* 16 (Winter 1983), pp. 141–50, and *The Leavises on Fiction* (London: Macmillan Press – now Palgrave, 1988). See also Greenwood on Q. D. Leavis's interest in the position of women. Edward Greenwood, 'F. R. Leavis (1895–1978)', in Ian Scott-Kilvert (ed.), *British Writers* (New York: Scribner, 1984), pp. 233–56. According to Terry Lovell, Q. D. Leavis was doubly marginalized: first in the context of Cambridge English and, secondly, in the context of her husband's journal *Scrutiny*. Terry Lovell, *Consuming Fiction* (London: Verso, 1987), p. 140. See also M. C. Bradbrook, 'Queenie Leavis: the Dynamics of Rejection', *Women and Literature 1779–1982* (Sussex: Harvester Press, 1982), pp. 124–31.
9. Samson, *F. R. Leavis*, p. 71.
10. Michael Bell, *F. R. Leavis* (London: Routledge, 1988), p. vii.
11. F. R. Leavis, 'Literature and Society', in M. H. Abrams (ed.), *The Norton Anthology of English Literature* (London: Norton, 1979), pp. 2350–60 (2360, 2351).
12. Carver, 'In Pursuit of the Fugitive Good', p. 52.
13. F. R. Leavis, *The Great Tradition* (Harmondsworth: Penguin in Association with Chatto & Windus, 1967).
14. Ibid., p. 10.
15. Ibid., pp. 17, 23, 27.
16. T. S. Eliot, 'Tradition and the Individual Talent', in Sean Burke (ed.), *Authorship: From Plato to the Postmodern* (Edinburgh: Edinburgh

University Press, 1995), pp. 73–80 (76). In his later career F. R. Leavis
came to disagree vehemently with T. S. Eliot's ideas. Bernard Bergonzi
gives a fascinating account of the internal dynamics of the F. R. Leavis–
T. S. Eliot relationship in 'Leavis and Eliot: the Long Road to Rejection',
Critical Quarterly 26/1–2 (Spring/Summer 1984), pp. 21–43.

17. Toril Moi, *Sexual/Textual Politics* (London: Methuen, 1985), p. 78.
18. Ibid., p. 78.
19. Samson, *F. R. Leavis*, p. 41.
20. Antony Easthope, *Literary into Cultural Studies* (London: Routledge,
1991), p. 5.
21. Carver, 'In Pursuit of the Fugitive Good', p. 52. I would like to add,
incidentally, that in his own time F. R. Leavis had a number of strong
opponents. One of them resorted to a type of amused irony which seems
to work quite well. In 1955 John Middleton Murry reviewed Leavis's
D. H. Lawrence and concluded 'never has he been so prodigal of eulogy;
never quite so pugnacious in downing the opposition, which consists, for
Dr Leavis, not only of those who have been in any way publicly critical of
Lawrence's work but even of the novelists who have had the misfortune
to be contemporary with him'. John Middleton Murry, 'Dr Leavis on
D. H. Lawrence', in John Gross (ed.), *The Modern Movement* (Chicago:
University of Chicago Press, 1992), pp. 44–51 (44).
22. Anita Loomba, 'Tangled Histories: Indian Feminism and Anglo-
American Feminist Criticism', *Tulsa Studies in Women's Literature* 12/2
(Fall 1993), pp. 271–5.
23. Perry Anderson, 'Components of the National Culture', *New Left Review*
50 (May/June 1968), pp. 3–57; Tom Nairn, *The Break-Up of Britain*
(London: New Left Books, 1977); Frances Mulhern, *The Moment of
Scrutiny* (London: Verso, 1981); Terry Eagleton, 'The Rise of English',
Literary Theory (Oxford: Blackwell, 1983), pp. 17–53.
24. Elaine Showalter, *A Literature of Their Own* (London: Virago, 1978); Moi,
Sexual/Textual Politics; Lovell, *Consuming Fiction*; Tae Haesook, 'Feminist
Criticism and F. R. Leavis's Literary Criticism', *Journal of English
Language and Literature* 39/1 (Spring 1993), pp. 63–80.
25. Peter Widdowson, 'W(h)ither "English"?', in Martin Coyle, Peter
Garside, Malcolm Kelsall and John Peck (eds), *Encyclopedia of Literature
and Criticism* (London: Routledge, 1990), pp. 1221–36; Stuart Hall, 'The
Emergence of Cultural Studies and the Crisis of the Humanities', *October*
53 (1990), pp. 11–90; Sarah Franklin, Celia Lurie and Jackey Stacy, *Off
Centre: Feminism and Cultural Studies* (London: Harper Collins, 1991);
Lawrence Grossberg, Cary Nelson and Paula Treichler (eds), *Cultural
Studies* (London: Routledge, 1992); Jessica Munns and Gita Rajan, *A
Cultural Studies Reader* (London: Longman, 1995).
26. Roland Barthes, *S/Z* (London: Cape, 1975); Antony Easthope, *British
Post-Structuralism* (London: Routledge, 1988); Bernand Harrison, 'How
to Reconcile Humanism and Deconstruction', *Inconvenient Fictions:
Literature and the Limits of Theory* (New Haven: Yale University Press,
1991), pp. 19–70; M. H. Abrams, *Doing Things with Texts: Essays in
Criticism and Critical Theory* (New York: Norton, 1991), pp. 237–392.

27. A public re-evaluation of Leavis's work took place from 1995 onwards. Ian McKillop's *F. R. Leavis* (London: Viking, 1995) was reviewed extensively: Nigel Spivey, 'Embattled Preacher with a Cult Following', *Financial Times* (15 July 1995), p. xiii; Nigel Williams, 'The Mystery of Doctor Leavis', *Independent Weekend* (15 July 1995), p. 6; Malcolm Bradbury, 'Whatever Happened to F. R. Leavis?', *Sunday Times* (9 July 1995), pp. 10–11; John Naughton, 'A Clash along the Great Rift', *Observer* (9 July 1995), pp. 2–3; Ronald Hayman, 'What Would He Say about Radio Three', *Daily Telegraph* (15 July 1995); Lorna Sage, 'The Culture Hero's Vision of Sameness', *Observer* (16 July 1995), p. 15; James Wood, 'Don't Mess with the Don', *Guardian* (21 July 1995), p. 5. Judging from the type of overviews published in the past years, academics have also returned to a discussion of Leavis's approach to literature. See Bell, *F. R. Leavis*; Samson, *F. R. Leavis*; Milner, *Contemporary Cultural Theory*.
28. A. S. Byatt, 'Either a Borrower or a Lender Be', *Guardian* (2 March 1992).
29. A. S. Byatt, 'The God I Want', in James Mitchell (ed.), *The God I Want* (London: Constable, 1967), pp. 71–87 (75).
30. Ibid., p. 72.
31. Byatt, 'Pleasure of Reading'.
32. Byatt, 'God I Want', p. 73.
33. 'Either a Borrower or a Lender Be', *Guardian* (2 March 1992).
34. Valentine Cunningham, 'The Greedy Reader: A. S. Byatt in the Post-Christian Labyrinth', *TLS* (16 August 1991), p. 6.
35. Aragay, 'Interview with A. S. Byatt'. In a subtle essay titled 'The Religion of Fiction', Michael Levenson discusses 'the religious sense' in A. S. Byatt's work. Byatt shares this interest in religion with Iris Murdoch. See Iris Murdoch, *Metaphysics as a Guide to Morals* (Harmondsworth: Penguin, 1992); *The Fire and the Sun: Why Plato Banished the Arts* (London: Chatto & Windus, 1977); 'Art and Eros: a Dialogue about Art', *Acastos: Two Platonic Dialogues* (London: Chatto & Windus, 1986), pp. 9–66.
36. Carver, 'In Pursuit of the Fugitive Good', p. 53.
37. Byatt, 'Either a Borrower or a Lender Be'.
38. A. S. Byatt, *Passions of the Mind: Selected Writings* (London: Chatto & Windus, 1991), p. 2.
39. A. S. Byatt, 'Identity and the Writer', in Lisa Appignanesi (ed.), *Identity: the Real Me*, ICA Documents 6 (London: Institute of Contemporary Arts, 1987), pp. 23–6 (23).
40. Juliet Dusinberre, 'A. S. Byatt', in Janet Todd (ed.), *Women Writers Talking* (New York: Holmes S. Meier, 1983), pp. 181–95 (188).
41. Aragay, 'Interview with A. S. Byatt'; Sonia Zyngier, 'The Passionate Act of Reading' (1992), p. 73. Unpublished. The idea of the writer as 'ventriloquist' appears often in Byatt's critical work. I owe the opposition between writers as 'ventriloquists' and 'soliloquists' to Virginia Woolf. See Virginia Woolf, 'Notes for Reading at Random', in Bonnie Kime Scott (ed.), *The Gender of Modernism* (Bloomington: Indiana University Press, 1990), pp. 673–9. Byatt admires Eliot's type of narrator. She disagrees with the idea that Eliot's narrative voice is too dominant: 'Eliot lays out her

evidence and conclusions, speaks sometimes as "I", sometimes to "you" and sometimes as "we". But despite her passionate morality, her reasonable proceedings leave room for dissent and qualification – indeed, she demonstrates and argues the case for independent thought, in reader as in characters and writer'. (*Passions of the Mind*, p. 4). See also Elizabeth Deeds Ermarth's emphasis on the multiplicity of Eliot's narrator: 'Realism and the English novel', in Martin Coyle *et al.* (eds), *Encyclopedia of Literature and Criticism*, pp. 565–75. However, Andrew Davies, writer of the screen script of *Middlemarch*, calls Eliot a 'control freak' for using the narrative voice to force her reader into agreement with her own point of view. According to Davies, any sympathy the reader may feel for Rosamund Vincy is pre-empted by the narrator's bitchiness about her (*The Late Show*, 9 February 1994).

42. A. S. Byatt, 'Insights Ad Nauseam', *TLS* (14 November 1986), p. 4363.
43. Tredell, 'A. S. Byatt', p. 73; George Greenfield, *Scribblers for Bread: Aspects of the English Novel since 1945* (London: Hodder & Stoughton, 1989), pp. 42–9.
44. Anne Sheppard, *Aesthetics* (Oxford: Oxford University Press, 1987), pp. 142–150; Andrew Milner, 'Culturalism', p. 37; David Storey, *Cultural Theory and Popular Culture* (London: Harvester, 1994). For a good overview of the differences between Marxist-oriented types of theories of art, see Stuart Shim, 'Marxism and Aesthetics', in Oswald Hanfling (ed.), *Philosophical Aesthetics* (Oxford: Blackwell, 1992), pp. 441–71.
45. Her review of *Romanticism, Writing and Sexual Difference* by Mary Jacobus may be read in this light. Byatt deplores Jacobus's use of deconstructionist methods to read Wordsworth's poetry. 'The Trouble with the Interesting Reader', *TLS* (23 March 1990), p. 310. In a letter to the *TLS*, Jacobus protested against Byatt's 'heavy burden of reproof' and said that her book's argument was meant as an antidote to 'the natural piety of this reading of Wordsworth, and, especially, against the burdensome implications of such Romantic teaching for women; implications which ought to be self-evident, for instance to any serious reader of George Eliot (as I imagine Byatt herself to be)'. *TLS* (20–6 April 1990), 419.
46. Michèl Foucault, 'What Is an Author?', in Josue V. Harari (ed.), *Textual Strategies* (New York: Cornell University Press, 1979), pp. 141–160; Roland Barthes, 'The Death of the Author', in Burke (ed.), *Authorship*, pp. 125–130; Donald E. Pease, 'Author', in Burke (ed.), *Authorship*, pp. 263–76.
47. Barthes, 'Death of the Author', p. 130.
48. Byatt, 'Trouble with the Interesting Reader'.
49. Carver, 'In Pursuit of the Fugitive Good', p. 48.
50. Byatt, *Passions of the Mind*, p. 1.
51. Byatt, 'Identity and the Writer', p. 24.
52. Tredell, 'A. S. Byatt', p. 67; *The Brains Trust* (8 January 1996).
53. Byatt, 'Identity and the Writer', p. 24.

54. Ibid., p. 25.
55. Ibid., p. 26. This ambivalence about post-structuralist ideas about identity and language may be typical of our postmodern times. As Allen Thiher writes in *Words in Reflection*: 'not the least interesting aspect of contemporary culture is that many believe simultaneously that language articulates the world and language cannot reach the world'. Quoted in Hans Bertens, 'Postmodern Characterization and the Intrusion of Language', in Matei Calinescu and Douwe Fokkema (eds), *Exploring Postmodernism* (Amsterdam: Benjamins, 1987), pp. 139–60 (158). One can see a comparable process at work in *Imagining Characters*: A. S. Byatt and Ignès Sodre discuss characters in novels by women writers as if they are real people – a traditional way of looking at literature – while simultaneously acknowledging that modern literary theories have replaced these traditional ideas (London: Chatto & Windus, 1995), p. 253.
56. Byatt, 'Identity and the Writer', p. 24.
57. Judith Mayne, 'A Parallax View of Lesbian Authorship', in Diana Fuss (ed.), *Inside/out: Lesbian Theories, Gay Theories* (London: Routledge, 1991), pp. 173–84 (177). Freeland gives examples of the feminist criticism of 'the death of the author' and its indifference to the gender of the speaking and writing subject: 'Isn't the language of pure indifference the latest ruse of phallocentrism?' (Naomi Schor); 'To my mind, there is something profoundly depressing in the spectacle of female critics avowing their eagerness to relinquish a mastery they have never possessed' (Tania Modleski); 'One cannot deconstruct a subjectivity that one has never been granted' (Rosi Braidotti); 'the postmodern decision that the author is dead, and subjective agency along with him, does not necessarily work for women and prematurely foreclosed the question of identity for them' (Nancy Miller). All of these feminist voices are quoted in Cynthia Freeland, 'Revealing Gendered Texts', *Philosophy and Literature* 15/1 (April 1991), pp. 40–58.
58. A. S. Byatt, 'George Eliot: a Celebration', *Passions of the Mind*, pp. 72–6; George Eliot, *Selected Essays, Poems and Other Writings*, eds A. S. Byatt and Nicholas Warren (Harmondsworth: Penguin, 1990). Byatt wrote introductions to Eliot's *The Mill on the Floss* (Harmondsworth: Penguin, 1988), pp. 27–40, and *Middlemarch* (Oxford: Oxford University Press, 1999).
59. Lyall argues that this is precisely the function of literature: 'in the end, we have direct access only to our own consciousness; but it is the peculiar function of literary texts to provide through the power of imagination a mediated insight into the innermost life of other human beings'. Roderick J. Lyall, *Understanding Difference: Issues and Challenges in Literary Studies Today* (Amsterdam: Free University, 1996), p. 6. *The Observer*, however, included Byatt's remark in its rubric 'Quotes of the Week', presumably finding it remarkable and funny. To A. S. Byatt the remark must have seemed perfectly sensible, especially in the context in which she made it.

60.   Lovell, *Consuming Fiction*, pp. 146, 145. Lentricchia and Simpson point to an anxiety on the part of male critics about the possible 'feminine' nature of literature. Frank Lentricchia, 'Patriarchy against Itself', *Critical Inquiry* 14 (1987), pp. 379–413; David Simpson, 'The Sublime: a Masculine Confusion', *Romanticism, Nationalism, and the Revolt against Theory* (London: University of Chicago Press, 1993), pp. 126–30. From the French Revolution onwards this anxiety resulted in a remasculinization of theory. According to Simpson, a theoretical concept such as 'the sublime' has received so much attention in literary criticism because of this anxiety. I will come back to the gender of 'the sublime' in the next chapter.

61.   F. R. Leavis, *Great Tradition*, pp. 54, 56.

62.   Ibid., p. 89, emphasis added. Some feminist critics agreed with Leavis in this evaluation of Dorothea Brooke. Ellen Moers compares *Middlemarch* to Sand's novel *Corinne* and writes about Dorothea: 'Dorothea Brooke is the worst kind of product of the myth of Corinne . . . for she is good for nothing *but* to be admired. An arrogant, spoiled, rich beauty, she does little but harm in the novel. Ignorant in the extreme and mentally idle, Dorothea has little to say, but an interesting voice to say it in . . . She has also what must be the most stunning wardrobe in Victorian fiction'. Ellen Moers, *Literary Women* (London: Women's Press, 1987), p. 194. Germaine Greer says of Dorothea Brooke: 'what goes wrong with Dorothea is that [Eliot] falls in love with Dorothea, she abandons her ironic stance and starts fawning on her and calling her beautiful when she called her anything but in the first few chapters' (Joseph Kestner, 'Interview with Germaine Greer', in Olga Kenyon (ed.), *Women Writers Talk* (Oxford: Lennard, 1989), p. 156.

63.   F. R. Leavis, *Great Tradition* p. 44.

64.   Ibid., p. 67, emphasis added.

65.   Ibid., p. 139.

66.   Ibid., p. 123. I want to thank Trev Broughton for pointing this out to me.

67.   Ibid., p. 51.

68.   I wish to thank Professor Luisa Flora for drawing my attention to Leslie Stephen's book.

69.   Dorothea Barrett, *Vocation and Desire: George Eliot's Heroines* (London: Routledge, 1989), p. x.

70.   Roberts is the only critic of *Passions of the Mind* who pays attention to this: 'one quibble: in a collection that isn't concerned with feminist criticism and which mixes Muriel Spark, George Eliot, Iris Murdoch et al. in with the men, why bother to have a tiny section called 'The female voice?' which reimposes marginality without discussing it?'. Michèle Roberts, 'Greed Reading', *New Statesman* 4/163 (9 August 1991), p. 38.

71.   A. S. Byatt, 'Distrusting the Intellect', *New Statesman* (19 May 1967), pp. 689–90 (689).

72.   Byatt, 'Introduction', in George Eliot, *Mill on the Floss*, p. 27.

73.   Hermione Lee, 'The Glory of Middlemarch', *Sunday Times* (16 January 1994).

74. A. S. Byatt, 'The "Placing" of Stephen Guest', in Eliot, *Mill on the Floss*, pp. 687–91 (690). Van de Ven has shown that George Eliot uses irony to undermine Deronda and describes him as a man thoroughly influenced by nineteenth-century attitudes towards women. Like Byatt, Van de Ven takes the social and historical background of Daniel Deronda into account and argues that George Eliot had feminist aims with the novel. Ariadne van de Ven, *Daniel Deronda: a Novel of Protest* (Utrecht: Department of English, 1985).

75. Byatt, *Degrees of Freedom*, pp. 203–4.

76. Byatt and Sodre, *Imagining Characters*, pp. 83–4.

77. A. S. Byatt, 'The Power of Learning', *New Statesman* (17 August 1979), pp. 239–40 (239).

78. Christien Franken, 'An Interview with A. S. Byatt' (Utrecht: Department of Women's Studies, 1991). Unpublished. In the interview Byatt gave an example of this kind of approach to her work: 'There is the famous example of a man making love in one of my novels. It says "in this position he thought, as he always did, of T. S. Eliot". This was a joke. I thought this was extraordinarily funny, but hundreds of reviewers have picked this sentence up and said, "this woman is so literary" . . . I was trying to say this about my hero. Also he actually preferred T. S. Eliot to making love which some people do, but that again is partly funny'.

79. Rosanna Greenstreet, 'Questionnaire: A. S. Byatt', *Weekend Guardian* (n. d.).

80. Byatt, *Passions of the Mind*, p. 76, emphasis added.

81. George Greenfield, *Scribblers for Bread* (London: Hodder & Stoughton, 1989), p. 48.

82. Tredell, 'A. S. Byatt', p. 69.

83. Dusinberre, 'A. S. Byatt'.

84. It is quite ironical that Byatt quotes Woolf's advocation of androgyny in an article that is wholly devoted to women writers. I found a proof of the article in A. S. Byatt's archive. It was originally published in the American journal *Harpers & Queen*. Byatt is one of many female critics discussing Woolf's concept of androgyny. Elaine Showalter condemns it vehemently. She reads in Woolf's plea for the androgynous nature of the writer a repression of women's anger and an escape from female experience. 'Virginia Woolf and the Flight into Androgyny', *Literature of Their Own*, pp. 263–97. Toril Moi accuses Showalter of applying bourgeois realist standards to Woolf's modernist writing strategies. 'Who's Afraid of Virginia Woolf?: Feminist Readings of Woolf', *Sexual/Textual Politics*, pp. 1–18. For widely divergent feminist evaluations of Woolf's concept of androgyny see Rachel Blau DuPlessis, *Writing beyond the Ending* (Bloomington: Indiana University Press, 1985); Cora Kaplan, *Sea Changes* (London: Verso, 1986); Barbara Johnson, *The Critical Difference* (London: Johns Hopkins University Press, 1987); Jane Marcus, 'Still Practice, A/Wrested Alphabet: Toward a Feminist Aesthetic', in Sari Benstock (ed.), *Feminist Issues in Literary Scholarship* (Bloomington: Indiana University Press, 1987), pp. 79–97; Makiko Minow-Pinkney, *Virginia Woolf and the Problem of the Subject* (New Brunswick: Rutgers University Press, 1987); Mary Jacobus,

'The Difference in View', in Catherine Belsey and Jane Moore (eds), *The Feminist Reader* (London: Macmillan, 1989), pp. 49–62; Peggy Kamuf, 'Replacing Feminist Criticism', in Marianne Hirsch and Evelyn Fox Keller (eds), *Conflicts in Feminism* (London: Routledge, 1990), pp. 105–11; Teresa De Lauretis, *Feminist Genealogies* (Utrecht: Anna Maria van Schuurman Centrum, Arts Faculty, 1991).

85.   Aragay, 'Interview with A. S. Byatt'.
86.   A. S. Byatt, 'Twenty Ways to Avoid Despair', *Weekend Telegraph* (24 April 1993), p. xxv.
87.   Aragay, 'Interview with A. S. Byatt'.
88.   Linda Alcoff, 'Cultural Feminism versus Post-Structuralism: the Identity Crisis in Feminist Theory', *Signs* 13/3 (1988), pp. 405–36.
89.   Belsey and Moore (eds), *Feminist Reader*, p. 245.
90.   Donna Haraway, 'Situated Knowledges', *Simians, Cyborgs and Women* (London: Free Association Books, 1991), p. 193.

2   *The Shadow of the Sun*: The Lady of Shalott or the writer as genius

1.   Byatt, *Shadow of the Sun*, p. 135.
2.   In 1964 the novel was published under the title *Shadow of a Sun*. C. D. Lewis, A. S. Byatt's publisher, preferred it. With the first reprint of the novel, A. S. Byatt rewrote history and chose the title she had had in mind all along: *The Shadow of the Sun* (London: Chatto & Windus, 1991).
3.   *Shadow of the Sun* (London: Vintage, 1991), p. xvi. Further references to this edition are included in brackets in the text.
4.   Olga Kenyon, 'Michèle Roberts', *Women Writers Talk*, p. 168. For an analysis of women's fiction from the fifties see Niamh Baker, *Happily ever after: Women's Fiction in Post-War Britain 1945–1960* (London: Macmillan, 1989). Showalter describes 1950s literature as 'conservative' – 'untouched by either modernism or a sense of personal experiment' – and 'passive'. *Literature of Their Own*, p. 34. Other critics have either chosen to write about the period leading up to the 1950s or the period following it when the women's movement strongly influenced women's fiction. Examples of the former are Nicola Beauman, *A Very Great Profession: the Woman's Novel 1914–1939* (London: Virago, 1983), and Alison Light, *Forever England: Femininity, Literature and Conservatism between the Wars* (London: Routledge, 1991). Examples of the latter are: Gayle Green, 'Women Writing in the Twentieth Century: the Novel and Social Change', *Changing the Story: Feminist Fiction and the Tradition* (Bloomington: Indiana Press, 1991), pp. 31–57; Rita Felski, *Beyond Feminist Aesthetics* (London: Hutchinson, 1989); and Maria Lauret, *Liberating Literature: Feminist Fiction in America* (London: Routledge, 1994).
5.   The high expectations and moral urgency that were at the heart of Leavis's critical practice undermined Byatt's own ambitions as a writer.

This feeling of awe returns again in *Possession*, published 35 years after her study at Cambridge. James Blackadder, a man who has become a professor of English Literature, still remembers the inferiority complex F. R. Leavis gave him: 'Leavis did to Blackadder what he did to serious students; he showed him the terrible, the magnificent importance and urgency of English literature and simultaneously deprived him of any confidence in his own capacity to contribute to, or change it'. *Possession*, p. 27. Byatt's mother went to Cambridge University – as the first woman in her lower middle-class family – and finished her study of English Literature successfully; her upbringing was not conducive to a love of literature, though: 'My mother's background, which she had rejected, was non-conformist and Puritanical. The best thing that had happened to her was English Literature, but in her misery she was suspicuous of it, tended to dismiss artists gloomily as exploiters, self-indulgent, frivolous'. Byatt, *Shadow of the Sun* (London: Chatto & Windus, 1991), p. x.

6. When asked why she signs her work with A. S. Byatt, instead of Antonia Byatt, she said: 'I just always did, really. It goes back to T. S. Eliot, when I began writing. I called my daughter Antonia because when she was born I thought I could never write anything, so she may as well have this very good name, and she might write something. I was twenty-three and suddenly I had this baby and I did feel that it was the end of my life. I gave her the name and then it wasn't. So I have done her rather a harm'. Zyngier, 'Passionate Act of Reading'. Byatt's passion for George Eliot's novel *Middlemarch* dates from this period: 'I suppose I was in my late twenties when I began teaching *Middlemarch*, and I taught it with passion because I perceived it was about the growth, use and inevitable failure and frustration of all human energy – a lesson one is not interested in at eleven, or eighteen, but at twenty-six, with two small children, it seems crucial'. 'George Eliot: a Celebration', *Passions of the Mind*, p. 73.

7. Claire Tomalin has sketched a vivid picture of the difficult time ambitious women had after graduating in the mid-1950s: 'Then, as young graduates, the husbands found jobs easily and contined to live much as they had before, but the wives had to struggle what "work" they could into any space left by childbearing and rearing and domestic duties . . . In fact one of my most vivid memories of the mid-1950s is of crying into a washbasin full of soapy grey baby clothes – there were no washing machines – while my handsome and adored husband was off playing football in the park on Sunday morning with all the delightful young men who had been friends to both of us at Cambridge three years earlier'. Claire Tomalin, 'Everything but the Truth', *Independent on Sunday* (9 October 1994), p. 32.

8. I have borrowed the phrase 'the house of fiction' from Lorna Sage who in turn borrowed the term from Henry James. Sage wrote a well-received study of British women novelists with the title *Women in the House of Fiction* (London: Macmillan, 1992).

9. Sandra Gilbert and Susan Gubar, *The Madwoman in the Attic* (New Haven: Yale University Press, 1979), p. 49.

10. These observations return in Byatt's novel *Babel Tower* (London: Chatto & Windus, 1996), pp. 211–17. Frederica teaches the novel to arts students, as Byatt did, and analyses D. H. Lawrence's work. In *Perfectly Correct*, Phillipa Gregory's satire on English academia, a feminist academic is thoroughly confused by Lawrence's story 'The Virgin and the Gipsy' (London: Harper Collins, 1996), pp. 8–9. For an analysis of the influence D. H. Lawrence's work had on women writers such as Woolf, Mansfield, H. D., Bowen, Stead and Welty see Carol Siegel, *Lawrence among the Women* (University Press of Virginia, 1992), and Elizabeth M. Wallace, 'Lawrence among the Women', *Women* 3/1 (Spring 1992), pp. 97–9.

11. In a literary survey for *Harpers & Queen*, A. S. Byatt defined 'sensibility' as the outstanding characteristic of the work of women writers in the 1950s: 'My own education in writing by and about women came, I suppose, largely from the generation that immediately succeeded Virginia Woolf – novelists of sensibility, delicate social discrimination, sexual hinting and stirring and inexplicit passions, telling much and leaving much to the imagination. Rosamond Lehmann, Elizabeth Bowen, E. Arnot Robertson. These novelists, unlike the great Victorians, even unlike Virginia Woolf, if you think very hard about it, tended to centre their novels very much on the sensibilities of their heroines . . . Because of the social shifts in the air the heroines tend to be victims'. Given her criticism of the sensibility of women's novels, it is ironical that Malcolm Bradbury praised Byatt's second novel *The Game* for its 'female sensibility'. Malcolm Bradbury, 'On from Murdoch', *Encounter* 31/1 (July 1968), pp. 72–4.

12. Gilbert and Gubar, *Madwoman in the Attic*, p. 49.

13. She listed Alice Munro's *The Progress of Love* as her 'book of the decade': 'I have a sense of recognizing a real artist when I read that. She handles the English language better than almost anyone else. I have learnt so much from her, how to structure a narrative, and what can be done with the English language now'. *Telegraph* (1 September 1992). Munro's novel *Lives of Girls and Women* contains a sentence which I think describes Byatt's own craft perfectly. In this book a girl with a novel in her mind is making lists to try and capture the world around her: 'and no list could hold what I wanted, for what I wanted was every last thing, every layer of speech and thought, stroke of light on bark and walls, every smell, pothole, pain, crack, delusion, held still and held together – radiant, everlasting'. (Harmondsworth: Penguin, 1982), p. 249.

14. There are many similarities between Byatt and Coleridge: both are erudite and intellectually curious people. Like Byatt, Coleridge created 'complex abstract structures of ideas' and as a critic he favoured unity and coherence in art. A. S. Byatt, *Unruly Times: Wordsworth and Coleridge in Their Time* (London: Hogarth, 1970), p. 34. A. S. Byatt's concept of the imagination is, indeed, Coleridgean: 'as being that part of your mind which very slowly forms an adequate image of the world outside, as a mirror and a lamp, to use Abrams' distinction'. Aragay, 'Interview

with A. S. Byatt'. She portrays with insight the loneliness Coleridge suffered from at school, another thing they have in common. As Byatt said on *Desert Island Discs*: 'I never spoke outside class, I never spoke to anybody. I was extremely lonely but in class I would say what I thought' (10 January 1991).

15. Tom Furniss, *Edmund Burke's Aesthetic Ideology: Language, Gender and Political Economy in Revolution* (Cambridge: Cambridge University Press, 1993), p. 25.
16. Ibid., p. 23.
17. Ibid., pp. 27, 25.
18. Edmund Burke, *Philosophical Enquiry in the Origin of Our Ideas of the Sublime and the Beautiful*, edited with an introduction and notes by J. T. Boulton (London: Routledge, 1958), p. 114.
19. Hélène Cixous, 'Sorties', in Elaine Marks and Isabelle de Courtivron (eds), *New French Feminisms* (New York: Schocken Books, 1981), pp. 90–8 (91). Originally published in French in *La jeune née* (1975).
20. Burke, *Philosophical Enquiry*, pp. 110, 111, 115, 116.
21. Timothy Gould, 'Intensity and Its Audiences', *Journal of Aesthetics and Art Criticism* 48/4 (Fall 1990), pp. 305–15 (306). For an analysis of the gender connotations of the sublime and the beautiful see Patricia Yaeger, 'Toward a Female Sublime', in Linda Kauffman (ed.), *Gender and Theory* (London: Blackwell, 1989), pp. 191–212; Terry Eagleton, 'Aesthetics and Politics in Edmund Burke', *History Workshop* 28 (Autumn 1989), pp. 53–63; Lee Edelman, 'At Risk in the Sublime', in Kauffman (ed.), *Gender and Theory*, pp. 213–24; Paul Mattick, 'Beautiful and Sublime: Gender Totemism in the Constitution of Art', *Journal of Aesthetics and Art Criticism* 48/4 (Fall 1990), pp. 293–304; Timothy Gould, 'Engendering Aesthetics: Sublimity, Sublimation and Misogyny in Burke and Kant', in Gerarld Bruns and Stephen Watsons (eds), *Aesthetics, Politics and Hermeneutics* (SUNY Press, 1991); Barbara Claire Freeman, 'The Rise of the Sublime: Sacrifice and Misogyny in Eighteenth-Century Aesthetics', *Yale Journal of Criticism* 5/3 (1992), pp. 81–100; Barbara Claire Freeman, *The Feminine Sublime: Gender and Excess in Women's Fiction* (Berkeley: University of California Press, 1995); Amanda Gilroy, 'The Discourse of Beauty and the Construction of Subjectivity in Edmund Burke's *A Philosophical Enquiry*', *Liverpool Studies in Language and Discourse* 1 (1993), pp. 45–70.
22. Burke, *Philosophical Enquiry*, p. 110, emphasis added.
23. Maaike Meijer, 'Binaire opposities en academische problemen' (Binary Oppositions and Academic Problems), *Tijdschrift voor Vrouwenstudies* (Dutch Journal of Women's Studies) 12/1 (1991), pp. 108–15 (109).
24. Patricia Yaeger, 'Toward a Female Sublime', p. 192.
25. Terry Eagleton, *The Ideology of the Aesthetic* (Oxford: Blackwell, 1990), p. 66.
26. Lawrence Meynell, *Wolverhampton Express* (10 January 1964); Bernard Share, *Irish Times* (11 January 1964); Frederic Raphael, 'Girl in a Trap', *Sunday Times* (12 January 1964).

27. Ferguson also provides the reader with an excellent historical survey of the place of the 'sublime' in philosophy and contemporary critical theory. Rachel Ferguson, *Solitude and the Sublime: Romanticism and the Aesthetics of Individuation* (London: Routledge, 1992), pp. 1–36.

28. Lies Wesseling, 'The Struggle for the Sublime', unpublished lecture (Utrecht: Department of Women's Studies, University of Utrecht, 1991); Annelies van Heijst, *Verlangen naar de val* (Kampen: Kok Agora, 1992), p. 176.

29. Ferguson gives an amusing eighteenth-century example of a woman who undermined any strict boundaries between 'the sublime' and 'the beautiful'. Coleridge describes her in 'On the Principles of Genial Criticism': 'many years ago, the writer [Coleridge himself, C. F.] in company with an accidental party of travellers was gazing on a cataract of great height, breadth, and impetuosity, the summit of which appeared to blend with the sky and clouds, while the lower part was hidden by rocks and trees; and on his observing that it was, in the strictest sense of the word, a sublime object, a lady present assented with warmth to the remark, adding – 'Yes! and it's not only sublime, but beautiful and absolutely pretty'. Quoted in Ferguson, *Solitude and the Sublime*, pp. 38–9. According to Ferguson, this anecdote presents both Coleridge and 'the lady present' in a bad light – 'the lady for gushing and Coleridge for being something of a pedant of tourism' – but I find the lady's irreverence rather refreshing.

30. Trev Broughton, 'The Froud–Carlyle Embroilment: Married Life as a Literary Problem', *Victorian Studies* 39/1 (Autumn 1995), pp. 551–85 (576).

31. God and Job were *the* symbols of 'the sublime' in the eighteenth century, but, as Ferguson points out, Job is far from the stable, sublime figure which for instance Edmund Burke makes him out to be: 'the use of Job as the example of a powerful man challenges our certainty about the firmness of the dividing lines. For Job in the passage that Burke cites . . . only memorializes his *past* power'. Ferguson, *Solitude and the Sublime*, p. 49.

32. Caroline's double view of Henry reminds me of a more contemporary source. In the film *Moonstruck* the actress Cher corrects a man who tells her that he is an artistic genius with a down-to-earth 'Oh yeah, how come you've got butter on your tie?'

33. Eagleton, *Ideology of the Aesthetic*, p. 264.

34. Quoted in Patricia Yaeger, 'The Language of Blood: Toward a Maternal Sublime', *Genre* XXV/1 (Spring 1992), pp. 5–24 (24).

35. Byatt has said that 'identity under pressure interests me most as a novelist. What happens when a personality slips into disintegration'. Olga Kenyon, 'A. S. Byatt', *Women Novelists Today* (Brighton: Harvester Press, 1988), pp. 51–84 (58). She describes the disintegration of Margaret in a surrealist, Buñuel-like way (*Shadow of the Sun*, pp. 181–2). Oliver treats Margaret cruelly and she has nothing left in her life to build an identity on that is different from a wife's. Her

breakdown is terrible. When Henry visits her, he has trouble not feeling involved but manages to distance himself by escaping into his writer's way of seeing (p. 185).

36. Mieke Bal, 'Delilah Decomposed: Samson's Talking Cure and the Rhetoric of Subjectivity', *Lethal Love: Feminist Literary Readings of Biblical Love Stories* (Bloomington: Indiana University Press, 1987), pp. 65, 66.

37. Kenyon, 'A. S. Byatt', p. 57; Flora Alexander, *Contemporary Women Novelists* (London: Edward Arnold, 1989), p. 3.

38. I would like to thank Denise de Costa for advising me to take Byatt's definition of Anna as the focus of my reading.

39. Byatt, 'Pleasure of Reading', p. 128. For an analysis of the importance of 'The Lady of Shalott' in Byatt's work see also Jane Campbell, 'The Hunger of the Imagination in A. S. Byatt's *The Game*', *Critique* (Spring 1988), pp. 147–62. In *Woman/Image/Text* Lynn Pearce discusses Tennyson's poem and paintings of the Lady of Shalott by Holman Hunt and John William Waterhouse (London: Harvester, 1991). For other feminist interpretations of 'The Lady of Shalott' in art and/or literature see Nina Auerbach, *Woman and the Demon* (Cambridge, Mass.: Harvard University Press, 1982); Isobel Armstrong, 'Tennyson's "The Lady of Shalott"', in J. B. Bullen (ed.), *The Sun Is God: Painting, Literature and Mythology in the Nineteenth Century* (Oxford: Clarendon Press, 1989), pp. 49–108; Jennifer Gribble, *The Lady of Shalott in the Victorian Novel* (London: Macmillan, 1983); Jan Marsh, *The Pre-Raphalite Sisterhood* (New York: St. Martin's Press, 1985), pp. 7–9; Dorothy Mermin, 'The Damsel, the Knight and the Victorian Woman Poet', *Critical Inquiry* 13/1 (Autumn 1986), pp. 64–8; Elaine Shefer, 'Elizabeth Siddal's "The Lady of Shalott"', *Women's Art Journal* 9/1 (1988), pp. 21–9; Elaine Jordan, *Alfred Tennyson* (Cambridge: Cambridge University Press, 1988); Karen Hodder, 'The Lady of Shalott in Art and Literature', in Susan Mendus and Jane Rendall (eds), *Sexuality & Subordination* (London: Routledge, 1989), pp. 60–88; Carl Plasa, ' "Cracked from Side to Side": Sexual Politics in The Lady of Shalott', *Victorian Poetry* 30 (Autumn/Winter 1992), pp. 247–63. Loreena McKennit has put 'The Lady of Shalott' to music from *The Visit* (Scarborough, Ontario: Warner Music, 1994) (I would like to thank Angelique van Vondelen for drawing my attention to this rendition). Elizabeth Bishop used 'The Lady of Shalott' as a source of inspiration for her poem 'The Gentleman of Shalott', *Complete Poems* (London: Chatto & Windus, 1991).

40. This is a quote from a radio lecture titled *Finding a Voice* (1978). I found a transcript of the lecture in A. S. Byatt's archive. She said elsewhere: 'I am obsessed with glass, for reasons I only partly understand'. See her essay on *The Djinn in the Nightingale's Eye* (address: http://asbyatt.com/essays.htm, 1999).

41. Linda Huf, *Portrait of the Artist as a Young Woman* (New York: Ungar, 1983), p. 9.

42. Rosalind Hursthouse, 'Truth and Representation', in Oswald Hanfling (ed.), *Philosophical Aesthetics* (Oxford: Blackwell, 1992), pp. 239–96 (266).
43. Willa Cather, 'Light on Adobe Walls', *Willa Cather on Writing* (Lincoln: University of Nebraska Press, 1976), p. 123.
44. Byatt, 'Pleasure of Reading', p. 128.
45. Tredell, 'A. S. Byatt', p. 66.
46. Luce Irigaray, 'Divine Women', *Sexes and Genealogies*, trans. Gillian C. Gill (New York: Columbia University Press, 1993), pp. 55–72 (72).
47. Plasa, ' "Cracked from Side to Side" '; Armstrong, 'Tennyson's "The Lady of Shalott" ', and *Victorian Poetry: Poetry, Poetics, Politics* (London: Routledge, 1993).
48. The art historian E. H. Gombrich – whose work Byatt admires greatly – has described a similar situation: 'our kitchen floor at home happens to have a simple black-and- white checkerboard pattern. As I was taking a glass of water from the tap to the table, I suddenly noticed the delightful and interesting distortions of this pattern visible through the bottom of the glass. I had never seen this transformation before, though I must have made this same movement hundreds of times'. *The Image and the Eye* (Ithaca: Cornell University Press, 1982), p. 32.
49. Byatt, 'Identity and the Writer', p. 26.
50. A. S. Byatt, 'The Djinn in the Nightingale's Eye', *The Djinn in the Nightingale's Eye: Five Fairy Stories* (London: Chatto & Windus, 1994), p. 275.
51. Quoted in Hélène Cixous, 'Reaching the Point of Wheat, or a Portrait of the Artist as a Maturing Woman', *New Literary History* 19/1 (Autumn 1987), pp. 1–22 (20).
52. Irigaray, 'Divine Women', p. 65.
53. Cixous, 'Reaching the Point of Wheat', p. 20.
54. Tredell, 'A. S. Byatt', p. 67.

3   *The Game*: Cassandra or the writer as proto-feminist visionary

1. Haraway, 'Situated Knowledges', p. 188. This chapter has benefitted greatly from comments made by Alexa Alfer.
2. Byatt, *The Game* (London: Chatto & Windus, 1967). All references are to this edition and will be included in brackets in the text.
3. A. S. Byatt, *The Virgin in the Garden* (London: Chatto & Windus, 1978), and *Possession* (London: Chatto & Windus, 1990).
4. See Joanne V. Creighton, 'Sisterly Symbiosis: Margaret Drabble's *The Waterfall* and A. S. Byatt's *The Game*', *Mosaic* 20 (Winter 1987), pp. 15–29; Giulianna Giobi, 'Sisters Beware of Sisters: Sisterhood as a Literary Motif in Jane Austen, A. S. Byatt and I. Bossi Fedrigotti', *Journal of European Studies* 22 (September 1992), pp. 241–58; Bradbury, 'On

from Murdoch', p. 386, emphasis mine. For a writer's view on the pitfalls of biographies see Margaret Atwood, 'Biographobia: Some Personal Reflections on the Act of Biography', in Laurence Lockridge (ed.), *Nineteenth-Century Lives* (New York: Cornell University Press, 1989), pp. 1–8.

5. Byatt, *Shadow of the Sun*, p. x.
6. Wallace Stevens, 'Notes towards a Supreme Fiction', *The Collected Poems of Wallace Stevens* (New York: Knopf, 1967), pp. 380–408 (404).
7. Evelyn Fox Keller, 'The Mind's Eye', in Sandra Harding and Merill B. Hintikka (eds), *Discovering Reality: Feminist Perspectives on Epistomology, Metaphysics, Methodology, and Philosophy of Science* (Norwell: Kleuwer Academic Publishers, 1983), pp. 207–24.
8. Ibid., p. 209.
9. Ibid., p. 213.
10. Patricia Yeager, *Honey-Mad Women: Emancipatory Strategies in Women's Writing* (New York: Columbia University Press, 1988), p. 183.
11. Donna Haraway gives examples of the way in which contemporary visualizing technologies are not passive at all, but devour our world in a cannibal-like way, in a feast of 'unregulated gluttony'. 'Situated Knowledges', p. 189. See also Braidotti for an analysis of the scopic drive in contemporary reproductive technologies as a means of domination and control. Rosi Braidotti, 'On Contemporary Medical Pornography', *Tijdschrift voor Vrouwenstudies* (Dutch Journal of Women's Studies) 12/3 (1991), pp. 356–71.
12. In *The Independent Magazine* Byatt wrote that the original idea for Simon's experiences in the jungle came from Aldous Huxley's essay 'Wordsworth in the Tropics': 'where the jungle represents the idea that Nature can be appalling, unmanageable and hostile . . . I wrote a rather wild description of how an unseen television cameraman was devoured by piranha fish'. 'Life in a Soap Opera', *Independent Magazine* (10 October 1992), pp. 30–5.
13. Todd, *A. S. Byatt*, p. 10.
14. Campbell, 'Hunger of the Imagination in A. S. Byatt's *The Game*', p. 155.
15. Bradbury, 'On from Murdoch', p. 73.
16. Byatt, *Still Life*, p. 109.
17. In its portrayal of the intense relationship between two sisters, *The Game* is remarkably similar to *Cassandra at the Wedding* (London: Virago, 1982; copyright 1962), a novel by the American writer Dorothy Baker, which A. S. Byatt read in the sixties, prior to the publication of *The Game*.
18. For an analysis of the canonical signs of the typical artist-hero in British literature see Christien Franken, 'Are These Missing Features Yours?: Gender, Genius and Artist-Novels', *Multiple Mythologies* (Utrecht PhD Department of Women's Studies, Utrecht University, NL, 1997), pp. 21–52.

19.   Rachel Ferguson, *The Brontës Went to Woolworths* (London: Virago, 1988), pp. iii–xiii (xi).
20.   Dusinberre, 'A. S. Byatt', p. 190.
21.   See Thane for a concise survey of this period in British feminism. Pat Thane, 'Towards Equal Opportunities? Women in Britain since 1945', in Terry Gourvish and Alan O'Day (eds), *Britain since 1945* (London: Macmillan, 1991), pp. 183–208. Thane describes for instance the influence of de Beauvoir's *The Second Sex* (1953) and Lessing's *The Golden Notebook* (1962) on individual women in Britain (p. 199). Byatt has written positively about de Beauvoir's *Les Belles Images*. She has been more ambivalent about Doris Lessing's later work, understanding Elaine Showalter's doubt: 'Ms Showalter ends by taking issue with Doris Lessing, as with Virginia Woolf, for running away from her own necessary sexuality, and joining groups, acquiring beliefs . . . that absolve her from the need to define or confront her female self. As literary criticism this does pinpoint some of one's anxieties about Doris Lessing – *The Golden Notebook*, her great novel, took on the female, and with it politics, the novel, language, modern life, in a way I think she has never managed again'. In the same breath, however, Byatt criticizes Showalter: 'As a woman novelist I am interested in [Showalter's] "female tradition": I wish to be female, not feminist, not imitation male. But she seems to assume that to achieve this I must study femaleness, use the support of women's groups, women's presses, women's groups – and I fear her groups as I fear Doris Lessing's'. Again the ambivalence that is so typical of Byatt's stance towards feminist literary criticism is apparent in this review (a typescript of which I found in A. S. Byatt's archive; to my regret I have been unable to trace its publication date).
22.   In an interview Byatt said, 'Cassandra sees writing as artifice and Julia sees writing as natural, and Cassandra writes better than Julia'. Tredell, 'A. S. Byatt', p. 66. The actual text of *The Game* leads me to disagree with this statement.
23.   Byatt and Sodre, *Imagining Characters*, pp. 247–8.
24.   See Jay Clayton, 'Narrative and Theories of Desire', *Critical Inquiry* (Autumn 1989), pp. 33–53 (36).
25.   Peter Brooks, *Reading for the Plot: Design and Intention in Narrative* (New York: Vintage, 1984), p. 7.
26.   The title is taken from Coleridge. In 1967 – the year in which *The Game* was published – Byatt wrote a contribution to *The God I Want*, referring to Coleridge's sense of glory as 'a sudden, apparently unsolicited flooding in of excessive light, energy, significance, which shakes the personality and creates an unexplained area of experience where the word God becomes useful. Pantheism and visionary experience come in here'. James Mitchell (ed.), *The God I Want* (London: Constable, 1967), p. 71. This description can be read alongside *The Shadow of the Sun*'s description of the sublime experiences of the visionary Henry Severell.
27.   'Identity and the Writer', p. 25.

28. Byatt and Sodre, *Imagining Characters*, pp. 247–8.
29. Ibid., p. 232. Byatt's desire for order is one of the reasons why she likes the fairy tale form: 'the fairy tale gives form and coherence to formless fears, dreads and desires. Recognizing a fairy tale motif, or an ancient myth, Cinderella or Oedipus, in the mess of a life lived or observed gives both pleasure and security and the sense – or illusion of wisdom'. Essay on *The Djinn in the Nightingale's Eye*.
30. Caryn Mctighe Musil, 'A. S. Byatt', in Jay L. Halio (ed.), *Dictionary of Literary Biography: British Novelists since 1960* (Detroit: Bruccoli Clark, 1983), pp. 194–205 (197).
31. 'Identity and the Writer', p. 24.
32. Clayton, 'Narrative and Theories of Desire', pp. 33–53 (35).
33. Campbell, 'Hunger of the Imagination in A. S. Byatt's *The Game*', p. 160.

4 *Possession*: Melusine or the writer as serpent woman

1. A. S. Byatt, *Possession* (London: Chatto & Windus, 1990), p. 7. All page references are to this edition and will be included in brackets in the text.
2. A. S. Byatt, *The Virgin in the Garden* (London: Chatto & Windus, 1978); *Still Life* (London: Chatto & Windus, 1985).
3. Danny Karlin, 'Prolonging Her Absence', *London Review of Books* (8 March 1990), pp. 17–18 (17). I found this information in a survey conducted by Oates. He looked at the 'Books of the Year' sections of *The Times, Sunday Times, Observer, Daily Telegraph, Independent, Independent on Sunday* and the *Spectator*. Quentin Oates, *The Bookseller* (14 December 1990), pp. 1786–7.
4. Richard Jenkyns, 'Disinterring Buried Lives', *TLS* (2–8 March 1990), pp. 213–14 (214).
5. Ibid., p. 214.
6. Todd, 'Interview with A. S. Byatt', p. 43; Tredell, 'A. S. Byatt', p. 58.
7. Franken, 'Interview with A. S. Byatt'.
8. Ibid.
9. Aragay, 'Interview with A. S. Byatt'; *The Late Show* (1990).
10. *The Late Show*. Browning inspired Byatt's short story 'Precipice Encurled', included in *Sugar* (London: Chatto & Windus, 1987), pp. 185–214. For an analysis of this story see Jane Campbell, ' "The Somehow May Be Thishow": Fact, Fiction and Intertextuality in Antonia Byatt's "Precipice-Encurled" ', *Studies in Short Fiction* 28 (Spring 1991), pp. 115–23. For Byatt's critical work on Robert Browning, see the long essay in *Passions of the Mind*, pp. 29–71, the foreword to Browning's *Dramatic Monologues* (London: Folio Society, 1991), pp. vii–xxxi, and a review of three academic studies on Browning, 'Prophet and Doubter', *New Statesman* (2 January 1970), p. 16. In 'My

hero: A. S. Byatt on Robert Browning' she explains her fascination with the Victorian poet at length. *Independent Magazine* (26 November 1988), p. 78.

11. Byatt also said that Christabel echoes Isobel Armstrong's name. Armstrong is Professor of English at Birkbeck College and a good friend of A. S. Byatt. In an interview Byatt said that as 'the best living Browning scholar' and as a feminist expert on nineteenth-century women poets, Armstrong 'seemed thoroughly the right person to dedicate *Possession* to'. Zyngier, 'Passionate Act of Reading'.

12. Todd, 'Interview with A. S. Byatt', p. 43.

13. Tredell, 'A. S. Byatt', p. 64. In another interview A. S. Byatt mentioned again the spilt milk poem: 'You do have contact with [LaMotte] when you read her poems. The spilt milk poem is the most violent and passionate statement anybody makes in the book, the reader has to actually do an act of reading to see how terrible that poem is. *I didn't exactly imagine I was her,* but I did imagine what it felt like to be a woman whose child had immediately been taken away the moment it was born. One of the problems of that *is* milk'. Franken, 'Interview with A. S. Byatt'. Emphasis added.

14. Franken, 'Interview with A. S. Byatt'.

15. Kenneth Asher, *T. S. Eliot and Ideology* (Cambridge: Cambridge University Press, 1995), p. 86.

16. As Showalter writes: 'The image of feminists as angels of death, vicious animals, or witches handing innocent young women the poison apple of knowledge, is not, of course new. These stereotypes derive from a long-standing tradition of anti-feminist caricature, whether its ostensible subject is the bluestocking, the New Woman, the suffragette, or the Women Studies Professor'. Elaine Showalter, 'Feminists under Fire: Images of the New Woman from the Nineties to the 1990s', *TLS* (25 June 1993), p. 14. Isobel Armstrong situates *Possession*'s description of feminist academics in an early period of feminism: 'Early feminism began to look like the parodies of the feminist which have begun to enter novels – into A. S. Byatt's *Possession,* or Carol Shield's *Mary Swann* to name some recent British and North American examples of the genre'. Isobel Armstrong, 'Postscript', in Susan Sellers (ed.), *Feminist Criticism* (Manchester: Harvester, 1991) p. 209.

17. M. H. Abrams, *A Glossary of Literary Terms* (New York: Holt, Rinehart and Winston, 1981), p. 167.

18. Rosemarie Buikema and Anneke Smelik (eds), *Women's Studies and Culture: a Feminist Introduction* (London: Zed Books, 1995), pp. 192–3.

19. Franken, 'Interview with A. S. Byatt'. Luce Irigaray, *This Sex Which Is Not One*, trans. Catherine Porter (New York: Cornell University Press, 1985). See the following bibliographies for the titles of English translations of Irigaray's work: Margaret Whitford, *Luce Irigaray: Philosophy in the Feminine* (London: Routledge, 1991), pp. 222–3; Carolyn Burke, Naomi Schor and Margaret Whitford, *Engaging with Irigaray* (New York:

Columbia University Press, 1994), pp. 401–6; Rosi Braidotti, *Patterns of Dissonance* (Cambridge: Polity Press, 1991), p. 304 n. 90.

20. Zyngier, 'Passionate Act of Reading'.
21. Ibid.
22. Byatt has mentioned her impatience with 'parrot writing', i.e. essays by undergraduates who adopt a theoretical approach to literature without having read the primary literature itself. See Aragay, 'Interview with A. S. Byatt'. When Leonora Stern is interviewed on television, she and her female interviewer are also described as 'gaudy parrots, talking about female sexuality and its symbols when repressed'. This description is in marked contrast to the way in which a conversation between Maud and Ariane Le Minier is described. I would like to suggest that the last part of the following quote explains the positive tone of the narrator: 'The two women liked each other; they shared a passionate precision in their approach to scholarship, and discussed liminality and the nature of Melusina's monstrous form as a "transitional area", in Winnicott's terms – an imaginary construction that frees the woman from gender-identification' (*Possession*, p. 334).
23. Valerie Grove, 'Academic Reflections in a Victorian Climate', *Sunday Times* (21 October 1990), p. 3. The Booker Prize ceremony 1990 was a remarkable example of the ways in which some critics cut women writers down to size. When Byatt won the Booker Prize on the evening of 16 October, Germaine Greer, Maggie Gee and Eric Griffiths commented upon the choice of the Booker judges. Here is a good example of Griffiths's generosity: '[*Possession*] is a novel written by somebody who is not an artist . . . who has done A-level courses, taught them, and taken them, in what novels are like . . . It is clearly the work of a thinking person. She is trying to think about some quite serious questions, about the ways in which people are trapped into the different ways in which they talk about love, that there is no freedom, no simply free discourse, but, I think, as a novel it is an absolute disaster'. Susannah Clapp, one of the Booker judges, later remarked, ' "beautifully written" is novel-reviewer's shorthand for "written by a woman". So is "slim". And "slender". I began to notice these casual condescensions when I was helping to judge last year's Booker Prize'. Susannah Clapp, 'Lovers on a Train', *London Review of Books* (10 January 1991), p. 19.
24. Aragay, 'Interview with A. S. Byatt'. The novelist Christine Brooke-Rose has lamented the tendency of English novelists to be critical of literary theory: 'English writers often seem to be against technique and against theory as if talent alone were all that mattered. It's a very strange notion which no one would ever dream of upholding in music, or in painting. But with writing they seem to think that a thorough grasp of theory blocks creation. In my case on the contrary it absolutely inspired me'. Maria del Sapio Garbero, 'A Conversation with Christine Brooke-Rose', in Theo D'haen and Hans Bertens (eds), *British Postmodern Fiction* (Amsterdam: Rodopi, 1993), p. 102.

25. Franken, 'Interview with A. S. Byatt'. In the interview with Sonia Zyngier A. S. Byatt also mentioned these seminars: 'wonderful seminars of Frank Kermode's on modern critical analysis and we went through Barthes and Derrida. It was my education in modern literary theory. It was done in the late sixties and early seventies when the theory was actually happening. I used to come out of those seminars and . . . make lists exactly like Roland, of words that couldn't be reduced to part of the theoretical system'. Zyngier, 'Passionate Act of Reading'.
26. Tredell, 'A. S. Byatt', p. 61.
27. Jean d'Arras, *Le Roman de Melusine ou l'Histoire des Lusignan* (Paris: Stock, 1991). For an extensive historical survey of the Melusine mythology, see Bea Lundt, *Melusine und Merlin im Mittelalter: Entwürfe und Modelle weiblicher Existenz im Beziehungs-Diskurs der Geschlechter* (München: Fink Verlag, 1991), and Jacques Le Goff and Emmanuel Le Roy Ladurie, 'Mélusine maternelle et défricheuse', *Les Annales* 26/3–4 (mai–août 1971), pp. 587–622. For studies on waterwomen see Anna Maria Stuby, *Liebe, Tod und Wasserfrau* (Opladen, 1992). Inge Stephan, 'Weiblichkeit, Wasser und Tod: Undinen, Melusinen und Wasserfrauen bei Eichendorff und Fouqué', in Renate Berger and Inge Stephan (eds), *Weiblichkeit und Tod in der Literatur* (Keulen: Böhlau Verlag, 1987).
28. Jan de Vries, 'Les contes populaires', *Diogène* 22 (avril–juin 1958), 13.
29. Stuby, *Liebe, Tod und Wasserfrau*.
30. Le Goff and Le Roy Ladurie, 'Mélusine maternelle et défricheuse', p. 614.
31. Lundt, *Melusine und Merlin im Mittelalter*, p. 33, translation mine.
32. Maurice Beebe, *Ivory Towers and Sacred Founts: the Artist as Hero in Fiction from Goethe to Joyce* (New York: New York University Press, 1964), p. 81.
33. A. S. Byatt, 'How Was It for Them?', *Sunday Times* (28 January 1990), p. 4.
34. Margaret Hallissy, 'Woman and the Serpent', *Venomous Woman: Fear of the Female in Literature* (New York: Greenwood Press, 1987), pp. 89–132; Agnès Vincenot, 'Genèse', in Agnès Vincenot, Marion de Zanger, Heide Hinterthur and Anne–Claire Mulder (eds), *Renaissance* (Amsterdam: Perdu, 1990), pp. 46–88; Lundt, *Melusine und Merlin im Mittelalter*; Irigaray, 'Divine Women'. 'Divine Women' is based on a reading of *Le Roman de Melusine* by Jean d'Arras, the related fairy tales by Andersen and Grimm, and Le Goff and Le Roy Ladurie's analysis of Melusine.
35. Mieke Bal, 'Myth à la lettre: Freud, Mann, Genesis and Rembrandt, and the Story of the Son', in Shlomith Rimmon-Kenan (ed.), *Discourse in Psychoanalysis and Literature* (London: Methuen, 1987), pp. 57–89.
36. Irigaray, 'Divine Women', p. 59.
37. Luisa Muraro, 'Female Genealogies', in Carolyn Burke, Naomi Schor and Margaret Whitford (eds), *Engaging with Irigaray* (New York: Columbia University Press, 1994), pp. 317–34 (322).

38. Vincenot, 'Genèse', p. 55.
39. Tredell, 'A. S. Byatt', p. 60.
40. Irigaray, 'Divine Women', p. 59.
41. Ibid., p. 71.
42. Ibid., p. 64.
43. Anne-Claire Mulder, 'Goddelijk worden' (Becoming Divine), Vincenot et al., *Renaissance*, pp. 140–60 (142), translation mine.
44. Vincenot, 'Genèse', p. 58, translation mine. Hallissey is quite witty in describing Melusine's building power. Melusine builds and builds, quickly and on her own accord, and the land prospers. Towns and castles grow under her hands to the point where Raymond has difficulties recognizing his home ground on coming back from one of his journeys, 'because she has built a whole town around it in his absence'. Hallissy, 'Woman and the Serpent', p. 104.
45. Todd, *A. S. Byatt*, pp. 59–60.
46. Vincenot, 'Genèse', pp. 69, 57, translation mine.
47. Quoted in Beebe, *Ivory Towers and Sacred Founts*, p. 99. A. S. Byatt is a great admirer of Cather's work. She persuaded Cather's American publishers to let Virago publish Cather in England and prefaced seven of the Virago editions. Byatt explained her 'passionate involvement' with Cather as follows: 'I think what I love about Cather is that she invented a new form of sentence, an apparently loose fluid and wandering sentence which is actually clear-cut and completely apt in saying what it wants. She combined so many levels of discourse'. Franken, 'Interview with A. S. Byatt'. Her description does remind me of Woolf's definition of Dorothy Richardson's style: 'She has invented, or, if she has not invented, developed and applied to her own uses, a sentence which we might call the psychological sentence of the feminine gender. It is of a more elastic fibre than the old, capable of stretching to the extreme, of suspending the frailest particles, of enveloping the vaguest shapes'. Virginia Woolf, 'Dorothy Richardson', *Women & Writing* (London: Women's Press, 1979), p. 191.
48. Franken, 'Interview with A. S. Byatt'.
49. Goldberg does not give titles of these artist-novels but seems to imply in an earlier paragraph that he is referring to Frances Moore Brooke's *The Excursion* (1777), Helen Maria Williams's *Julia* (1790), Elizabeth Inchbald's *Nature and Art* (1796) and William Beckford's *Modern Novel Writing* (1796). Gerald Jay Goldberg, 'The Artist-Novel in Transition', *English Fiction in Transition* 4/3 (1961), pp. 12–27 (12).
50. Jonathan Coe is the only reviewer of *Possession* to notice that 'a debate about gender' is at the heart of the novel. 'Byatt's Pendulum', *Guardian* (11 March 1990), p. 23. Even Roland, who is quite sympathetic towards LaMotte, suggests at one point that *The Fairy Melusine* may have been written by Ash.
51. Rachel Blau DuPlessis, 'To "Bear My Mother's Name": Künstlerromane by Women Writers', *Writing beyond the Ending: Narrative Strategies of Twentieth-Century Women Writers* (Bloomington: Indiana University

Press, 1985), pp. 104, 93. Perhaps it is possible to construct an auto-biographical interpretation of *Possession*'s emphasis on art as a bridge between women, between a mother and a daughter. A. S. Byatt has always been quite outspoken about the difficult relationship she had with her mother. However, in the radio programme *Desert Island Disks* she evoked art as a bridge between herself and her mother. She said that when her mother died she 'felt an immense space, I felt a huge amount of brilliantly coloured air coming into the window, if I'm going to be absolutely truthful. And I also felt that she could stop hurting herself. That there was peace in a corner of my mind where there had always been turmoil. After that I started thinking about her as a young woman and I started mourning, not for my mother, but for the girl who had gone to Cambridge and had been so brilliant. I began to be able to imagine her because she wasn't there shouting at me. I began to imagine what she was like when she used to read Keats to herself and I do grieve a lot for that woman. I miss *her*' (10 January 1999). Like *Possession* this touching statement evokes art as a bridge and an intermediary between a mother and a daughter.

52. Elaine Feinstein, 'Eloquent Victorians', *New Statesman* (16 March 1990), p. 38.
53. Huf, *Portrait of the Artist as a Young Woman*, p. 153.
54. Blau DuPlessis, *Writing beyond the Ending*, p. 104.
55. Toni Morrison, 'Rootedness: the Ancestor as Foundation', in Mari Evans (ed.), *Black Women Writers* (New York: Anchor Press, 1984), p. 343. A. S. Byatt has said that she admires Toni Morrison's work 'inordinately'. 'The Man in the Back Row Has a Question V', *Paris Review* 146 (Spring 1998), p. 171. She has written about *Beloved* in *Passions of the Mind*, pp. 255–8, and *Imagining Characters* (with Ignès Sodre), pp. 192–229.
56. Byatt, *Djinn in the Nightingale's Eye*, p. 72.
57. Tredell, 'A. S. Byatt', p. 66.
58. Ibid., p. 60.
59. Andre Brink, 'Possessed by Language: A. S. Byatt: *Possession*', *The Novel: Language and Narrative from Cervantes to Calvino* (Houndmills: Macmillan – now Palgrave, 1998), pp. pp. 288–308 (305). Brink inter-prets Melusine as a symbol of female autonomy (p. 295), but is less interested in the connection with art and authorship. His analysis is particularly good on *Possession* as a Romance. See also Elisabeth Bronfen, 'Romancing Difference, Courting Coherence: A. S. Byatt's *Possession* as Postmodern Moral Fiction', in Ahrens-Rudiger (ed.), *Why Literature Matters* (Heidelberg: Winter, 1996), pp. 117–34, and Roberts, 'Passionate Reader'.
60. Blau DuPlessis, *Writing beyond the Ending*, p. x.
61. Helen Dunmore, 'Magic in the Palm of a Hand', *Observer* (1 January 1995), p. 17.
62. I only know of one other fiction writer who rewrites the Melusine motif in the same way as A. S. Byatt does, who takes Melusine's 'monstrous' side and turns it inside out as an image of women's creativity. In her

short story 'Anger' Michèle Roberts rewrites the Melusine motif in artist-novel style. Alison Fell (ed.), *The Seven Deadly Sins* (London: Serpent's Tail, 1988), pp. 13–40. Roberts came across the story of Melusine in a newspaper article she read in Italy 'about a folktale heroine called Melusina . . . she turns into a monster-artist every Saturday night. Her husband is forbidden to spy on her, but he does, so loses her'. Olga Kenyon, 'Michèle Roberts', *Women Writers Talk* (Oxford: Lennard Publishing, 1989), p. 168.

Art made me: conclusion

'Art Made Me' is the title of a sketch by Marlene Dumas which I encountered at the exhibition 'Miss Interpreted', Stedelijk van Abbemuseum Eindhoven 15 March–3 May 1992.

1. Byatt, *Babel Tower*, p. 244.
2. Martha Nussbaum, 'Transcending Humanity', *Love's Knowledge: Essays on Philosophy and Literature* (Oxford: Oxford University Press, 1990), pp. 365–92 (379). In her reading of Tiptree's 'A Momentary Taste of Being', Inez van der Spek revises 'transcendence' as an activity which points 'to transformation, to the power to cross over, make new connections; it indicates an imaginative movement from the existent to the possible'. *Alien Plots: Female Subjectivity and the Divine in the Light of James Tiptree's 'A Momentary Taste of Being'* (Liverpool: Liverpool University Press, 2000).
3. Nussbaum, 'Transcending Humanity', p. 379.
4. Ibid., p. 381.
5. Yaeger, *Honey-Mad Women*, p. 183.
6. Morrison, 'Rootedness', p. 341.
7. Barbara Johnson, quoted in Nancy Miller, *Getting Personal* (London: Routledge, 1991), p. 88.

Bringing Language and Thought to Life: Select Bibliography of A. S. Byatt's Fiction and Criticism, 1965–2000

All items within each section of the bibliography are arranged by their date of publication.

Primary sources

I   Novels

Shadow of a Sun (London: Chatto & Windus, 1964). Reprinted as *The Shadow of the Sun* with a foreword by the author (London: Vintage, 1991).
The Game (London: Chatto & Windus, 1967).
The Virgin in the Garden (London: Chatto & Windus, 1978).
Still Life (London: Chatto & Windus, 1985).
Possession (London: Chatto & Windus, 1990).
Babel Tower (London: Chatto & Windus, 1996).
The Biographer's Tale (London: Chatto & Windus, 2000).

II   Short stories

'Daniel', *Encounter* (April 1976), pp. 3–8.
'On the Day that E. M. Forster Died', *Encounter* 61 (1983), pp. 3–9; also in Patricia Craig (ed.), *The Oxford Book of Modern Women's Stories* (Oxford: Oxford University Press, 1995), pp. 442–55.
'The Changeling', *Encounter* 64/5 (May 1985), pp. 3–7.
Sugar (London: Chatto & Windus, 1987).
'Precipice Encurled', *Encounter* 68/4 (April 1987), pp. 21–31.
'Medusa's Ankles', in Giles Gordon and David Hughes (eds), *Best Short Stories 1991* (London: Heinemann, 1991), pp. 73–86; *Independent on Sunday* (19 February 1993), pp. 38–40.
Angels and Insects (London: Chatto & Windus, 1992).
'Art Work', in Malcolm Bradbury and Judy Cooke (eds), *New Writing* (London: Minerva, 1992), pp. 263–90.
'The Story of the Eldest Princess', Christine Park and Caroline Heaton (eds), *Caught in a Story: Contemporary Fairytales & Fables* (London: Chatto & Windus, 1992), pp. 12–28.

The Djinn in the Nightingale's Eye: Five Fairy Stories (London: Chatto & Windus, 1994).
The Matisse Stories (London: Chatto & Windus, 1994).
'Baglady', *Daily Telegraph* (15 January 1994), p. 11.
'Dragon's Breath', *Index on Censorship* 4/5 (1994), pp. 89–95.
'The July Ghost', in Hermione Lee (ed.), *The Secret Self: a Century of Short Stories by Women* (London: Phoenix, 1995), pp. 420–32.
'A Lamia in the Cevennes', in Christopher Hope and Peter Porter (eds), *New Writing 5* (London: Vintage in association with the British Council, 1996), pp. 1–17.
Elementals: Stories of Fire and Ice (London: Chatto & Windus, 1998).
'Crocodile Tears', *Paris Review* 146 (Spring 1998), pp. 43–84.

III   Poems

'A Dog, a Horse, a Rat', *TLS* (24 May 1991), p. 22.
'Working with Cliches', in Elisabeth Maslen (ed.), *The Timeless and the Temporal: Writings in Honour of John Chalker by Friends and Colleagues* (London: University College, Queen Mary and Westfield, 1993), pp. 1–3.
'Dead Boys', *TLS* (2 December 1994), p. 27.

IV   Academic studies

Degrees of Freedom: the Novels of Iris Murdoch (London: Chatto & Windus, 1965; New York: Barnes and Noble, 1965). Reprint (London: Vintage, 1994).
Unruly Times: Wordsworth and Coleridge in Their Time (London: Hogarth, 1970; Vintage, 1989).
Wordsworth and Coleridge in Their Times (New York: Crane, Russak, 1973).
Iris Murdoch: a Critical Study (London: Longman for the British Council, 1976).
Passions of the Mind: Selected Writings (London: Chatto & Windus, 1991).
On Histories and Stories (London: Chatto & Windus, 2000).

V   Lectures

'Identity and the Writer', in Lisa Appignanesi (ed.), *Identity: the Real Me*, ICA Documents 6 (London: Institute of Contemporary Arts, 1987), pp. 23–6.

VI   Academic articles and essays

'The Lyric Structure of Tennyson's Maud', in Isobel Armstrong (ed.), *The Major Victorian Poets: Reconsiderations* (London: Routledge, 1969), pp. 69–92.
Iris Murdoch: the Black Prince (London: The British Council, 1977).
'Wallace Stevens: Criticism, Repetition, and Creativity', *Journal of American Studies* 12/3 (1978), pp. 369–75.

'People in Paper Houses: Attitudes to "Realism" and "Experiment" in English Postwar Fiction', in Malcolm Bradbury and David Palmer (eds), *The Contemporary British Novel* (London: Edward Arnold, 1979), pp. 19–41.

'Still Life/Nature Mort', in David Kelley and Isabelle Clasera (eds), *Cross References: Modern French Theory and the Practice of Criticism* (London: Society for French Studies, 1986), pp. 9–20.

'The Omnipotence of Thought: Frazer, Freud and Post-Modernist Fiction, 1990', in Robert Fraser (ed.), *Sir James Frazer and the Literary Imagination* (London: Macmillan, 1990), pp. 270–308.

'A Sense of Religion: Enright's God', in Jacqueline Simms (ed.), *Life by Other Means: Essays on D. J. Enright* (Oxford: Oxford University Press, 1990), pp. 158–74.

'Reading, Writing, Studying: Some Questions about Changing Conditions for Writers and Readers', *Critical Quarterly* 35/4 (1993), pp. 3–7.

'A New Body of Writing: Darwin and Recent British Fiction', in Alan Hollinghurst and A. S. Byatt (eds), *New Writing 4* (London: Vintage in Association with the British Council, 1995), pp. 439–48.

'A Riddle Around the Edges of Vision', in David Sylvester (ed.), *Patrick Heron* (London: Tate Gallery, 1998), pp. 13–17.

VII Introductions/afterwords

Elizabeth Bowen, *The House in Paris* (Harmondsworth: Penguin, 1976).

Grace Paley, *Enormous Changes at the Last Minute* (London: Virago, 1979).

Willa Cather, *A Lost Lady* (London: Virago, 1980).

Willa Cather, *My Antonia* (London: Virago, 1980).

Grace Paley, *The Little Disturbances of Man* (London: Virago, 1980).

Willa Cather, *Death Comes for the Archbishop* (London: Virago, 1981).

Willa Cather, *My Mortal Enemy* (London: Virago, 1982).

Willa Cather, *The Song of the Lark* (London: Virago, 1982).

Willa Cather, *O Pioneers* (London: Virago, 1983).

Willa Cather, *Shadows on the Rocks* (London: Virago, 1984).

Ford Madox Ford, *The Fifth Queen* (Oxford: Oxford University Press, 1984), pp. xiv, 592.

Willa Cather, *Lucy Gearhart* (London: Virago, 1985).

Pamela Handsford Johnson, *An Error of Judgement* (Oxford: Oxford University Press, 1987).

George Eliot, *The Mill on the Floss* (Harmondsworth: Penguin, 1988).

Rachel Ferguson, *The Brontës Went to Woolworths* (London: Virago, 1988).

George Eliot, *Selected Essays, Poems and Other Writings* (Harmondsworth: Penguin, 1990), pp. ix–xxxv.

Robert Browning, *Dramatic Monologues* (London: Folio Society, 1991), pp. vii–xxxi.

A. L. Barker, *A Case Examined, John Brown's Body, The Gooseboy* (London: Vintage, 1992).

'Willa Cather', *Keepsake* (London: Virago, 1993), pp. 16–19.

Wim Bronzwaer and H. Verdaasdonk (eds), *Kees Fens: Finding the Place: Selected Essays on English Literature* (Amsterdam: Rodopi, Costerus, 1994).

The Song of Solomon (Edinburgh: Canongate, 1998), pp. vii–xviii.

George Eliot, *Middlemarch* (Oxford: Oxford University Press, 1999).

VIII   Reviews and articles

a.   Daily Mail

Daily Mail (22 April 1992). Review of Jack Zipes (ed.), *Spells of Enchantment: the Wondrous Fairy Tales of Western Culture.*

'The Feminine Forster: Can a Woman's Intuition Really Give Us New Insight?', *Daily Mail* (6 May 1993), p. 49. Review of Nicola Beauman, *Morgan: a Biography of E. M. Forster.*

b.   Encounter

'Evil is Commonplace', *Encounter* 27/6 (June 1966), pp. 64–8. Review of Graham Greene, *The Comedians.*

'Mess & Mystery', *Encounter* 27/1 (July 1966), pp. 59–61. Review of Kingsley Amis, *The Anti-Death League.*

'The Obsession with Amorphous Mankind: Marguerite Young's Strange Best-Seller', *Encounter* 27 (September 1966), pp. 63–9. Review of Marguerite Young, *Miss MacIntosh, My Darling.*

'The Battle between Real People and Images', *Encounter* 28 (February 1967), pp. 71–8. Review of Patrick White, *The Solid Mandala.*

'Subversion and Stubbornness: On Culture and its Critics', *Encounter* 67 (1986), pp. 46–51. Essay on the work of Lionel Trilling, William Empson and Cristopher Prendergast.

c.   Evening Standard

Evening Standard (22 April 1992). Review of Patrick O'Brian, *Clarissa Oakes.*

'Beware the Aisles of Plenty', *Evening Standard* (3 September 1992), p. 32. Review of Lawrence Stone, *Uncertain Unions: Marriage in England 1660–1753.*

d.   The Guardian

The Guardian (October 1987). Review of Toni Morrison, *Beloved.*

e.   Independent

'The Dangerous Belief that There Is No Such Thing as Knowledge', *Independent* (29 April 1988), p. 16. On the knowledge vs. skills debate.

'My Hero: A. S. Byatt on Robert Browning', *Independent Magazine* (26 November 1988), p. 78. Explanation of Byatt's admiration for Robert Browning.

'America's Double Voice', *Independent* (14 October 1989), p. 32. Review of Hermione Lee, *Willa Cather: a Life Saved Up.*

'The Names of the Rose', *Independent* (14 February 1991), p. 13. Parody on deconstruction.
'Life in a Soap Opera', *Independent Magazine* (10 October 1992), pp. 30–5. Report on a visit to Brazil.
'In Mine Age the Owls, after Death the Ghouls', *Independent* (10 April 1993). Review of Peter Levi, *Tennyson*.
'The Colour of Feeling', *Independent* (10 July 1994), pp. 30–1. Review of Andrew Graham-Dixon, *Howard Hodgkin*.

f. Listener

'Imagining the Worst', *Listener* 96 (15 July 1976), pp. 35–7. On images of disaster, the power of the imagination, Nietzsche, reality in art.
'Examination Fever', *Listener* 96 (22 July 1976), pp. 66–8. On exams and Byatt's own experiences as an examinee.
'Who Are the English', *Listener* 96 (5 August 1976), pp. 130–1. On (theories of) culture, a multicultural society, science/art.
'Some Call it Democracy', *Listener* 96 (19 August 1976), pp. 204–5. On education and the state.
'Flair Criticism', *Listener* 99 (19 January 1978), pp. 80–1. On taste and 'flair' for literature.

g. Literary Review

Literary Review (May 1979). Review of William Golding, *Darkness Visible*.
'First Novels: Judging the David Higham Award', *Literary Review* (16–29 November 1979), pp. 8–9.

h. Modern Painters

'Noel Forster's Work', *Modern Painters* 4/1 (Spring 1991), pp. 29–35. On the work of the British painter Noel Forster.
'Woman Unafraid', *Modern Painters* (Summer 1993), pp. 22–4. On the work of Georgia O'Keeffe and Alfred Stieglitz.

i. New Review

'Bible Readings', *New Review* 2/21 (1975), pp. 67–9. Review of E. S. Shaffer, *Kubla Khan and the Fall of Jerusalem*.
'Give Me the Moonlight, Give Me the Girl', *New Review* 2/15 (1975), p. 67. Review of Monique Wittig, *The Lesbian Body*.

j. New Statesman

'Distrusting the Intellect', *New Statesman* (19 May 1967), pp. 689–90. Review of George Levine, *The Emergence of Victorian Consciousness*, Laurence Lerner, *The Truth-Tellers*, and J. Killham, *Critical Essays on the Poetry of Tennyson*.
'Of Things I Sing', *New Statesman* (2 June 1967), p. 763. Reviews of William Golding, *The Pyramid*, and Mark Kinkead-Weeks (ed.), *William Golding*.

'Punch and Judy', *New Statesman* (14 July 1967), p. 53. Review of Sheila Graham, *College of One*.

'Connoisseur of Order', *New Statesman* (4 August 1967), p. 146. Review of Frank Kermode, *The Sense of an Ending*.

'Crumbling the Text', *New Statesman* (17 November 1967), p. 763. Review of Barbara Hardy (ed.), *Middlemarch*, and Bernard C. Meyer, *Joseph Conrad*.

'Whittled and Spiky Art', *New Statesman* (15 December 1967), p. 848. Review of Muriel Spark, *Collected Stories I*, and *Collected Poems I*.

'Tempest in my Mind', *New Statesman* (22 September 1967), p. 371. Review of A. D. Nuttall, *Two Concepts of Allegory*.

'Life Lies', *New Statesman* (5 January 1968), p. 15. Review of Simone de Beauvoir, *Les Belles Images*, Daniel Ford, *Incident at Muc Wa*, Vincent Burgess, *Second-Hand Persons*, and Earl Lovelace, *The Schoolmaster*.

'Kiss and make up', *New Statesman* (26 January 1968), pp. 113–14. Review of Iris Murdoch, *The Nice and the Good*.

'The Half-Fiction Novel', *New Statesman* (16 February 1968), pp. 209. Review of Julian Mitchell, *The Undiscovered Country*. Andrew Salkey, *The Late Emancipation of Jerry Stoves*, S. Menon Marath, *The Sale of an Island*, Robert Stone, *A Hall of Mirrors*, Gwyn Griffin, *An Operational Necessity*, and Joel Lieber, *How the Fishes Live*.

'Trapped', *New Statesman* (29 March 1968), pp. 421–2. Review of Andrew Hall, *Safe behind Bars*, Sue Walton, *Here before Kilroy*, Jean Rhys, *Tigers Are Better-Looking*, Joan Lindsay, *Picnic at Hanging Rock*, and John Reid, *Horses with Blindfolds*.

'Substitutes for Reading', *New Statesman* (12 April 1968), p. 491. Review of *Literature in Perspective, Profiles in Literature, English Library*, and F. A. Scott, *Close Readings*.

'Elegiac Saga', *New Statesman* (17 May 1968), pp. 654–5. Review of Pamela Hansford Johnson, *The Survival of the Fittest*, and Isabel Quigly, *Pamela Hansford Johnson*.

'Empty Shell', *New Statesman* (14 June 1968), pp. 807–8. Review of Muriel Spark, *The Public Image*.

'The Victorian Balancing Act', *New Statesman* (26 July 1968), pp. 111–12. Review of Raymond Chapman, *The Victorian Debate*.

'The Rage for Order', *New Statesman* (1 November 1968), p. 584. Review of Frank Kermode, *Continuities*.

'Energetic Doubts', *New Statesman* (6 December 1968), p. 800. Review of Gertrude Himmelfarb, *Victorian Minds*, and David Mathew, *Lord Acton and His Time*.

'The Spider's Web', *New Statesman* (17 January 1969), p. 86. Review of Iris Murdoch, *Bruno's Dream*.

'Mythical Analogies', *New Statesman* (24 January 1969), pp. 120–1. Review of Honor Matthews, *The Hard Journey*.

'Daughter of Debate', *New Statesman* (16 May 1969), pp. 693–4. Review of Antonia Fraser, *Mary, Queen of Scots*.

'Prophet and Doubter', *New Statesman* (2 January 1970), p. 16. Review of Maisie Ward, *Robert Browning and His World*, Mary Sullivan, *Browning's*

Voices in 'The Ring and the Book', and Leonard Burrows, *Browning the Poet.*

'A Man of Balance', *New Statesman* (18 December 1970), pp. 839–40. Review of *The Letters of Thomas Mann 1889–1942, 1943–1955.*

'Mirror, Mirror on the Wall', *New Statesman* (23 April 1976), pp. 541–2. Review of Sylvia Plath, *Letters Home.*

'The One Life', *New Statesman* (26 January 1979), pp. 118–19. Review of John Beer, *Wordsworth in Time and Wordsworth and the Human Heart.*

New Statesman (May 1979). Review of Arnold Fruman, *Coleridge: the Damaged Archangel.*

'Downstream', *New Statesman* (4 May 1979), p. 646. Review of Charles Rycroft, *The Innocence of Dreams.*

'The Greedy Reader', *New Statesman* (18 May 1979), p. 724. Review of V. S. Pritchett, *The Myth Makers.*

'The Power of Learning', *New Statesman* (17 August 1979), pp. 239–40. Reviews of Gordon S. Haight, *Letters: Vols VIII and IX by George Eliot,* Michael Wheeler, *The Art of Illusion in Victorian Fiction,* Andrew Sanders, *The Victorian Historical Novel,* and Michael Irwin, *Picturing: Description and Illusion in the Nineteenth-Century Novel.*

k. Nova

'The Agony of the Middle Class Liberal', *Nova* (May/June 1969), p. 46.

'Georgette Heyer Is a Better Writer than You Think', *Nova* (August 1969), p. 14.

'Monica Dickens: the Lady Is Not for Moaning', *Nova* (March 1970), p. 26.

l. Sunday Times, Sunday Times Magazine, The Times

'Unhappily Ever After', *Sunday Times Magazine* (9 February 1969), p. 7.

'Such Stuff as Dreams Are Made of', *Sunday Times Magazine* (16 February 1969), pp. 40–1.

'A Murder in Hell', *Times* (24 September 1970), p. 14. Review of Muriel Spark, *The Driver's Seat.*

'The Ferocious Reticence of Georgette Heyer', *Sunday Times Magazine* (5 October 1975), p. 28.

'Unfaithful to Marian', *Sunday Times* (16 July 1989). Review of Ina Taylor, *George Eliot: Woman of Contradictions.*

'How Was It for Them?', *Sunday Times* (28 January 1990), p. 4. Review of Ruth Brandon, *The New Women and the Old Men: Love, Sex, and the Woman Question.*

'A Leave out of His Own Book', *Sunday Times* (8 November 1992), pp. 8–9. Review of David Lodge, *The Art of Fiction.*

'The New Romantics', *Sunday Times* (6 June 1993), p. 7. Review of Jerome J. McGann, *The New Oxford Book of Romantic Period Verse.*

'Identity Crises', *Sunday Times* (1 October 1995), p. 13. Review of Iris Murdoch, *Jackson's Dilemma.*

'Testament to a Soul in Torment', *Sunday Times* (25 February 1996). Review of Ronald de Leeuw (ed.), *The Letters of Vincent van Gogh*.
'Passionate Tale of the Unexpected', *Times* (4 April 1996), p. 39. Review of Doris Lessing, *Love, again*.
'Planet of the Japes', *Sunday Times* (15 December 1996). Byatt explains the delight she finds in reading Terry Pratchett's work.

m.   *Times Literary Supplement*

'Yearning for Jerusalem', *TLS* (6 October 1978), p. 1110. Review of Amos Oz, *The Hill of Evil Counsel*.
'Cannibals, Scholars and Artists', *TLS* (25 April 1980), p. 466. Review of *The Rear Column* (BBC TV).
'The Isle Full of Noises', *TLS* (26 September 1980), p. 1057. Review of Penelope Fitzgerald, *Human Voices*.
'Working by Intuition', *TLS* (23 January 1981), p. 86. Review of Walter Nash, *Designs in Prose*.
'Impressions in Their Rendering', *TLS* (13 February 1981), pp. 171–2. Review of *The Bodley Head Ford Madox Ford*.
'Flourishing Fleshily', *TLS* (23 October 1981), p. 1231. Review of A. N. Wilson, *Who Was Oswald Fish?*
'The Architecture of the Emotions', *TLS* (11 December 1981), p. 1446. Review of V. Pritchett (ed.), *The Oxford Book of Short Stories*.
'The Raj and the Great Tradition', *TLS* (1981), p. 33. Review of the television adaptation of Paul Scott's novel.
'Imaging the Past', *TLS* (28 May 1982), p. 591. Review of Mary Lascelles, *The Story-Teller Retrieves the Past*.
'An Assorted Life', *TLS* (2 December 1983), p. 138. Review of John Carswell, *The Exile: a Life of Ivy Litvinov*.
'The Ideal of Public Woman', *TLS* (12 October 1984), p. 1160. Review of the film *The Bostonians*.
'The Mechanics of Evil', *TLS* (3 May 1985), p. 496. Review of *The Cenci*, by Bristol New Vic.
'Viewpoint: the Resistant Element', *TLS* (17 May 1985), p. 548. On war and the literature of war.
'Harsh Light on the Web', *TLS* (9 August 1985), p. 875. Review of Fay Weldon, *Polaris and Other Stories*.
'Neglected Fictions', *TLS* (18 October 1985), p. 1186. On A. L. Barker.
'Natural and Unnatural Causes', *TLS* (6 December 1985), p. 1397. Review of the film *Turtle Diary*.
'Standing and Falling with the Body', *TLS* (20 December 1985), p. 1463. Review of David Plante, *The Catholic*.
'Wisdom after the Event', *TLS* (7 March 1986), p. 258. Review of Philip Gardner (ed.), *E. M. Forster's Commonplace Books*.
'The Disreputable Other Half', *TLS* (4 April 1986), p. 357. Review of Patrick White, *Memoirs of Many in One*.

'Suffering and Creating', *TLS* (13 June 1986), p. 637. Review of Elaine Scarry, *The Body in Pain: the Making and Unmaking of the World*.

'Marginal Lives', *TLS* (8 August 1986), p. 862. Review of Barbara Pym, *An Academic Question*, and Robert Long Emmett, *Barbara Pym*.

'Insights ad nauseum', *TLS* (14 November 1986), p. 4363. Review of Timothy Peltason, *Reading* 'In Memoriam', David Albright, *Tennyson: the Muses' Tug-of-War*, Susan Shatto (ed.), *Tennyson's* 'Maud': a Definitive Edition, and Alan Sinfield, *Alfred Tennyson*.

'The Real Made Sense', *TLS* (16 January 1987), p. 65. Review of Nicholas Boyle, *Realism in European Literature*, and Barbara Foley, *Telling the Truth: the Theory and Practice of Documentary Fiction*.

'Hearths in the Wilderness', *TLS* (15 May 1987), pp. 507–8. Review of Sharon O'Brien, *Willa Cather: the Emerging Voice*, and Susan J. Rosowski, *The Voyage Perilous: Willa Cather's Romanticism*.

'Beginning in Craft and Ending in Mystery', *TLS* (13 May 1988), p. 527. Review of Malcolm Bradbury (ed.), *The Penguin Book of Modern British Short Stories*, V. Pritchett (ed.), *The Oxford Book of Short Stories*, W. Somerset Maugham, *The Dragon's Head*, Dan Davin (ed.), *The Killing Bottle*, T. S. Dorsch (ed.), *Charmed Lives*, and Roger Sharrock (ed.), *The Green Man Revisited*.

'Control of the Life-Sources', *TLS* (12 August 1988), p. 890. Review of Peter Redgrove, *The Black Goddess and the Sixth Sense*, *The Moon Disposes* and *In the Hall of the Saurians*.

'Writing and Feeling', *TLS* (18 November 1988), p. 1278. On poetry and language.

'Obscenity and the Arts: a Symposium', *TLS* (12–18 February 1988), pp. 159–61. Contributors: A. S. Byatt, Anthony Burgess, Clark Glymour, Marina Warner, Melvyn Bragg, A. W. Price and Mary Lefkowitz.

'Theoria', *TLS* (30 December 1988–5 January 1989), p. 1443. On Malcolm Bull's review of Peter Fuller's *Theoria*.

'A Word Play', *TLS* (5 May 1989), p. 487. Review of Iris Murdoch's play *The Black Prince*.

'Chosen Vessels of a Fraud', *TLS* (2 June 1989), p. 605. Review of Alex Owen, *The Darkened Room: Women, Power and Spiritualism in Late Victorian England*.

'The Trouble with the Interesting Reader', *TLS* (23 March 1990), p. 310. Review of Mary Jacobus, *Romanticism, Writing and Sexual Difference*.

'After the Myth, the Real', *TLS* (29 June 1990), pp. 683–5. Review of Ken Wilkie, *The Van Gogh File*, Martin Bailey, *Young Vincent*, David Sweetman, *The Love of Many Things: a Life of Vincent van Gogh*, and Tsukasa Kodera, *Vincent van Gogh*.

'Amatory Acts', *TLS* (31 August 1990), p. 913. Review of John Fuller (ed.), *The Chatto Book of Love Poetry*, and Amandie McCardie (ed.), *The Collins Book of Love Poetry*.

'Savage Londoners', *TLS* (1990), p. 146. Review of Doris Lessing's play *In Pursuit of the English*.

(With Ignès Sodre) 'The Dislikable Gwendolen: a Conversation between A. S. Byatt and Ignès Sodre, TLS (6 October 1995), pp. 19–20.

n.   *Weekend Telegraph*

'Twenty Ways to Avoid Despair', *Weekend Telegraph* (24 April 1993), p. xxv.

'Fast, Thick Warbles of Delicious Notes', *Weekend Telegraph* (10 July 1993). Review of Richard Mabey, *Whistling in the Dark: In Pursuit of the Nightingale*.

IX   Editor

George Eliot, *The Mill on the Floss* (Harmondsworth: Penguin, 1988); with an introduction, notes and 'The "placing" of Stephen Guest'.

(With Nicholas Warren), George Eliot, *Selected Essays, Poems and Other Writings* (Harmondsworth: Penguin, 1990); Introduction, pp. ix–xxxv.

(With Alan Hollinghurst), *New Writing 4* (London: Vintage in Association with the British Council, 1995).

(With Peter Porter), *New Writing 6* (London: Vintage in Association with the British Council, 1997).

X   Varia

'The God I Want', in Mitchell, James (ed.), *The God I Want* (London: Constable, 1967), pp. 71–87. Autobiographical essay on religion, literature and myth: chapter in Mitchell 'A. S. Byatt'.

'Fear and Loathing in Putney', *Evening Standard* (28 February 1988). On being robbed.

'The Call of the Coast', *Country Homes and Interiors* (November 1990), pp. 50–4. Autobiographical piece on the importance of Yorkshire to Byatt's work.

'Safe from Grave-Robbers and Ghouls', *Daily Telegraph* (3 November 1990), p. 17. Extract from *Possession* on biographers.

'Favourite Books of the Year', *Independent* (24 November 1990), p. 30. Byatt's list: Angela Carter, *Virago Book of Fairy Tales*; Gesualdo Bufalino, *Night's Lies*; Alice Munro, *Friend of My Youth*; Ruth Fainlight, *The Knot*.

'Voices from Her People', *Independent on Sunday Review* (25 November 1990), pp. 3–4. On Margaret Thatcher.

'In the Second-Hand Bookshops', *Sunday Telegraph* (3 December 1990), p. 12. On books bought at the Richmond Bookshop.

'In Memoriam', *Poetry in Motion 2* (London: Channel 4, 1992), pp. 54–70. On elegies and personal poems about death.

'The Pleasure of Reading', in Antonia Fraser (ed.), *The Pleasure of Reading* (London: Bloomsbury, 1992), pp. 127–32. On the pleasure of reading, including a list of favourite books.

'Either a Borrower or a Lender Be', *Guardian* (2 March 1992). On reading, literature and public libraries.

'In a Still Life, a Garden of Possessions', *Times Saturday Review* (22 August 1992), pp. 26–7. On the influence of books read in childhood.

'Books of the decade' (Salman Rushdie' *Shame* and Alice Munro's *The Progress of Love*), *Telegraph* (1 September 1992).

Introduction to 'Recurrent Dreams and Visions', an exhibition of water-colours by Norman Adams, R.A. (31 March–23 April 1993).

'Author's Picture Choice', *National Gallery News* (November 1993). On the painting *Kitchen Scene with Christ in the house of Martha and Mary*, by Velázquez.

'Books of the Year 1993', *Daily Telegraph* (27 November 1993). Byatt's choice: Roberto Calasso's *The Marriage of Cadmus and Harmony*, Steve Jones's *The Language of Genes*, and Pat Barker's *The Eye in the Door*.

'The Glory of *Middlemarch*', *Sunday Times* (16 January 1994). Short comment on George Eliot's *Middlemarch*.

(With Ignès Sodre), *Imagining Characters: Six Conversations about Women Writers* (London: Chatto & Windus, 1995).

'In the Grip of *Possession*', *Independent* (2 February 1995), p. 26. On the artistic choices that gave *Possession* its form and content.

'Could It Be We're Falling in Love?', *Independent* (14 February 1995), p. 20. On the charm of London.

'Female Poets: Talented or Talentless?', *Independent* (14 September 1995), p. 50. Comment on Germaine Greer's study *Slip-shod Sybils*.

'A Woman of Great Importance', *Daily Telegraph* (24 September 1995), p. 8. A tribute to Harriet Harvey Wood, the British Council's Literature Director.

'However much he had to drink at lunch, he went on writing', *Guardian* (23 October 1995), p. 3. Short comment on Kingsley Amis.

'I Was a Wembley Virgin', *Observer* (30 June 1996). Report on the match in which Germany beat England in the World Championship Football.

'Fashion for Squares', *Observer* (3 August 1997), pp. 14–17. On the use of Mondriaan's images in fashion.

'Pink', *Observer* (5 April 1998), pp. 18–19. On the colour pink.

'The Man in the Back Row Has a Question V', *Paris Review* 146 (Spring 1998), pp. 163, 165, 169, 171, 173, 175, 177. A. S. Byatt's opinions on the 'Britishness' of literature, tradition, American literature, the Booker Prize.

Secondary sources

I Bibliographies

Alexa Alfer (School of English and Drama, Queen Mary and Westfield College, University of London) and Michael D. Crane (Department of English, University of Otago, Dunedin, New Zealand), with contributions by Michael J. Noble (Department of English, University of Southwestern Louisiana) and Christien Franken (Department of English, Vrije Universiteit Amsterdam), *A. S. Byatt: an Annotated Bibliography* (address: http://asbyatt.com/biblio/index.htm, 2000), Part I: Works by A. S. Byatt; Part II: About A. S. Byatt: Biography, Criticism and Comment.

Robert Hosmer, Janice A. Rossen and Lisa D. Mossman, 'A Bibliography of Writings by A. S. Byatt', in Robert E. Hosmer Jr. (ed.), *Contemporary British Women Writers* (New York: St. Martin's Press, 1992), pp. 61–4.

Christien Franken, 'Bringing Language and Thought to Life', *Multiple Mythologies: A. S. Byatt and the British Artist-Novel* (Utrecht: PhD Department of Women's Studies, Utrecht University, NL, 1997), pp. 223–54. Primary and secondary bibliography of A. S. Byatt's fiction and criticism 1965–97.

II   General

Caryn Mctighe Musil, 'A. S. Byatt', in Jay L. Halio (ed.), *Dictionary of Literary Biography: British Novelists since 1960* (Detroit: Bruccoli Clark, 1983), pp. 194–205.

Anthony Burgess, 'The Courage of the Clear Eye', *Fiction Magazine* 4 (August–September 1985), p. 31.

Olga Kenyon, 'A. S. Byatt', *Women Novelists Today* (Brighton: Harvester Press, 1988), pp. 51–84.

Flora Alexander, *Contemporary Women Novelists* (London: Edward Arnold, 1989), pp. 34–41.

Nicci Gerrard, *Into the Mainstream* (London: Pandora, 1989), pp. 71–2, 97, 100, 102–3, 107, 108–9.

Gabriele Griffin, 'A. S. Byatt', in Janet Todd (ed.), *Dictionary of British Women Writers* (London: Routledge, 1989), pp. 116–117.

Virginia Blain, Patricia Clements, Isobel Grundy (eds), 'A. S. Byatt', *The Feminist Companion to Literature in English* (London: Batsford, 1990), p. 166.

Christopher Hope, *A. S. Byatt* (London: British Council, 1990).

Alan Massie, 'The Moral Imperative', *The Novel Today: a Critical Guide to the British Novel 1970 to 1989* (London: Longman in association with the British Council, 1990).

'A. S. Byatt', *Current Biography* 52/9 (September 1991), pp. 10–14.

Flora Alexander, 'A. S. Byatt', in Hans Bak, Geert Lernout, Richard Todd and Wil Verhoeven (eds), *Post-War Literatures in English: a Lexicon of Contemporary Authors* (Groningen: Nijhoff, 1992); biography pp. 1–2; critical essay pp. 3–10; bibliography A1 and B1.

D. J. Taylor, 'The Rise and Rise of Antonia Byatt', *Sunday Times* (15 January 1995), pp. 8–9.

Kathleen Coyne Kelly, *A. S. Byatt* (New York: Twayne, 1996).

Bookmark on A. S. Byatt (BBC Television, March 1996).

Jan Dalley, 'A Time to Be Serious: Profile of A. S. Byatt', *Independent on Sunday* (14 March 1996).

Harry Richie, 'Fame at Last', *Telegraph Magazine* (May 1996).

Richard Todd, *A. S. Byatt* (Plymouth: Northcote House in Association with the British Council, 1997).

'A. S. Byatt', *New Writing from Britain: the European Connection, 23–28 Nov 98* (London: The British Council, 1998), p. 13.

Alexa Alfer, ' "A Second That Grows First, a Black Unreal/In Which a Real
Lies Hidden and Alive": the Fiction of A. S. Byatt', *Anglistik* 10 (September
1999), pp. 27–40.

III   Interviews

Juliet Dusinberre, 'A. S. Byatt', in Janet Todd (ed.), *Women Writers Talking*
(New York: Holmes S. Meier, 1983), pp. 181–95.
George Greenfield, *Scribblers for Bread: Aspects of the English Novel since 1945*
(London: Hodder & Stoughton, 1989), pp. 42–9.
Robert Carver, 'In Pursuit of the Fugitive Good: Criticism and the Arts on the
Air. A. S. Byatt in Conversation with Robert Carver', in Robert Carver (ed.),
Ariel at Bay: Reflections on Broadcasting and the Arts (Manchester: Carcanet,
1990), pp. 45–54.
Anne Chisholm, 'A Withering Look at the Scavengers', *Sunday Telegraph* (25
February 1990).
D. J. Taylor, 'Treasure Hunt with Spasmodic Poets', *Independent* (3 March
1990), p. 28.
Kate Kellaway, 'Self-Portrait of a Victorian Polymath', *Observer* (16 September
1990), p. 45.
Ysenda Maxtone Graham, 'The Literary Part of Life's Rich Pattern', *Sunday
Telegraph* (21 October 1990), p. 11.
Valerie Grove, 'Academic Reflections in a Victorian Climate', *Sunday Times*
(21 October 1990), p. 3.
Christien Franken, 'An Interview with A. S. Byatt' (Utrecht: Department of
Women's Studies, 1991). Unpublished.
Desert Island Disks, 10 January 1991.
Richard Todd, 'Interview with A. S. Byatt', *NSES: Netherlands Society for
English Studies* 1/1 (April 1991), pp. 36–44.
Richard Rosenfeld, 'A Childhood: A. S. Byatt', *Times Saturday Review* (27 April
1991), p. 54.
Mireila Aragay, 'An Interview with A. S. Byatt' (Barcelona 1992).
Unpublished.
Sonia Zyngier, 'The Passionate Act of Reading' (1992). Unpublished.
Sally Vincent, 'A. S. Byatt', *Sunday Times* (5 December 1993), pp. 28–32.
Eva Millet, 'Continental Assortment', *Guardian* (18 November 1993), pp. 8–9.
Nicolas Tredell, 'A. S. Byatt', *Conversations with Critics* (Manchester: Carcanet,
1994), pp. 58–74.
Jo Ind, 'An Open-and Closed-Book', *Birmingham Post* (15 April 1996), p. 19.
Marianne Brace, 'That Thinking Feeling', *Guardian* (9 May 1996), pp. 6–7.

IV   On the novels

a. Shadow of a Sun

Olivia Manning, 'Eagle in Flight', *Spectator* (27 December 1964).
Guardian Journal (9 January 1964).

Rosaleen Whately, 'The Rough with the Smooth', *Liverpool Daily Post* (9 January 1964).
'New Novels', *Times* (9 January 1964), p. 13.
TLS (9 January 1964).
Yorkshire Post (9 January 1964).
Manchester Evening News (10 January 1964).
Lawrence Meynell, *Wolverhampton Express* (10 January 1964).
Glasgow Herald (11 January 1964).
Bernard Share, *Irish Times* (11 January 1964).
Isabel Quigly, *Sunday Telegraph* (12 January 1964).
Frederic Raphael, 'Girl in a Trap', *Sunday Times* (12 January 1964), p. 38.
Maggie Ross, 'New Novels', *Listener* (16 January 1964).
Michael Wolfers, *Northern Echo* (17 January 1964).
Vernon Fane, *Sphere* (18 January 1964), p. 102.
Scotsman (19 January 1964).
Lady (23 January 1964).
R. G. Price, *Punch* (29 January 1964).
S. Hugh-Jones, *Tatler* (29 January 1964).
Richard Church, 'A New Talent', *Country Life* (30 January 1964).
Daily Telegraph (21 February 1964).
Irish *Independent* (29 February 1964).
Duncan Rice, *Press & Journal Aberdeen* (29 February 1964).
James Gordon, *Good Housekeeping* (April 1964).

b.   The Game

R. G. G. Price, 'New Novels', *Punch* 252 (18 January 1967), p. 100.
Martin Levin, 'Reader's Report', *New York Times Book Review* (17 March 1968), p. 36.
Malcolm Bradbury, 'On from Murdoch', *Encounter* 31/1 (July 1968), pp. 72–4.
Joanne V. Creighton, 'Sisterly Symbiosis: Margaret Drabble's *The Waterfall* and A. S. Byatt's *The Game*', *Mosaic* 20 (Winter 1987), pp. 15–29.
Jane Campbell, 'The Hunger of the Imagination in A. S. Byatt's *The Game*', *Critique* (Spring 1988), pp. 147–62.
Giulianna Giobi, 'Sisters Beware of Sisters: Sisterhood as a Literary Motif in Jane Austen, A. S. Byatt and I. Bossi Fedrigotti', *Journal of European Studies* 22 (September 1992), pp. 241–58.
Patsy Stoneman, 'Jane Eyre as Mirror and Monster: Intertextual Strategies in Women's Self-Representation', in Vita Fortunati and Gabriella Morisco (eds), *The Representation of the Self in Women's Autobiography* (Bologna: University of Bologna, 1993), pp. 84–106.
D. J. Taylor, *After the War: the Novel and England since 1945* (London: Chatto & Windus, 1993), pp. 185–206.
Brian Fallon, *Irish Times* (21 November 1993).

c.   The Virgin in the Garden

Michael Irwin, 'Growing up in 1953', *TLS* (3 November 1978), p. 1277.

J. M. Blom and L. R. Leavis, 'Current Literature 1978', *English Studies* 60 (1979), p. 631.

Juliet Dusinberre, 'Forms of Reality in A. S. Byatt's *The Virgin in the Garden*', *Critique*, 24/1 (1982), pp. 55–61.

Kuno Schumann, 'English Culture and the Contemporary Novel', in Jorg Hasler (ed.), *Anglistentag 1981* (Frankfurt am Main: Lang, 1983), pp. 111–27.

d.   Still Life

Adam Mars-Jones, 'Doubts about the Monument', *TLS* (28 June 1985), p. 720.

Peter Kemp, 'Still Life with Books', *Sunday Times* (30 June 1985).

N. Miller, *Antioch Review* 44/1 (1986), p. 118.

P. Lewis, *Strand Magazine* 27/2 (1986), pp. 38–44.

C. Matthews, *Malahat Review* 80 (1987), pp. 131–2.

New Statesman 114 (November 1987), p. 33.

Catherine Civello, 'George Eliot: From Middlemarch to Manhattan', *George Eliot Fellowship Review* 20 (1989), pp. 52–6.

Michael Westlake, 'The Hard Idea of Truth', *PN Review* 15/4 (1989), pp. 33–7.

Tess Cosslett, 'Childbirth from the Woman's Point of View in British Women's Fiction: Enid Bagnold's *The Squire* and A. S. Byatt's *Still Life*', *Tulsa Studies in Women's Literature* 8/2 (1989), pp. 263–86.

Hazel K. Bell, 'Indexing Fiction: a Story of Complexity', *Indexer* 17/4 (October 1989), pp. 251–6.

D. J. Taylor, 'Reading the 1950s: A. S. Byatt's *The Virgin in the Garden* and *Still Life*', *After the War: the Novel and England since 1945* (London: Chatto & Windus, 1993), pp. 90–102.

e.   Possession/Booker Prize

Vintage Reading Group Guide: *Possession*, by A. S. Byatt. London: Vintage, 1990.

Anne Smith, 'Sifting the Ash', *Listener* (1 March 1990), p. 29.

Nicola Murphy, 'A Romance of Literary Crit', *Times* (1 March 1990), p. 17.

Richard Jenkyns, 'Disinterring Buried Lives', *TLS* (2–8 March 1990), pp. 213–14.

Nicolas Shrimpton, 'Victorian Eco-Chamber', *Independent on Sunday* (4 March 1990), p. 18.

Peter Kemp, 'An Extravaganza of Victoriana', *Sunday Times* Books (4 March 1990), p. 6.

Danny Karlin, 'Prolonging Her Absence', *London Review of Books* (8 March 1990), pp. 17–18.

Jonathan Coe, 'Byatt's Pendulum', *Guardian* (11 March 1990), p. 23.

Elaine Feinstein, 'Eloquent Victorians', *New Statesman* (16 March 1990), p. 38.

J. Parini, Jr., 'Unearthing the Secret Lover', *New York Times Book Review* (October 1990), p. 9.

Philip Howard, 'Booker Winner Lets Her Hair Down', *Times* (7 October 1990), p. 3.

D. J. Taylor, 'Booker: Musical Chairs with Quirky Corners', *Independent* (20 October 1990), p. 27.

Peter Kemp, 'Academic Questions: Passionate Solutions', *Sunday Times* (21 October 1990), p. 6.

Kate Saunders, 'One Party That Proves a Best-Seller', *Sunday Times* (21 October 1990), p. 5.

Biba Kopf, 'Raze the Value of the Word', *City Limits* (7 February 1991).

'A. S. Byatt and the Random House Horror', *Sunday Telegraph* (17 February 1991), p. 21.

Kate Saunders, *Sunday Telegraph* (17 March 1991).

Brenda K. Marshall, 'Parallel Lives', *Women's Review of Books* 8/8 (May 1991), p. 6.

Scarlet Cheng, 'A Time of Purple Passions', *Belles Lettres* (Spring 1991), p. 17.

Christien Franken, 'Possession', *Netherlands Society for English Studies* 1 (November 1991), pp. 51–6.

Anne Hulbert, 'The Great Ventriloquist', in Robert E. Hosmer Jr. (ed.), *Contemporary British Women Writers* (New York: St. Martin's Press, 1992), pp. 55–65.

Louise Yelin, 'Cultural Cartography: A. S. Byatt's *Possession* and the Politics of Victorian Studies', *Victorian Newsletter* 81 (Spring 1992), pp. 38–41.

Janice Rossen, *The University in Modern Fiction* (London: Macmillan, 1993).

Elaine Showalter, 'Feminists under Fire: Images of the New Woman from the Nineties to the 1990s', *TLS* (25 June 1993), pp. 14–15.

Margaret A. Rose, 'Contemporary Late-Modern and Post-Modern Theories and Uses of Parody', *Parody: Ancient, Modern and Post-Modern* (Cambridge: Cambridge University Press, 1994), pp. 230–2.

Caroline Webb, 'History through Metaphor: Woolf's Orlando and Byatt's *Possession*', in Mark Hussey and Vara Neverow (eds), *Virginia Woolf* (New York: Pace University Press, 1994).

Giuliana Giobbi, 'Know the Past: Know Thyself. Literary Pursuits and Quest for Identity in A. S. Byatt's *Possession* and in F. Duranti's *Effetti Personali*', *Journal of European Studies* 24/1 (March 1994), pp. 41–54.

Ann Ashworth, 'Fairy Tales in A. S. Byatt's *Possession*', *Journal of Evolutionary Psychology* 15 (March 1994), pp. 1–2.

Stephen J. Fountain, 'Ashes to Ashes: Kristeva's Jouissance, Altizer's Apocalypse, Byatt's *Possession* and "The Dream of the Rood" ', *Literature and Theology* 8/2 (June 1994), pp. 193–208.

Kelley A. Marsh, 'The Neo-Sensation Novel: a Contemporary Genre in the Victorian Tradition', *Philological Quarterly* 74 (1995), pp. 99–123.

Maureen Sabine, ' "Thou Art the Best Of Me": A. S. Byatt's *Possession* and the Literary Possession of John Donne', *John Donne Journal* (1995), pp. 127–48.

Richard Todd, 'The Retrieval of Unheard Voices in British Postmodernist Fiction: A. S. Byatt and Marina Warner', in Theo D'haen and Hans Bertens (eds), *Liminal Postmodernisms* (Amsterdam: Rodopi, 1995), pp. 99–114.

Elisabeth Bronfen, 'Romancing Difference, Courting Coherence: A. S. Byatt's *Possession* as Postmodern Moral Fiction', in Ahrens-Rudiger (ed.), *Why Literature Matters: Theories and Functions of Literature* (Heidelberg: Winter, 1996), pp. 117–34.

Steven Connor, *The English Novel in History 1950–1995* (London: Routledge, 1996).

Richard Todd, 'A. S. Byatt's *Possession*', *Consuming Fictions: the Booker Prize and Fiction in Britain Today* (London: Bloomsbury, 1996), pp. 25–43.

Jackie Buxton, ' "What's Love Got to Do with It": Postmodernism and *Possession*', *English Studies in Canada* 22/2 (June 1996), pp. 199–219.

Andre Brink, 'Possessed by Language: A. S. Byatt: *Possession*', *The Novel: Language and Narrative from Cervantes to Calvino* (Houndmills: Macmillan – now Palgrave, 1998), pp. 288–308.

Michèle Roberts, 'The Passionate Reader: *Possession* and Romance', *Food, Sex & God* (London: Virago, 1998), pp. 47–69.

Christien Franken, 'De Melusine mythologie in *Possession* van A. S. Byatt', *Bzzlletin* 28 (December 1998), pp. 261–2, and (January 1999), pp. 27–33.

f. *Babel Tower*

Hugo Barnacle, 'Has A. S. Byatt Lost the Plot?', *Independent Weekend* (4 May 1996).

Lucy Hughes-Hallett, 'Swinging in the Sixties', *Sunday Times* (5 May 1996).

Kate Kellaway, 'Tall Stories', *Observer* (5 May 1996), p. 14.

Caroline Moore, 'Of Love, Loss and Depravity', *Sunday Telegraph* (5 May 1996), p. 14.

Penelope Lively, 'Truth in Many Tongues', *Times* (9 May 1996), p. 40.

D. J. Taylor, 'My Generation', *Guardian* (10 May 1996), p. 11.

Miranda Seymour, 'An Idea too Big for Its Plot', *Financial Times* (11 May 1996).

Victoria Glendinning, 'Only Connect the Prose and the Passion', *Sunday Telegraph* (12 May 1996).

V On novellas and short stories

a. *Sugar and Other Stories*

Anne Duchene, 'Ravening Time', *TLS* (1987), p. 395.

T. Hargreaves, *Hermathena* 142 (1987), pp. 77–8.

Patricia Craig, 'The Grace of Accuracy', *Sunday Times* (12 April 1987).

Francis Spufford, 'The Mantle of Jehova', *London Review of Books* (June 1987).

L. S. Schwartz, *New York Times Book Review* (July 1987), p. 5.

New Directions for Women (November 1987), p. 22.

British Book News (December 1987), p. 792.

Bloomsbury Revue 8 (January 1988), p. 17.

Belles Lettres 3 (March 1988), p. 8.

K. Cushman, *Studies in Short Fiction* 25/1 (Winter 1988), pp. 80–1.

Jane Campbell, ' "The Somehow May Be Thishow": Fact, Fiction and Intertextuality in Antonia Byatt's "Precipice-Encurled" ', *Studies in Short Fiction* 28/1 (Winter 1991), pp. 115–23.

b.   Angels and Insects

Marilyn Butler, 'The Moth and the Medium', *TLS* (16 October 1992).

Nicci Gerrard, 'Butterfly Netted', *Observer* (18 October 1992).

Peter Kemp, 'A Near Myth', *Sunday Times* (18 October 1992), p. 13.

Paul Taylor, 'A Mixed Blessing from Tennyson', *Independent on Sunday* (25 October 1992), p. 28.

Kathryn Hughes, 'Repossession', *New Statesman* (6 November 1992), pp. 49–50.

Victoria Glendinning, 'Angels and Ministers of Graciousness', *Times Saturday Review* (7 November 1992), p. 45.

David Robson, 'Politics, Prickles and Perversity', *Sunday Telegraph* (8 November 1992).

John Lanchester, *Guardian* (10 November 1992).

Godfrey Hodgson, 'A Struggling Society Well-Read in Tooth and Claw', *Independent* (14 November 1992).

Caroline Moore, 'A Rare Specimen', *Daily Telegraph* (14 November 1992).

John Barrell, 'When Will He Suspect?', *London Review of Books* (19 November 1992), pp. 18–19.

Valentine Cunningham, 'In a Little Room', *British Book News* (July 1993), p. 422.

Michael Levenson, 'The Religion of Fiction', *New Republic* (2 August 1993), pp. 41–4. Reprinted in A. S. Byatt, *Degrees of Freedom* (London: Chatto & Windus, 1994).

Tess Lewis, 'Metamorphoses', *Belles Lettres* (Fall 1993), pp. 28–9.

Nicholas Lezard, *Guardian* (2 November 1993).

Janet Watts, 'The Word Made Fresh', *Guardian* (8 December 1995), p. 8. On the cooperation between A. S. Byatt and Philip Haas, the director of *Angels and Insects*.

Marion Shaw, 'Remembering the Victorians in the Nineties', in Nicole Rowan (ed.), *(W)righting the Nineties* (Ghent: English Department, University of Ghent, 1995), pp. 63–74.

Christien Franken, 'The Gender of Mourning: Tennyson's *In Memoriam* and A. S. Byatt's "The Conjugial Angel" ', in Ton Hoenselaars and Paul Franssen (eds), *The Author as Character: Representing Historical Writers in Western Literature* (Madison: Fairleigh Dickinson University Press, 1999), pp. 243–52.

Margaret Pearce, ' "Morpho Eugenia": Problems with the Male Gaze', *Critique* 40(4) (Summer 1999), pp. 399–411.

c.   The Matisse Stories

Lucy Hughes-Hallet, *Vogue* (December 1993).

Cressida Connolly, *Tatler* (January 1994), p. 16.

Helen Dunmore, 'Demolish, then Rebuild with Care', *Observer* (2 January 1994), p. 17.

Hilary Spurling, 'The Art of the Sensual', *Daily Telegraph* (8 January 1994), p. 9.

Tom Adair, *Scotland on Sunday* (9 January 1994).

Candida McWilliam, 'Death, Decay and Hairdos', *Independent on Sunday* (9 January 1994).

David Robson, 'Painting in Prose', *Sunday Telegraph* (9 January 1994).

Geoff Dyer, 'Precious in the Pink', *Guardian* (11 January 1994).

Penelope Fitzgerald, *Evening Standard* (13 January 1994).

Alex Clark, 'Artist and Models', *TLS* (14 January 1994), p. 21.

Anita Brookner, 'It's Nicer, Much Nicer, than Nice', *Spectator* (15 January 1994), p. 28.

Peter Kemp, 'Still Lives', *Sunday Times Books* (21 January 1994), p. 1.

Alan Massie, 'A Painterly Piece of Work', *Scotsman* (22 January 1994).

Michèle Roberts, 'Matisse: All the Nudes That's Fit to Print', *Independent* (22 January 1994).

Digby Durrant, 'Square Pegs', *London Magazine* (February/March 1994), pp. 157–8.

d.   *The Djinn in the Nightingale's Eye*

Andy Beckett, 'Confessions of a Stout Scheherazade', *Independent on Sunday* (1 January 1995), p. 34.

Helen Dunmore, 'Magic in the Palm of a Hand', *Observer* Review (1 January 1995), p. 17.

Alev Adil, 'Obeying the Genie', *TLS* (6 January 1995).

David Holloway, 'Princess and Boris Becker', *Daily Telegraph* (7 January 1995), p. 7.

Jane Shilling, 'The Powerful Magic of the Fairy Tale', *Sunday Telegraph* (15 January 1995).

Francis Spufford, 'A Djinn in the Tale', *Guardian* (17 January 1995).

e.   *Elementals*

Katy Emck, 'The Consolations of a Kindly Genie', *TLS* (1998).

Emily Perkins, 'Naming Nimes', *Observer* (22 November 1998).

VI   On essays and academic writing

a.   General

Christien Franken, 'The Turtle and Its Adversaries: Gender Disruption in A. S. Byatt's Critical and Academic Work', in Richard Todd and Luisa Flora (eds), *Theme Parks, Rain Forests and Sprouting Wastelands: European Essays on Theory and Performance in Contemporary British Fiction* (Amsterdam, Atlanta: Rodopi, 2000), pp. 195–214.

b. (With Ignès Sodre) Imagining Characters (London: Chatto & Windus, 1995).

Michèle Roberts, 'Bringing Back the Author', *Independent* (9 December 1995).

c.   Passions of the Mind

Alan Massie, 'Electrified by the Hard Idea of Truth', *Weekend Telegraph* (3 August 1991), p. xix.

James Wood, 'A. S. Byatt: a Mind too Fine for Detail', *Sunday Telegraph* (4 August 1991).

Michèle Roberts, 'Greed Reading', *New Statesman* 4/163 (9 August 1991), p. 38.

Declan Kibert, 'A Critic's World of Books Tells a Superb Story', *Sunday Tribune* (11 August 1991).

Valentine Cunningham, 'The Greedy Reader: A. S. Byatt in the Post-Christian Labyrinth', *TLS* (16 August 1991), p. 6.

Peter Kemp, 'Chapter and Verses', *Sunday Times* (18 August 1991).

John Bayley, 'Glutton for a Good Read', *Evening Standard* (22 August 1991), p. 34.

Stephen Davy, 'Revelations concerning Genesis', *Times* (25 August 1991).

Amanda Craig, 'The Donnish Appetites of a Greedy Reader', *Independent* (28 August 1991).

Max Davidson, *Weekend Telegraph* (28 August 1993).

VII   On the editor A. S. Byatt

a.   Oxford Book of English Short Stories

Karl Miller, 'Thinking of England', *Observer* (19 April 1998), p. 15.

Elizabeth Lowry, 'The Nouvellle Cuisine of the Turnover', *TLS* (26 June 1998), pp. 23–4.

Index